Lust &
Loyalty

Also by Shelly Ellis

Chesterton Scandal series

To Love & Betray
Lust & Loyalty
Best Kept Secrets
Bed of Lies

Gibbons Gold Digger series

Can't Stand the Heat
The Player & the Game
Another Woman's Man
The Best She Ever Had

Published by Dafina Books

Lust & Loyalty

SHELLY ELLIS

KENSINGTON PUBLISHING CORP.
www.kensingtonbooks.com

DAFINA BOOKS are published by

Kensington Publishing Corp.
119 West 40th Street
New York, NY 10018

All Kensington titles, imprints, and distributed lines are available at special quantity discounts for bulk purchases for sales promotions, premiums, fund-raising, and educational or institutional use. Special book excerpts or customized printings can also be created to fit specific needs. For details, write or phone the office of the Kensington Special Sales Manager. Kensington Publishing Corp., 119 West 40th Street, New York, NY 10018, attn: Special Sales Department, Phone: 1-800-221-2647.

Dafina and the Dafina logo Reg. U.S. Pat. & TM Off.

ISBN-13: 978-1-4967-0879-3
ISBN-10: 1-4967-0879-2
First Kensington Trade Edition: April 2017
First Kensington Mass Market Edition: September 2018

eISBN-13: 978-1-4967-0880-9
eISBN-10: 1-4967-0880-6
First Kensington Electronic Edition: April 2017

10 9 8 7 6 5 4 3 2 1

Printed in the United States of America

To Andrew and Chloe—my North and my South . . .
To Mom and Dad—my East and my West . . .
Thanks for helping to give me a sense of direction.

Acknowledgments

Nina Simone once said, "An artist's duty, as far as I'm concerned, is to reflect the times." Maybe it's about time that I start to do the same. But when writing commercial lit, I'm always wary of being too heavy-handed with the allegories and messaging. This is supposed to be escapism, isn't it? People have a lot to deal with in their everyday lives and may just want to have a good time laughing, sighing, and rolling their eyes at all the drama on a novel's pages. But, when I really thought about it, I realized I've tried to do a little of it in the past. In *Can't Stand the Heat*, I talked about physical abuse in romantic relationships. In *Another Woman's Man*, I explored a character finding out that her father was dying of cancer, and the feelings of loss and frustration she experienced soon after his death. In *Bed of Lies*, I talked about depression and plan to explore it even more in this book, the follow-up, *Lust & Loyalty*. Also, considering the times and current events, from the current political environment to #BlackLivesMatter protests, it's hard not to put any of that in your work. Police brutality, especially within the black community, is always a concern. How black people, particularly how black men, are viewed and subsequently treated by cops regardless of their socioeconomic status can be alarming. In the real world, the Murdoch brothers, even with all their money, influence, and status, wouldn't be immune. I chose to reflect that in this entry of the Chesterton Scandal saga. I tried not to be heavy-handed with it, but hopefully I still get my point across.

I wouldn't have the ability to write, to take *any* chances with my work, if it wasn't for those around me who help me to get words on page. The person I always acknowledge first is my husband, Andrew, who was there before the books made it from my laptop to the bookshelf. He pep-talked me through each rejection letter and helped me keep the faith even when my belief in myself faltered.

I also want to thank my former editor, Mercedes Fernandez, for seeing the talent in me, and my new editor, Esi Sogah, for seeing it, too, and believing in the stories that I write. Having a champion for your work in a publishing house is immeasurable, and I'm grateful for every time you ladies go before the editorial board and say, "I really like this. We should acquire it." I'm even more grateful for the doors you have opened for other writers of color. We really appreciate you!

I also want to thank my agent, Barbara Poelle. You can make as many martinis and goofy jokes as you want . . . I know you definitely have your stuff together. You're an agent who I know has my back and will make sure I'm taken care of. I come to you with ideas and you always say, "I love it! Now let's make that idea reality." Thank you so much for all that you do.

Prologue

Hospitals weren't usually happy places, especially the Wilson Medical Center ICU, where many of the patients hovered near death's door and a pall of sickness seemed to hang over every surface. But today the ICU staff at least *tried* to be festive in honor of the new nurse's birthday. Meredith, the plump nurse with the springy red curls and freckles, was turning thirty. The other nurses figured the big 3-0 deserved, at minimum, a small party in their break room. They had even brought a cake and candles for her. One of the nurses, Rhonda, had brought balloons and streamers that were left over from her nephew's birthday earlier that week. By the time they had finished decorating that sad-looking room, with its bare white walls, lone microwave, coffeemaker, and two tables, it looked like a completely different place. A small two-tiered cake sat at the center of one of the tables on a cotton bedsheet they used as a makeshift tablecloth.

They decided to hold the party midday when visiting hours were at a lull because many of the patients' families would leave to eat lunch and return in an hour or so to stand vigil at their loved ones' bedsides. The five nurses on that shift had agreed to take turns at the front desk and keep an ear out for buzzing from patients' rooms, though most of the patients were so sedated they wouldn't be buzzing anything. Not Mr. J. Hinkler in room 402, who was dying of cirrhosis of the liver, or Mrs. C. Reynolds in room 410, who had suffered multiple strokes and was now little more than a vegetable connected to a respirator, and certainly not Mr. D. Turner in room 406.

Turner was the youngest patient in the ICU, and if it weren't for the gunshot wound to the stomach that he had suffered a week ago, he probably wouldn't have found himself in the ward at all. He looked fit and handsome. The nurses had speculated that he had been quite the heartbreaker before the shooting. A few of them had even whispered about his six-pack abs and muscular arms, and admired and giggled about another appendage they had noticed while changing the dressing on his wound.

"No wonder his name is Dante," Rhonda had murmured ruefully as she pointed to his bare crotch. "A man *that* fine wielding *that* thing could certainly drag a girl through hell and back!"

But Mr. Turner wouldn't be putting any women through hell or breaking any hearts any time soon. He remained heavily sedated while his body repaired itself. And unlike the other patients, he'd had few to no visitors in his room.

Nurse Kelly took the first shift while the rest attended Meredith's birthday party. She glanced through the glass doors of each hospital room, including Mr. Turner's, as she walked from the break room to the front desk, carrying her slice of carrot cake. She passed an old woman who gave her a wan smile before entering room 403.

"Hello, Mrs. O'Shea," Kelly said, giving her greeting from the doorway.

"Good afternoon," Mrs. O'Shea said as she dragged a chair toward the bed to sit next to her husband, who was dying of end-stage lung cancer.

A minute later, Kelly plopped into her rolling chair and dug into her carrot cake, finishing the entire slice in less than three minutes and licking the remaining icing off the plastic fork tongs and the tips of her fingers. She looked longingly at her empty paper plate. She could use a second slice.

A moment on the lips, a lifetime on the hips, she thought, glancing down at her wide hips that were encased in blue scrubs. She had been trying to lose her last ten pounds of baby weight for ages. Plus, she was supposed to be staffing the front desk while the other nurses were at the birthday party.

But then Kelly ran her tongue over her lips, tasting the remains of the cream cheese icing, and she almost shuddered in ecstasy. She remembered how fluffy the cake itself had been, how the bits of carrot had been so crisp.

"Just one more," she mumbled, rising from the chair. "I'll be quick."

With the exception of Mrs. O'Shea, it was dead as a doornail around the ward—no pun intended. None of the patients would miss her.

It was just seconds after Kelly walked out of the break room and plunged her fork into her second slice of carrot cake that she heard the alarm, a piercing beep to alert them at the nursing station that a patient was in distress. She rushed down the corridor, still holding her plate of cake in one hand and fork in the other, wondering if it was Mrs. Reynolds or poor Mr. O'Shea.

That's when she spotted something black jump out of room 406 and flash past her, like a wraith in a horror movie. She screamed and dropped her cake and fork to the floor. It was only after a few blinks that she realized it wasn't some ghost that had flown out the room, but a person—a living, breathing person dressed head-to-toe in black—hoodie, cap, and sweatpants—who was racing with breakneck speed down the hospital hallway.

"Hey!" she shouted after him—or her. She couldn't tell the sex of the person at this distance. "Hey, what were you—"

Her words died on her lips when the person slammed into the metal doors, shoving them open and disappearing into the adjoining hall. The door slammed shut behind them.

Kelly stared in shock at the closed door until the alarm shook her out of her daze. She turned back to room 406 and saw a pillow slumped on the linoleum floor. Her eyes raised and she saw Mr. Turner. His head was now tilted to the side instead of sitting forward and upright in its proper position, and it looked like his breathing tube had been partially removed. The white tape below his nose now flapped limply, revealing the peach fuzz above his lip. His mouth hung open like that of a catfish on a slab of ice.

"Oh, God," she whispered, feeling the carrot cake and bile rise in her throat as she realized what had happened. She rushed into the room and heard thunderous footsteps behind her as the other nurses and doctors came to assist.

It looked like someone had tried to kill Dante Turner—*again*.

Chapter 1
Evan

Evan Murdoch tried not to wince with discomfort as he watched the doctor do his handiwork. He didn't want to worry his little brother, Terrence, who was already nervous and had already tried to back out of the consultation and fitting twice before Terrence's girlfriend and Evan had finally talked him into it. But now, watching it less than five feet away from him, Evan was starting to feel put off by the whole procedure. The twelve-by-twelve-foot office was starting to feel stuffy and claustrophobic, and Evan longed to open one of the windows on the other side of the room. But he tamped down that impulse and instead valiantly painted on his best impression of a polite smile as the ocularist fiddled around in Terrence's eye socket with the piece of plastic that was molded and painted to be a replica of Terrence's left eye—the eye that was mangled in a car accident nearly five months ago.

"All right, Terrence," the technician said, turning Terrence around in his chair and blocking Evan's view. "The scleral cover shell is now in place. How does it feel?"

"Uh, okay, I . . . I guess."

Evan could hear the apprehension in his brother's voice.

"Okay, I want you to open and close your eyes," the technician said. "Good. Look up . . . Look down . . . Look right. . . . Now look left, please." There was another pause. "Does it still feel okay?"

"Yeah, it feels fine," Terrence said with a nod.

Evan leaned forward, trying desperately to see Terrence's new eye, but having little success. He had a perfect view of the back of his brother's head, though.

He needs a haircut, Evan noted.

"Good. Good! Now you can have a look," the technician said, extending a small handheld mirror to Terrence. He sat back in his rolling chair and smiled. "What do you think?"

Terrence held the mirror in front of his face. "Goddamn!" he shouted.

"What?" Evan asked, finally tired of waiting. He got visions of scenes from old-fashioned movies where the bandages are slowly unwound from around a patient's head, revealing a new, horrifying face, making the patient scream out in agony. He hopped out of his chair and raced to his brother's side. "What's wrong?"

"Nothing," Terrence said, turning to him. "Nothing's wrong!"

"Goddamn," Evan echoed, breaking into a grin.

It was like the ocularist had given Terrence his eye back; it didn't look like a replica but like the real thing. Terrence now had two perfect, caramel-colored irises. He had two eyes that winked and shifted simultaneously. Evan would challenge anyone to know which eye was real and which one was not.

"I know, right?" Terrence laughed. "It looks good."

"It doesn't look good; it looks fucking perfect!" Evan exclaimed.

"You get a tap for this one, doc," Terrence said, holding his fist up to the elderly, white-haired man who looked like he could've starred in an AARP ad. The technician chuckled, pushed his glasses up the bridge of his nose, and gave Terrence a fist bump.

"I'm glad you like the final product," the man said.

"So . . . so that's it?" Terrence asked, lowering his fist and the mirror. "I can just walk out with it? Just like that?"

The technician nodded. "Just like that. I'll send you home with a cleanser and instructions. I'll probably schedule a follow-up to make sure everything is okay with the new prosthetic, but that's it. You're done!"

"I'm done," Terrence said softly, and Evan knew instantly he was talking about more than just today's appointment.

His younger brother had completed the last step to making a full recovery from his accident. He no longer walked with his cane. Now he no longer had to wear the eye patch over his damaged eye. He had returned to the gym and lost the weight he had put on from sitting alone at home, staring at the television all day and all night, and drinking and eating his way through his depression. He was even no longer seeing a therapist on a weekly basis. His mild depression seemed to have waned; he readily joked and laughed more now than he had in months.

Evan gazed at his brother and nodded. "You're done, Terry."

"Damn, how many times are you going to look at yourself, pretty boy?" Evan asked as Terrence pulled his silver Porsche roadster to a stop at the red light and flipped down his visor for the umpteenth time to gaze in the small mirror at his reflection.

Terrence chuckled and flipped the visor up again. "Come on, man! I just got to the point where I could look at myself and not wince. Give a brotha a break!"

"I'm just messing with you, Terry." Evan punched his shoulder playfully. "I'm glad he was able to give you such a good prosthetic eye. You've been through a lot. It looks like you're finally on the comeback."

"You sound like C. J.," Terrence said, referring to his girlfriend. He pulled off when the light turned green. "She said my eye was the last missing puzzle piece."

"She's probably right."

Terrence tightened his hold around the leather steering wheel. His smile disappeared. "I'm not sure that she's . . . well . . . totally happy about it, though. I mean with me getting the prosthesis."

"What do you mean? Why wouldn't she be happy? I thought she talked you into doing it!"

"She did, but . . . it's not just the eye. It's my whole recovery. She told me once that she was worried that when I finally got better, I would . . . that I would go back to my old ways—hooking up with all types of chicks, caring more about money, cars, and clothes than I do about her . . . about *us*. I told her there's no chance of that happening. I'm not that guy anymore."

Evan could understand why C. J. was worried. Terrence had been the love 'em and leave 'em type for many, *many* years prior to the accident. And the women he had dated had been nothing like the smart, sensible, plain-Jane girlfriend he had now.

In the old days, Terrence had seemed disgusted by the idea of love and commitment. Evan had expected his brother to die at the ripe old age of eighty in some sex ranch in Las Vegas with a smile on his face and Viagra in his system. But the car crash had caused Terrence's life to veer in another direction. Terrence had become introspective and thoughtful. He did seem to be genuinely in love with C. J. But even Evan wondered how long all of this would last.

"Well, I guess time will tell," Evan said thoughtfully.

Terrence snapped his head around to glare at him. "What the hell do you mean 'Time will tell'? You think I'm going to cheat on her . . . that I'm going to *dump her*?"

"No, I didn't say that! I just think—"

"Good! Because it's not gonna happen!" Terrence drew to a stop at another stoplight. "C. J. is the only woman for me and to hell with anybody who says any differently!"

Just then, the sound of pounding dance beats filled the car. The two men turned to find a Toyota pulling up beside them at the light. It was the source of the music. The driver lowered her tinted window and raised her dark shades, revealing her comely brown face. She leaned in her driver's seat toward their car and tossed her long, dark hair over her shoulder.

"Damn!" she shouted to Terrence over the sound of the music as her eyes scanned Terrence's Porsche from headlights to rear bumper. "That's a sweet ride, baby!"

"Thanks," Terrence called back.

"It looks brand new!"

"That's because it is," he said, tapping the buttery smooth leather along the dashboard. "Just got it a little over a month ago."

"Well, you look good in it!"

Terrence chuckled. "Hell, girl, you're making me blush!"

Evan cocked an eyebrow as he watched their exchange. He wondered if his brother realized that his voice had deepened as he spoke to her, that he was smiling ear-to-ear. He wondered if his brother realized it seemed a lot like he was flirting with this woman when he had professed only seconds ago that C. J. was the only woman for him.

"I can make you do a lot more than blush if you let me test drive that car," the driver said, licking her plump, red lips.

"Whoa!" Terrence exclaimed, laughing even harder, making Evan sigh with irritation. "That's some big talk!"

"Big talk that I can back up." She gave a saucy wink. "Don't believe me?"

"Oh, I believe you!"

"So take a girl out to dinner next week and let me prove it."

"The light's green, Terry," Evan muttered.

Terrence turned away from the beautiful driver and glanced up at the stoplight. "Oh, shit. Uh, maybe some other time," he mumbled before giving her a quick wave good-bye, pressing the accelerator, and pulling off.

As he drove, he glanced at Evan, who silently stared out the windshield.

"Don't say it," Terrence ordered tightly, reading Evan's mind.

Evan held up his hands in mock defense. "Hey, I'm not saying a damn thing!"

"No, but you're thinking it!" Terrence pointed his finger at Evan. "Look, she and I were *just* talking! She was just some random chick I met on the street. It's not like I was really going to follow through and have dinner with her. I told you I would never cheat on C. J.!"

"I'm not saying you would cheat"—Evan inclined his head—"per se."

"What the fuck? *Per se?* Really, Ev? Are you serious?"

"I'm just saying that people grow apart, Terry. Couples grow apart."

"We've only been together for a few months! How the hell could we grow apart already?"

"But *a lot* has happened in those few months. You have to admit that. And people change. It's a fact of life! Maybe C. J. is more realistic about that than you are. That's what I meant."

"Well, how do you know you and Lee won't 'grow apart'?" he asked, referring to Evan's fiancée Leila. "If C. J. and I are doomed, why the hell aren't you guys? You've got a lot more odds stacked against you than we do! That's for damn sure," he spat as he turned onto another street.

Evan narrowed his eyes at his little brother.

Evan and Leila had been through a lot in the past year or so. In fact, they had been through a lot in the past *ten* years. Their relationship had traversed several ups and downs, including false accusations, misunderstandings, marriages to other people, their clandestine affair, and a painful breakup before they finally reunited. They were now living together, engaged, and having a baby, which should have meant they had finally reached their happy ending. But Evan was encountering a major glitch in the form of his current recovering alcoholic wife, Charisse, who was refusing to grant him a divorce. Charisse insisted that now that she was clean and sober she wanted him back. She had even threatened to drag out the divorce proceedings for years, until Evan and Leila's baby was well into kindergarten.

Evan hadn't told Leila any of this—at least, not yet, anyway. He didn't want to crush her dreams of getting married in the near future. She said she didn't want to be anyone's mistress anymore, but it looked like she would have to be that—indefinitely.

Evan knew Leila loved him and he loved her, but all these obstacles could wear down even the most loyal of couples. He worried sometimes when it would all get to be too much, and if the foundation they had tried so hard to build together would eventually crumble.

"We'll make it through," Evan said firmly, shoving down his inner doubts. "Don't you worry about us."

"Don't you worry about me and C. J., either," Terrence argued as they pulled onto the short road leading up to Murdoch Mansion. As Terrence steered onto the circular driveway, they both noticed two cop cars parked in front of the stone steps, their blue-and-white emblems glistening in the afternoon sun.

"What the hell . . ." Evan whispered, unlocking and shoving open the Porsche's passenger side door even before the roadster pulled to a full stop.

His mind leapt to the worst conclusion. He wondered if something had happened to Leila— who he thought was at a meeting at the Chesterton Country Club today with his sister Paulette. Or maybe something had happened to Leila's daughter, Isabel, or her mother, Diane, both of whom lived at the mansion.

He charged up the stairs, taking them two at a time. He flung open the French doors. Terrence was only a few steps behind him.

"What's wrong?" he yelled, rushing over the marble tiles of his three-story foyer, his shout echoing off the wooden, coffered ceiling. Two officers stood near the staircase to the east and west wings, talking to his housekeeper, who looked scared and confused. "What the hell happened? Is Lee o—"

"Ah, so it's *both* the Murdoch boys!" Evan heard a voice call across the foyer, stopping him in his tracks. "Good! I can kill two birds with one stone."

Evan chafed at the sound of the familiar backwater drawl. Not only was he annoyed at being called "boy"—the last he checked, he was thirty-three, *not* three years old—but he also had no desire to talk to the owner of that drawl.

He turned to find a man in an oversize gray suit and a gray-and-white-striped tie striding toward them, chomping on a sandwich the size of his fist. The police detective lowered the sandwich from his mouth and smiled, revealing a smear of mustard on his upper lip.

"Just grabbed a quick bite to eat in your kitchen. Your cook was nice enough to make me a ham and cheese." He licked the mustard off his lip after he stopped chewing. "Hope you don't mind."

Evan crossed his arms over his broad chest. "How can I help you, Detective Morris?" he answered flatly even though, truth be told, he had no interest in helping this man at all. In fact, he had hoped to never see Detective Morris again.

They had spoken before in a sterile-looking room at the state police barracks soon after Dante had been shot. Evan had sat on one side of the table with one of his lawyers and Detective Morris had sat on the other.

"I understand that you and your brother Dante were going through kind of a row before he up and got shot. Is that right, Mr. Murdoch?" the detective had asked, leaning back in his metal folding chair.

"He wasn't one of my favorite people, if that's what you mean," Evan had quipped.

"I heard he was even screwing your wife. I know if it were me, I'd be mad as hell at him. Maybe even mad enough to kill him."

"Excuse me, but just what are you insinuating?" Evan's lawyer had barked. "Unless you're planning to charge my client with attempted murder, I suggest you keep your questions to—"

Evan had held up his hand, silencing the man beside him. "It's all right, Ben."

Unlike his lawyer, Evan hadn't been shaken by the detective's flagrant insinuations. Evan hadn't shot Dante and he had an alibi to prove it. The detective could insinuate all he wanted.

"Honestly, Detective, considering the state of my marriage at that time, Dante did me a favor by screwing my wife. I didn't want to kill him. If he wasn't such an asshole, I would have sent him a fruit basket to show my gratitude."

The detective had burst into laughter. "Oh, that's funny! That was a good one! You're a comedian, Mr. Murdoch. You should be on late-night TV!"

He had chuckled a bit longer before finally letting his laughter taper off. He had then become somber. His gray eyes had gone cold.

"You know what? I've got a joke, too . . . a real funny one." He had shifted in his chair, leaned one elbow on the table between them, and tapped the edge of his Styrofoam coffee cup as he spoke. "I was talking the other day to another detective, Detective Nola at the Mannock County Sheriff's Office. I found out that he's been questioning your sister Paulette in another investigation. This time . . . a homicide."

At the mention of his sister's name in connection with the word "homicide," Evan had stilled. His confident façade had faltered. He had felt his stomach clench.

"Turns out that one of her ex-boyfriends, Marques Whitney, was strangled to death just eight months ago. Detective Nola said he thinks Marques may have been extorting money out of your sister, but he can't say for sure. She hasn't been very . . . shall we say . . . helpful, in that regard."

Evan could no longer meet the detective's eyes. As he sat there, he had felt his panic rise, making him shift in his chair and restlessly tap his foot. Even his lawyer had noticed the difference in him. The balding man had started to eye Evan warily and frown, as if asking, *"What's wrong?"*

Evan had realized what he was doing, giving all the tells that made him look guilty as sin, that made him look like he had something to hide. Because he *did* have a secret to hide—though it wasn't about himself.

Paulette's husband, Antonio, had confessed to him a mere week before Dante's shooting that he had murdered Marques Whitney when he found out that Marques had blackmailed Paulette into giving him money and having an affair. Evan had been shocked by the revelation and immediately wondered if it had been prudent to let it slip to Antonio that Dante had also bullied and black-mailed Paulette, that the whole family would be more than happy to see Dante disappear.

Now that Dante had nearly been killed and the assailant hadn't been caught, Evan had started to wonder even more whether he'd made a mistake by blabbing about family drama to Antonio. In retaliation, in some misguided attempt to protect his wife and her family, had Antonio shot Dante, too?

"Detective Nola can't make heads or tails of his investigation. Frankly, I couldn't, either. But I find it awfully funny how people who cross the Mur-dochs end up in the hospital—*or dead,*" the detec-tive had observed with a smile before taking a sip from his coffee cup. "Don't you?"

Yes, I do, Evan had thought, but he didn't say it aloud.

Unable to get any more information out of Evan, Detective Morris had ended the interview soon after saying that he would keep in touch. Today it looked like he was following through with that promise.

"You can help me by telling me where you were at twelve thirty p.m. today," Detective Morris now said as he stood in front of Evan. He glanced up at Terrence and took another bite of his sandwich, spitting bits of wheat bread as he spoke. "You can tell me where you were, too."

That lupine smile was on his face again. He looked like the Big Bad Wolf who had just spotted two plump little pigs.

"I don't have to tell you shit!" Terrence snarled with a curl in his lip, not looking remotely intimidated by the detective. But Evan knew something Terrence didn't. He knew their family had something to lose.

"Terry," Evan said warningly to his little brother, shaking his head.

"No, Ev!" Terrence shouted. "These cops can't just barge up in here, harass your staff, eat your damn food," he said as he gestured to the detective's sandwich, "and start asking questions like we owe them somethin'. I don't care who the hell he is! Doesn't he need a fucking warrant or some shit to do this? We've got rights, man!" He glared at the detective. "I may be black, but my name's not Trayvon or Freddie! Fuck this shit!"

"Terry, calm down," Evan ordered, holding up his hand.

"You'd be smart to listen to your brother," the detective said. The smile had disappeared and was now replaced with a stony scowl. He tossed his ham sandwich aside so that it landed on Evan's marble console table, smearing it with mustard. "Don't let all that barking land you in handcuffs, boy! Your money can get you out of a lot of things, but this ain't one of them."

Evan watched as Terrence took a step forward, his face contorting with barely contained rage. Evan immediately placed a hand on his brother's chest, holding him back in more ways than one.

He knew when he was being baited into slipping up and doing something stupid, and this detective was dangling the ultimate lure by constantly referring to them as "boys," walking around Murdoch Mansion as if he owned the place, and having a dick-measuring contest with Terrence. But this wasn't Evan's first time at the rodeo; he had dealt with assholes like this before in the boardroom, just not in his foyer. He would remain calm and keep a level head though he was just as pissed as Terrence. He would do it—for his family's sake.

"Just tell us what this is about, Detective," Evan said evenly. "Maybe we can answer your questions if you explain to us why you're asking them."

"Oh, there's no 'maybe.' You're *both* gonna tell me where the hell you were this afternoon! It's probably no surprise to you that there was another attempt on your brother Dante Turner's life today. Someone tried to smother him with a pillow in his hospital room. He would've died if the doctor and nurses hadn't gotten to him in enough time."

"Damn," Terrence said with a snicker while casually leaning back against a newel post, "that dude's having a rough year."

"You find this funny?" the detective spat, scrutinizing Terrence again.

"Yeah, kinda," Terrence said with a shrug. "I sure as hell didn't try to kill him, but as far as I'm concerned, he's getting what he deserves. Dante's made plenty of enemies from the shit he's done. You've probably got a long line of people who'd want to take him out."

"*Including you?*" The detective took a menac-

ing step toward Terrence. "He represented a
woman who filed a lawsuit against you not too
long ago, am I right? That sounds a lot like mo-
tive to me. Were *you* anywhere near Wilson Medical Center at twelve thirty today?"

"No," Evan answered for his brother. "Terry
and I were at a doctor's office in Arlington. I'm
sure several people in the waiting room, the receptionist, and the ocularist himself can vouch for our
alibis." He reached into his jeans pocket and pulled
out a business card. "Here's the number to the ocularist. Ask him yourself if you don't believe me."

The detective leaned back and fixed his eyes on
Evan. Evan could see Terrence's mouth twitch,
like he was holding back a laugh. The detective
stared down at the card extended to him, then
snatched it out of Evan's hand.

"I'll give him a call," he mumbled.

"Yeah, you do that," Terrence said, sucking his
teeth.

"You know," the detective said, still gazing down
at the laminated card, "I asked around town about
you, Evan Murdoch."

"Did you now?"

Detective Morris nodded. "I most certainly did.
I like to know who and what I'm dealing with when
I'm conducting my investigations," the detective
explained. "A lot of folks in Chesterton admire
you. They say you're a good businessman . . . an
honest guy. But frankly, I don't think any man who
gets to where you've gotten in this world can do it
without getting his hands a little dirty, without
doing some things that aren't so honest." He glow-

ered at Evan again, boring into him like a hand drill. "I don't think you shot Mr. Turner or tried to kill him today, but I *do* think you know who did it. I think there's something you're not telling me."

Evan swallowed, ordering himself to control his breathing, to control his features so that he didn't reveal anything, but he felt like a hot spotlight was shining down on him, showing every flaw in the mask he was wearing.

Don't break, he told himself. *Don't you dare break!*

He couldn't be the reason Antonio went to jail. Paulette needed her husband and her infant son, Nate, needed his father. Evan would be damned if he was the one who helped destroy their family.

"I'm sorry," he finally answered, "but I don't know what you mean, Detective."

The detective chuckled and pointed the card at Evan. "Oh, I think you do! And at some point, you'll be ready to talk. Until then . . ."

He didn't finish. Instead, he abruptly turned away and walked toward the oversize French doors.

"We're done here!" the detective barked over his shoulder to the two uniformed police officers. They seemed to reluctantly follow him across the foyer.

Evan and Terrence watched as the detective and the officers opened the door and left, slamming the front door behind them.

Terrence whipped around to face his brother. "What the fuck was that?"

"He doesn't know who's trying to take out Dante, so he came to us. That's all. If he was with the Chesterton sheriff's office, I would have told the sheriff to call off his dog by now. But he's state police. I've got no connections over there."

Terrence waved his hand in a shooing motion. "I'm not talking about him. Fuck that redneck! I'm talking about *you*, Ev! Why'd you act so . . . so strange?"

"What do you mean? I wasn't acting strange."

"Yes, you were! You went robotic as hell! I know that look. That's the look you get when you're lying. You don't know who shot Dante, *do you?*"

Evan paused. It was on the tip of his tongue to tell Terrence the truth, to pull him aside into his nearby study, shut the door, and unload everything he knew and everything he secretly suspected. But he didn't want to drag his little brother into this. He hadn't even told Paulette that she was sharing a home with a murderer—even if Antonio had murdered in order to avenge her. He couldn't place a burden this big on Terrence's shoulders. With his recovery from his accident, Terrence had enough to deal with. No, Evan would carry this burden alone.

"Of course not," he lied. "That detective is just beating bushes, seeing what scuttles out. I guess I'm the best lead he has, but he's wasting his time. I didn't do it and I don't know who did."

Terrence still didn't look convinced.

"I swear," Evan added halfheartedly as an after-thought.

"Okay, Ev," Terrence murmured.

"It'll be fine." He clapped his brother on the shoulder. "Don't worry. They'll find whoever did it and this'll all blow over. In the meantime, you focus on your recovery and on keeping C. J. happy so she doesn't dump *your* ass."

Evan knew by saying Terrence's girlfriend's name he had uttered the magic word. All talk of Dante, secrets, and murder was a forgotten memory. Terrence smiled.

"I *would* focus on her if she were here. She's in North Carolina doing another meet-and-greet with her dad at his megachurch."

"*Again?*"

Terrence nodded and rolled his eyes. "Don't get me started! She's down there so much I only get to see her on the weekends. It's taking up so much of her time that she had to take a sabbatical from the newspaper."

Evan laughed. "Well, that's not such a bad thing. You know how I feel about her reporting."

C. J. had been a hard-hitting investigative journalist before she and Terrence hooked up. While working at the *Chesterton Times*, C. J. had written several far from complimentary stories about Murdoch Bank and Murdoch Conglomerated, even going so far as following Evan around to get an interview for one of her pieces. He had no idea the day he threatened her with a restraining order that she would one day be Terrence's lady.

Life is strange like that, I guess, Evan inwardly mused.

"Look, I'll let you get to work," Terrence said, walking toward the front door. "I know you. It's Saturday, but you've probably got some conference call or meeting scheduled, right?"

Evan nodded. "I've got a call at three thirty, actually."

Terrence grabbed the door handle. "I figured. Peace out!" He paused just after swinging open the front door. "And uh, thanks for going to that appointment with me. I won't fake. I probably wouldn't have gone through it without you being there."

Evan shook his head. "It's no big deal, Terry. You knew I would. All you had to do was ask."

Because he would do anything for his family— including telling a little white lie about a murder.

Terrence nodded and waved before stepping into the afternoon sunshine and shutting the door behind him.

Chapter 2

Leila

"All right," Paulette Murdoch said, adjusting her dark-tinted sunglasses and her glossy curls. She pulled to a stop in between the orange cones in front of the Chesterton Country Club and then turned to Leila. "Are we ready?"

Leila gnawed her pink lower lip as she gazed across the asphalt driveway to the country club's glass doors. She felt queasy, and for once she was sure she wasn't nauseated due to her pregnancy. She was finally past the first trimester—that annoying period when she was always rushing to the nearest restroom to puke or pee. She knew her queasiness today had more to do with nerves than anything else. She glanced at her future sister-in-law. "Maybe we could . . . uh . . . skip the whole committee meeting," she whispered, rubbing at the fluttering in her stomach that was either nerves or the baby—or both. Leila watched as Paulette smiled.

"You'll be fine, Lee. Really, don't worry!"

Easy for you to say, Leila thought ruefully.

Paulette had grown up with or knew socially most of the women on Chesterton Country Club's fund-raising committee. And she was one of the M&Ms, the Marvelous Murdochs. The Murdochs were one of, if not *the*, richest and most esteemed family in Chesterton. Even if people disliked Paulette, they knew it was better to keep those feelings to themselves or, at the very least, not say anything within earshot of her or her brothers.

But Leila hadn't grown up that way. She had grown up poor and, after much hard work, moved up to middle class when she got older. And she wasn't even a Murdoch—technically. She may have been engaged to and having a baby with one but she knew no one had a problem gossiping about her. She knew everyone in town saw her as Evan's live-in mistress and suspected she would be met with open disdain from some of the women today.

So why am I even doing this?

She'd rather be hanging out with her eight-year-old daughter, Isabel, who had run away not too long ago, only to be found wandering around Dulles International Airport hoping to catch a flight across the country to see her father. Leila knew her time with Isabel was precious. She longed to redevelop the stable relationship with her daughter they had once had. Or, if she wasn't with Isabel, Leila would rather be working on one of the elaborate invitations she handcrafted for her clients, poring over paper samples, ribbons, and typefaces. Hell, she'd rather be sitting on the couch in a T-shirt and a pair of Evan's old gym shorts, stuffing her face with butter pecan gelato and watching a marathon of the television show *Empire!* But she was here instead, about to put herself through this ordeal because she wanted to be a true partner to Evan, and that meant being part of his world. Unfortunately, his world included hobnobbing with snooty, judgmental rich folks like the ones she'd meet today.

Leila watched as the valet walked toward the driver's side door. Her grip on her leather handbag tightened as he swung the door open. Paulette climbed out of her Mercedes and Leila reluctantly opened her door and climbed out, too. The valet nodded and handed Paulette her ticket while Leila waited, adjusting the hem of her plum-colored maternity dress, which she had been forced to wear today because none of her other dresses fit anymore.

"Stop fussing with your clothes. You look amazing," Paulette told her.

"I feel fat," Leila said, still tugging at her dress. She then peered at her reflection in the gleaming car door. "I *look* fat!"

"You look *pregnant,* which is what you are. Come on!"

She then linked her arm through Leila's. Leila grumbled.

"Lee, if I'm not nervous, you shouldn't be," Paulette whispered as they walked arm in arm out of the sweltering August sun that was baking the asphalt driveway to the shaded brick pathway leading to the entrance. "Remember, you weren't the one who gave birth to a baby boy when no one knew you were even pregnant." She sighed and patted her stomach and the scars from her emergency caesarian. "I'm sure they had a good ol' time gossiping about that one."

Paulette had given birth to her son, Nate, less than a month ago, after hiding her pregnancy from everyone—including her husband. She had done it because she didn't know the paternity of the baby, whether it belonged to her husband, Antonio, or her blackmailing ex, Marques. As far as Leila could discern, Paulette *still* didn't know for sure who the father was. But Antonio didn't seem to mind.

"But you know what, Lee, after having Nate, it put all this stuff in perspective. I could have lost him in childbirth. Tony could have divorced me," she confessed as they walked down a series of walnut-paneled corridors lined with gold award plaques and portraits showing the founders of Chesterton Country Club and their families. "But that stuff didn't happen, and I'm forever grateful. Nate was released from the NICU last week, and Tony and I are stronger than ever! I thank God every day for sparing me, for sparing *us.* I'm a changed woman, Lee! I don't care about my reputation and what people think about me anymore. I don't have to prove myself to them—and neither do you!"

Leila absently nodded. Out of the corner of her eye, she spotted a portrait on the wall set off by itself and lit from below. It was of a man who looked very familiar. She looked again more closely. He was pale with hazel eyes and a black handlebar mustache. He leaned against a stone fireplace mantel with a wooden-and-ivory pipe in his hand. He bore a striking resemblance to Evan's late father, George Murdoch. The name plaque read, "The Venerable Judge Thomas J. Murdoch, First Chair of the Chesterton Country Club, 1919–1923."

Leila released a beleaguered breath as Paulette continued to speak. Of course Paulette didn't have to prove herself to any of these women—her damn great-great-grandfather was the granddaddy of the whole place!

They climbed a carpeted staircase and entered a large, sun-filled banquet room where more than two dozen women stood around a long table laughing and chatting with one another. The combined smells of their expensive perfumes permeated the space, burning Leila's nose and making her nauseated all over again.

Less than a year ago, Leila had been in this room serving as Evan's assistant, meticulously checking every detail and making sure all the party guests were happy. This time she was one of the guests, and she didn't know what to do with herself.

"Let me introduce you to everyone," Paulette said, guiding Leila to where a group of women stood.

Meanwhile, Leila fought the urge to go running back out the door.

"Sonya, hi! How have you been?" Paulette called

out, making one of the women turn—a slim, dark-skinned woman with a gray bob who was wearing a trim red suit.

"Paulette, sweetheart!" the woman gushed. "I haven't seen you in ages!"

They leaned forward and kissed each other's cheeks with a practiced air that was almost amusing, letting their lips hover millimiters away from their skin so that neither smeared lipstick on the other's cheek.

"How have you been?" The woman took a step toward her and dropped her voice down to an exaggerated whisper. "I was so shocked when I heard you had a baby, honey! I didn't even know you were pregnant!"

"Oh, I'm fine, just fine," Paulette answered breezily, not missing a beat. "Enjoying new motherhood." She then turned to Leila. "Let me introduce you to Leila Hawkins, Sonya. She's my brother Evan's fiancée, a long-time family friend, and she's joining our committee."

Sonya turned to Leila and slowly looked her up and down.

Leila could tell by the woman's assessing gaze that she already knew who she was, but mercifully, she pretended that she didn't know her for Paulette's sake. She extended her hand. "Pleasure to meet you."

"Same here," Leila said, shaking her hand stiffly.

And that's how the introductions went for the rest of the afternoon. As she and Paulette made their way around the banquet room, some of the women seemed genuinely pleased to meet Leila, but most fixed her with a withering stare or a barely contained aloofness that let her know what they thought about her. She silently told herself to keep a far distance from those women.

"Okay, everyone," Tilda, the committee chair, called out while standing at the head of the table. She was so willowy thin that her hips seemed to jut through the fabric of her off-white pencil skirt. "Grab a chair, ladies! Grab a chair! Enough socializing! We should finally get down to business."

The women did as Tilda ordered. The cacophony of voices in the room finally quelled to a soft murmur as all of them took their leather-padded seats. Leila took the chair next to Paulette at the long oak table. As she sat down, the door to the banquet room was flung open. Leila glanced toward the doorway and blinked in surprise as she watched a tall blonde in a pale blue sundress and gray stilettos glide into the room. Leila's throat tightened. Her body temperature shot up by about two degrees.

"What the hell is she doing here?" Paulette whispered, gaping.

They both watched in horror as Evan's wife, Charisse, walked toward the gathering while whipping off her sunglasses. Charisse pulled out the chair directly across from Leila and Paulette and loudly dropped her ostrich-skin handbag onto the tabletop.

"I'm not late, am I?" she asked, sitting down.

"Of . . . of course not, Charisse," Tilda replied nervously, glancing between her and Leila. "You're . . . you're right on time! The m-m-more the merrier!"

"Good," Charisse said flatly before glaring at Leila.

Leila forced herself to stare right back at her.

The table fell silent, like everyone was witnessing two gunslingers in a Mexican standoff.

Paulette had told Leila that there was no chance Charisse would be here today.

"Charisse hasn't been to any of the committee meetings in more than a year, and even then she only half-assed it when she was there," Paulette had confessed a week ago. "Charisse was so hung over most of the time that I don't think she even realized what the hell was going on."

Knowing Charisse wouldn't show up was the only reason Leila had agreed to come to the country club today. She didn't want to cause any drama or give the town gossips more to gossip about, but it looked like she and Charisse would be doing just that.

"Well," Tilda resumed, looking down at a sheet of paper in front of her. "I think we should . . . uh . . . address the first item on our agenda, namely the florist for the Thanksgiving—"

Charisse loudly cleared her throat and raised her hand. "Excuse me, Tilda. Before we start on the agenda, can I ask something?"

Tilda halted and began to tensely twirl the fountain pen in her hands. "Uh, s-sure, Charisse. What would . . . would you like to ask?"

"It was my understanding that committee membership was limited to members of the country club, their children, and their *wives*," she said, putting an emphasis on the last word. "Have the rules for committee membership changed as of late?"

Leila gritted her teeth. She knew where Charisse was going with this.

"Well, uh . . . no. N-no, I don't believe so," Tilda answered.

"So can I ask," Charisse continued, casually tossing her blond locks over her shoulder, "what Leila Hawkins is doing sitting at this table?"

The entire room fell eerily silent. Several eyes widened. One of the women hid a smile behind her hand.

"She's here because I invited her," Paulette answered tightly.

"You may have invited her," Charisse said, puckering her collagen-injected lips, "but as Tilda just confirmed, Leila is not eligible for committee membership. She is neither a member nor the child of a member, and she certainly isn't *married* to any member of the country club! She shouldn't be here."

"You are one petty bitch, Charisse," Paulette snapped, making several around her do a quick intake of breath.

Even Leila stared at Paulette in amazement. Maybe there was something to Paulette's assertion that she was a changed woman. She never would have said something like that a month ago.

Charisse released a caustic laugh. "Guilty as charged! But I'd rather be a petty bitch than a whore . . . which is what you have sitting beside you."

This time, Leila shoved herself up from the table. Her nostrils flared. *"Excuse me?"*

She would put up with many things in the name of love—would go out of her way to show support for Evan—but she wouldn't be openly disrespected by the likes of Charisse.

Charisse wanted to play the scorned woman, but she had conveniently forgotten that she had openly loathed her husband before they had separated and had been happy to have a marriage in name only. She forgot about that reckless affair she'd had with Evan's half-brother, Dante, long before Evan and Leila's affair had even started. Charisse and Dante had even *continued* their affair after Leila had broken things off with Evan when she refused to be the other woman in his life.

"Ladies! *Ladies*!" Tilda shouted, frantically banging her palm against the table as voices of discord rose around her. "This is a country club, *not* a nightclub! Please show some class, some decorum. Don't . . . please don't use language like that in here!"

"Allowing that woman in here shows no class, Tilda!" another shouted. "Charisse is right. Leila Hawkins shouldn't be here!"

"Oh, you're one to talk, Candy! We all know what *you* do behind closed doors," someone countered, making Candy's mouth drop open with outrage.

The shouts grew louder. Charisse sat in her chair, looking so smug that Leila wanted to slap the smile right off her face. She was seconds away from marching around the table and doing just that when a voice called out, "I motion that we open committee membership!"

Several of the women fell silent at the sound of that voice. Leila stared at the front of the table and realized that it was the pretty, petite woman sitting next to Tilda who had said those words. Leila recognized her as Lauren Gibbons-Weaver, the wife of Crisanto Weaver, the mayor of Chesterton.

"I think we should allow anyone to become a member who's invited to join," Lauren said. "It seems incredibly antiquated and cumbersome to place those kinds of restrictions on committee membership. It's hard enough to get members to join and stay active as it is."

"But what about *tradition*?" one of the older women squawked, making her double chin tremble. "We've had these bylaws in place for . . . for decades!"

"And some traditions are made to be broken," Lauren said, shrugging her silk-clad shoulders. "As vice chair of the committee, I motion that we change the bylaws to open up membership. I say we deal with this right now and put it to a vote. Those for the change?" she asked, raising her small hand.

Paulette's hand shot up, too.

Leila could see that several of the women hesitated, looking between the mayor's wife, whom they wanted to stay in the good graces of, and Charisse, who looked utterly furious at the change of events.

Ever so slowly, another hand pointed to the ceiling, then another. They gradually increased in number. Leila fell back into her chair, shocked to see how many hands were up.

Lauren smiled. "That looks like majority of the vote. Good! Now let's get back to the agenda and focus on what we're really here for."

Leila grinned, basking in the afterglow of victory, using it as a shield to fend off the arrows Charisse was now mentally shooting at her from across the table.

"Well, I guess we covered everything," Tilda said more than an hour later. "This meeting of the Chesterton Country Club fund-raising committee is adjourned!"

"Thank God," Paulette whispered as several of the women at the table began to rise from their chairs and the swell of conversations filled the reception room again. She tiredly rubbed her temples. "I need a drink after that debacle, but I'm breastfeeding Nate, so I guess I'll have to settle for an aspirin instead." She turned to Leila. "Well, we survived! Ready to get the hell out of here?"

Leila nodded and tossed the strap of her purse over her shoulder. "Sure, right after I do one quick thing, though."

"Okay. While you do that I'm going to call home to check on Nate," Paulette said, reaching into her purse for her phone. "I haven't gotten any panicked calls from Tony or my mother-in-law, but I just want to make sure."

Leila nodded, then walked down the length of the table, ignoring the frigid glares some of the women shot her as she passed. She tapped Lauren on the shoulder. The other woman was gathering her things and whispering something to Tilda.

When she saw Leila, she rewarded her with a stunning smile.

"Hello, Ms. Hawkins, how can I help you?" Lauren asked.

"Oh, you've helped enough!" Leila gushed. "Please call me Leila, and thank you so much for doing what you did. I wasn't expecting it at all!"

"Don't mention it," Lauren said, shaking her head and waving her hand. "My husband and Evan are friends. Evan helped Crisanto during his mayoral election. Plus"—she stood on the balls of her feet and leaned toward Leila's ear—"I know what it's like to be the odd girl out around here. I still am some days. These sanctimonious, hypocritical bitches can put you through the ringer, girl! But don't let it get you down." She leaned back and chuckled.

Leila joined her in her laughter. She watched as Lauren glanced down at her waist.

"Congratulations on the baby, by the way. I bet Evan is so excited," Lauren said. "It'll be his first, right?"

"Yep!" Leila nodded. "And excited is putting it lightly. He's ecstatic to become a dad."

"I bet he is! Is it a boy or a girl?"

Leila dropped her hand to her stomach and cradled the burgeoning lump growing there. "We don't know yet. We find out next week at my next appointment."

"Well, congratulations again and welcome to the committee, Leila!" She offered Leila her hand for a shake.

"Thank you," Leila said, shaking her hand. She then watched as Lauren waved and turned to head across the room. Leila turned also to walk back toward Paulette, feeling a lot better now than she had when she strode into the country club. As she turned, she ran smack into Charisse, who stood behind her with her arms crossed over her chest and a sneer on her lips. When Leila saw her, her smile faded. Her bright mood darkened.

"What do you want?" she snarled.

"So it seems you've got an ally now," Charisse said. She shrugged. "I'm not surprised. With the reputation Lauren has, you two should be like two peas in a pod. She comes from a family of gold-digging whores, after all, and she was one for many years until she managed to latch onto Mayor Weaver."

Several women were staring at them again. The added attention made Leila even more furious.

"Look, I'm going to keep it classy because of where we are," Leila whispered, "but don't keep coming at me like this, Charisse. I know what you are and *everything* that you've done! You keep throwing around that word, calling people whores, but I'd be careful using it if I were you. If I'm a whore, then so the hell are you!"

"That may be true. But you see, Leila," she said, taking another step toward her, "I'm a *married* whore and you're just the whore who managed to get knocked up by a very rich man—and that's all you'll ever be. He's never going to marry you."

"Is that what you've been telling yourself? That he'll never marry me?" Leila shook her head in disgust. "I hate to break it to you, but Evan does want us to get married, Charisse. He wants it more than anything!"

"Really?" She chuckled.

"*Yes,* really! He's done with the lie that you guys called a marriage, and as soon as you sign those goddamn divorce papers—"

"Oh, Evan didn't tell you?" Charisse raised her brows with mock innocence. "I'm not giving him a divorce. I told him in unequivocal terms that whatever settlement he offers me, I'm dismissing it. I did it more than a month ago."

Leila paused. Her stomach dropped. Evan hadn't mentioned a damn thing to her! She knew Charisse was dragging her feet, but he hadn't told her his wife had outright refused the divorce.

"I'm going to hold out as long as I possibly can, filing motions and counter motions, and if a judge finally decides to grant Evan a divorce, I'll simply file an appeal with a higher court. You will *never* be his wife, Leila. You will *never* take my place. Either he'll give up on the idea or you will. I'll make sure of it. I will make your life a living hell, and I'm only getting started."

She then primly raised her nose into the air and walked around Leila with hips swaying and the hem of her dress swishing around her long legs. She strode toward the door, leaving Leila stupefied.

"What the hell did she have to say to you?" Paulette asked, snapping Leila out of her daze.

Leila turned to Paulette and sighed, rubbing her belly again. "Oh, nothing," she muttered. "Nothing short of saying she's starting a war with me."

Chapter 3

Terrence

Terrence awoke to the sound of pounding thunder and the chime of his doorbell followed by a wall-rattling knock at his front door. He frowned as he raised his head from his pillow. He pushed himself up on his elbows and stared out his partially drawn curtains at the torrential rain outside his window. Terrence turned, bleary-eyed, to look at the alarm clock on his night table. It was a little after one a.m., *way* too late for a visit and for someone to be making such a ruckus.

"Who the hell . . ." he grumbled as he threw back his sheets and staggered to his feet. He reached for his eye patch that sat adjacent to his alarm clock and quickly put it on. His new prosthetic eye shield floated in a solution on his bathroom counter.

The doorbell rang yet again, this time in quick succession, like someone was holding their finger on the button.

"I heard you!" he shouted irritably, though his voice was drowned out by the chimes.

Terrence took unsteady steps out of his bedroom and down the hall. His wobbly gait wasn't due to the bad leg that he had injured in his car crash. With the exception of a barely discernible limp, he walked perfectly fine. No, it had more to do with the veil of sleep that was still hanging over him. He stumbled into the edge of his coffee table at one point, cursing to himself and grabbing his shin.

Finally, Terrence reached the front door. The person on the other side of the door was now knocking and ringing the bell simultaneously.

"This better be goddamn important!"

For a fleeting moment, he wondered if it had something to do with Dante again. Did someone try to kill that bastard a *third* time? He undid the locks and threw the door open. "What the hell is . . ."

When he realized who was standing in front of him, his lethal rant died on his lips. His anger dissipated. *"C. J.?"*

His girlfriend waved at him timidly and gave a small smile. "Hi, Terry." She glanced down at his pajama bottoms and then raised her gaze to his bare chest. Her smile faded. "Oh, I'm sorry, honey! Were you sleeping?"

He chuckled in exasperation and tiredly wiped his hand over his face. "Of course I was sleeping, babe! It's one o'clock in the damn morning! The way you were ringing my doorbell I thought something was really wrong! I thought you might be the cops."

She squinted at him in confusion. "Why would I be the cops?"

"Forget it." He waved his hand dismissively, not wanting to get into what had happened that day with Detective Morris at his brother's home. "It's a long story and not one worth retelling."

"Well, anyway, I'm sorry if I scared you," she said, shrugging out of her raincoat.

"You don't have to apologize." He gestured her inside his condo. "Why didn't you tell me you were coming?"

"I thought I might surprise you. The thing I had to do today in North Carolina ended a lot earlier than I thought it would. I thought I'd drive up here . . . you know . . . stop by and visit you for a few hours since we haven't seen each other in days."

She stepped through the doorway, set down a small overnight bag on the floor, and handed him her coat, revealing a prim gray suit and pink blouse underneath. Her hair was done in a simple bun at the nape of her neck.

Terrence tried not to cringe at or comment on her conservative look. Instead, he turned and opened the coat closet door. The truth was he much preferred C. J. in a tank top and jeans or negligee and a thong, but she wore her church lady clothes all the time now to appease her family, or, more specifically, her father, the esteemed Reverend Pete Aston, a.k.a. the sanctified hypocrite.

"I thought I could make it here by nightfall," C. J. continued, facing him after he hung up her coat. She stared at him sheepishly. "A bad traffic jam on the interstate and the rain kinda shut down those plans, though. Sorry."

"I told you, you don't have to apologize." He closed the front door and locked it. He grinned. "I'm glad you're here. I missed you."

"I missed you too, baby," she whispered.

They gazed at each other. He made a move to reach for her, to give her the kiss and the hug that he had been longing to give all week, but she lunged forward, spun him around, and shoved him back against the door before planting her lips on his.

"Goddamn," he murmured against her hungry mouth as she wrapped her arms around his neck and seared him with one heated kiss after another. She tore her mouth away, then licked his ear before nipping his ear lobe.

"Goddamn," he moaned. She took a step back and began to unbutton her suit jacket. She tossed it aside, then yanked open her blouse, sending pearl buttons flying in all directions and landing on Terrence's rug and hardwood floor.

He stared at her in amazement—and with sheer lust.

"I missed you a lot, Terry," she said as she kissed him again, "so, *so* much."

This time, he kissed her back just as fiercely, helping her take off her shirt while pulling down the zipper of her skirt.

"Let's finish this in the bedroom," he ordered

huskily as he tugged her skirt over her hips and down her legs. It pooled at her feet and she kicked it aside.

"No, I can't wait that long. Let's finish it here," she whispered back before tugging his bottom lip between her teeth. She then took his hand and led him toward his leather sofa.

Terrence cocked an eyebrow and allowed himself to be steered across his foyer and through his living room.

It was hard to believe that a little more than a month ago C. J. had been a timid, twenty-six-year-old virgin.

"I have to be eased into this," she had told him then, and Terrence had thoroughly enjoyed doing just that, introducing her to every carnal pleasure that came with foreplay and eventually sex. Watching her now take the reins made him a proud teacher. It also made him a horny one.

She had stripped down to a black lace bra, thong, and thigh-highs, finishing the ensemble with prim high heels, a simple string of pearls around her neck, and her bun, making her look like a naughty librarian. His eyes focused on her plump brown ass as she walked, and he reached out and squeezed it, but she quickly batted his hand away while giving him a saucy wink.

"Ah-ah! Not yet. Sit down first," she said, motioning toward his leather sofa.

This time he raised both eyebrows. "Are you asking me or telling me?"

Instead of answering him, she stepped forward and kissed him again, letting her tongue slide enticingly across his lips and inside his mouth. "What do you think?"

"I think I don't care either way," he said as she placed her hands on his chest and shoved him back onto the couch. He landed with his arms out-stretched and with an audible *oomph*.

Her brow wrinkled with concern. "I didn't hurt your leg, did I? Do we need to stop?"

"Hell no!" He reached up and pulled her down so that she fell on top of him, making her giggle. She straddled his lap and evidence of his arousal jutted eagerly between her thighs.

She kissed him again. "You know I've been fan-tasizing about doing this *all* day," she whispered as she reached behind her and unclasped her bra. "I've played it out over and over again . . . the things I wanted to do to you . . . and for you to do to me."

She languidly tugged her bra straps off her shoulders, removing the lace cups with a slow ease that was almost torturous before finally tossing the entire bra to the other side of his living room, where it fell near his coffee table. She sat in front of him, glorious, beautiful, and topless, and it took all Terrence's willpower not to throw her back on the leather cushions and shove his dick into her at that very moment.

"I thought about it even during the meeting at church," she said as she ground her pelvis against his erection, subjecting him to yet another form of delicious torture. "Sister Walters started staring at me. I started to get paranoid that she could read my mind." She held his face and lightly kissed his nose, mouth, and cheeks. "I was worried she'd put her healing hands on me to get the devil out."

He gazed at her breasts, leaned forward, and flicked his tongue across one of her hardened nipples, making her moan. He grinned. "Well, I guess we'd better do everything you fantasized about so you don't have those kinky thoughts in church again."

He then took the entire nipple into his mouth and began to suckle her. He eased aside her thong and used his expert hand and fingers to make her wet between the thighs, massaging her clit with a mix of brisk and slow strokes. She let out a guttural growl that sounded almost like a purr, telling him he was definitely on the right track.

Terrence shifted his attention to the other breast, this time lightly clamping the nipple between his teeth, making her subdued moans become even louder.

C. J. may have been reserved in other aspects of her life, but she certainly wasn't in bed. He figured his condominium neighbors had heard her screams enough times by now that they weren't fazed by them anymore.

He felt her hips begin to move rhythmically against his fingers, much like they did whenever she made love to him. C. J. closed her eyes and arched her back, enjoying every second of what he was doing.

He was enjoying it just as much as she was, feeling her tense and squirm against him, watching how he was pushing her to the edge. Even from the early days when he first started tutoring her about lust and desire, checking off the long list of

sexual pleasures they could enjoy together, he had
always loved watching her face and her body at moments like this, seeing her lose control just before
she came.

And he had every intention of letting her
come, of seeing her ride the wave as he guided her
to climax, but she turned the tables on him. She
reached down, pulled back the waistband of his pajama pants, wrapped her hand around his dick, and
began to stroke him. The move caught him completely by surprise.

Terrence's breathing deepened. His heart
began to thud wildly in his chest and his blood
started to whistle in his ears. He stopped massaging
her, no longer able to focus on pleasing her anymore. Instead, he sank further and further into the
haze of pleasure she was giving him.

"I thought about this all day, Terry," she
breathed into his ear. "Show me what I was fantasiz-
ing about. Don't hold back," she urged before nipping his ear again, then trailing her wet tongue
along his neck. "I can take it."

And that's when he lost it—lost the measured
control he had been tenuously holding on to.

He shoved her back onto the adjacent cushion
and sat himself between her legs, kneeling on the
carpet in front of the sofa. He tossed one of her
calves over his shoulder and wrapped the other leg
around his waist. He then roughly tugged the
crotch of her thong aside before plunging inside
her over and over again.

Instead of being taken aback by his roughness,
C. J. grinned with naughty delight. She began to

move her hips again, meeting him thrust for thrust, lifting her bottom so that it was almost completely off the couch cushion. She keened and moaned.

"Is this what you wanted, baby?" he asked, driving even harder, grabbing onto her hips and pounding into her, loving the warm, wet feel of her around him. "Huh? Is this what you wanted?"

She couldn't answer him. She could only respond with another strangled moan and a shout that made him smile.

He could see she was almost there, and thank God she was, because he didn't know how much longer he could hold this pace before he came. Her back began to arch even more and her thighs began to wobble. Her calf fell off his shoulder and her leg dangled limply to the side. He watched as her eyes rolled to the back of her head, as her mouth went slack before she shouted his name.

He came seconds later with a euphoric rush. He lowered his lips to hers as he did it, and she captured his groan of bliss and agony with her mouth. After a few more pumps of his hips, he wilted on top of her.

"Don't you dare fall asleep on me, Terry!" C. J. ordered an hour and a half later as they lay on his California king, sweaty, satiated, and snuggled beneath the Egyptian cotton sheets. "I haven't seen you in almost a week. I don't want to lie around watching you snore!"

Terrence chuckled and opened his weary eye.

"It's three o'clock in the morning, and we just had sex three times in less than two hours. A man's allowed to be a little bit tired."

She shifted so that she was lying on top of his chest and gazing down at him.

At that moment, she might look like an absolute mess to some but she seemed gorgeous to him. Her makeup was smeared and hair was no longer in a neat bun but was now disheveled, like she had been in a windstorm. And they had been in a bit of a windstorm—or at least, it felt like it from all the enthusiastic sex they'd enjoyed.

"*Talk* to me!" she whined playfully, making him laugh again. "Tell me what you've been up to. What'd I miss?"

He sighed gruffly. He just couldn't say no to this woman.

"Not much," he said with a yawn. "I almost got arrested yesterday."

She frowned. "You're joking, right?"

"Not really." He tucked his hands behind his head and reclined on the down pillows braced against his leather headboard. "Some asshole detective came to Evan's house, questioning us about our brother Dante, thinking he could bully a black man into saying something. I guess someone tried to kill Dante again."

"*Really?* A second time?" she asked, raising her brows, her face now alight with keen interest. "Are they closer to having a list of potential suspects for the first attempt or are they still just putting out feelers at this point?"

He rolled his eye heavenward. "Slow your roll,

Lois Lane! Remember, you don't work at the *Chesterton Times* anymore."

"I took a *break* from the *Chesterton Times*," she clarified, nudging his shoulder. "I didn't quit! And it's not like I'm whipping out my notebook, pen, and recorder, Terry. I'm just . . . just curious, that's all."

"Uh-huh," he replied dryly, knowing how her reporter's "curiosity" had caused friction in their relationship in the past. "Look, I don't know if they have any potential suspects, but the detective seemed to think we knew something . . . well, that *Evan* knew something."

She squinted. "Why Evan?"

He shook his head. "I don't know."

But that wasn't completely true. Terrence could sense, just like the detective, that Evan was hiding something about the shooting. He didn't know what it was, but a gnawing part of him suspected it was bad, *very* bad. He just hoped it wasn't something that could land his brother behind bars.

"That's odd," C. J. said, still frowning. "I hope it doesn't turn into anything."

"It won't. We both had alibis. Evan was with me at the ocularist's office. We were there all morning and most of the afternoon. We were there when that thing happened to Dante."

"Oh! Your appointment!" She broke into a smile. "I can't believe I forgot to ask about it. How did it go? Did you get your prosthesis?"

"Yeah."

"Well?" She pushed herself to her elbows and

sat up in bed beside him. "So let me see it then! Show it to me!"

"Babe, I am tired as hell. Can't we just—"

"Please, Terry. Just for a minute?" she asked, clasping her hands together and poking out her bottom lip. She then gave him the full blast of doleful puppy eyes. *"Pretty please?"*

Terrence hesitated. He was reluctant to put on the prosthesis, not because he was tired, but because he still wasn't sure what C. J.'s reaction would be when she saw him looking so much like his old self. Would her insecurities and worries about him and their relationship come back?

When they first started dating, C. J. reminded him of the man he once had been: a shallow, rich playboy who had literally walked right past her one day, almost hitting her with a door because he was more concerned with the model type he had on his arm. But the car accident and its aftermath had humbled Terrence. It had pummeled his ego and made him into a new man—a man he was finally proud of. He knew he had changed on the inside, but how would C. J. react if he looked like the old, shallow playboy again? Would she think they weren't compatible anymore? Would she seriously consider dumping *him*?

She laughed and placed a light kiss on his shoulder. "Come on! If you put it on, I won't ask you for anything else tonight. I'll leave you alone and let you sleep. I promise!"

After a few seconds, he reluctantly pushed himself up from the mattress and rose to his feet. "All right. Fine," he said, tossing off the bedsheets. "I'll let you see it. I'll be right back."

"If it's better than the view I'm looking at right now," she joked as she stared at his sculpted backside, "then I bet it looks amazing!"

He returned to the bedroom a minute later and when C. J. saw him, she gaped.

"Baby," she whispered breathlessly, pushing herself off the bed and walking naked across the room toward him. She raised her hand to his face and tenderly rested her palm on his cheek. "It looks so good!"

"It does, doesn't it?" he asked, relieved to see her happy.

"The doctor did a great job!" For some reason, tears were in her eyes. She cupped his face and kissed him. "I'm so happy for you, honey."

"You are?"

"Of course I am!" A lone tear trickled onto her cheek and down her chin, and he quickly wiped it away with his thumb. "Why wouldn't I be? I know you wanted this. I'm happy for you!" She sniffed and linked her arms around his neck. "We should celebrate!"

He gave her an impish smile and wrapped an arm around her waist, pulling her flat against him. "Give me a few hours to regain my strength and we can do that."

She giggled and shook her head. "Not *that* kind of celebrating! I mean the kind of celebrating that involves wearing clothes, maybe eating some dinner over candlelight."

"Okay. How about this coming weekend? I can

make reservations and take you out to a romantic dinner, and we can come back here later and celebrate my way."

"This weekend?" She grimaced and removed her hands from around his neck. "Sorry, baby, but I can't. Daddy has this thing on Saturday that I—"

Terrence sucked his teeth with annoyance, stopping her midsentence. He dropped his arm from around her and took a step back. "Damnit, C. J., when the hell are you *not* down there?"

"Terry, we talked about this," she began calmly, annoying him even more. "I told you my father was running for office now. Because of that and his church publicity crisis, I have to be in Raleigh more. You think I don't want to be here with you? *I do!* But I promised my family that I would—"

"But why can't you tell them no sometimes? I mean . . . Goddamn! You have a life, too!"

"Why are you yelling?"

"Because I'm trying to make a point! You need to stand up to your family, dammit!"

"Well, do you ever stand up to yours? Do you tell *your* family no? Of course not! You Murdochs always stick together!"

"Don't bring up my family! Don't turn this around on me! You know this shit is different!"

"No, it isn't!"

"Yes, it is! You know what your family—your father—is asking you to do. They're asking you to put on a fake smile and those ugly-ass church lady clothes and pretend to be the perfect preacher's daughter, to be part of the perfect Christian family! And you know it's all bullshit! What else are they gonna ask you to do, C. J.? Huh? When are you finally gonna put your foot down and say no?"

She bit down hard on her bottom lip, looking bewildered and hurt. "Terry, I didn't . . . I didn't come here to argue with you. I came here to see you, to *be* with you. I missed you, baby! Why are you trying to pick a fight with me? Why are you so angry?"

He lowered his head and rubbed the tense muscles along the back of his neck.

The truth was that Terrence wasn't angry at C. J. so much as he was angry at their circumstances.

"Sometimes people grow apart, Terry," Evan had told him today.

Terrence didn't want to admit it, but he could feel the distance growing between him and C. J., and that distance could be measured in more than the miles between Chesterton, Virginia, and her family's church in Raleigh. It was a lot wider than that. Things were changing. He was healing and getting back into the swing of things, regaining his old life. She was drawing closer to her old family circle, her old church, and more specifically her ex-fiancé Shaun Clancy, who still worked at Aston Ministries, serving as assistant pastor at the flagship church and functioning as one of her father's right-hand men.

C. J. hadn't mentioned Shaun tonight, but she had in the past, and every time she did Terrence's jaw would tighten. He would unwittingly clench his fists at his sides, like he was preparing for a fight. He just couldn't help himself.

C. J.'s father had been the one to coax her into

dating and getting engaged to Shaun six years ago, and he had almost succeeded in bullying her into marrying Shaun, too, until she finally woke up, rebelled, and fled the prison her family had constructed for her. Terrence worried if C. J. wasn't vigilant, if she didn't keep her guard up this time around, her family could play the same mind games and convince her to hook up with Shaun again.

That's not something she would do, Terrence would tell himself whenever that worry entered his mind. *Give her more credit than that!*

C. J. wouldn't fall prey to her family's manipulations again. She loved Terrence and he loved her. No one could come between them, no matter how much distance they had from each other.

So why did he still worry so much about the prospect of losing her?

"Do you want me to leave?" she now asked quietly, gazing up at him. "If we're just going to fight, I can go home . . . really. I don't want to—"

"No!" He took a deep breath, telling himself to get a grip. "No, I don't want you to go. I'm . . . I'm sorry," he whispered, taking her hand in his own. "I didn't mean to yell at you. I don't want to fight with you, either. It's just . . . it's just been a long day. I'm tired."

She nodded. "Okay, let's go to sleep then."

A few minutes later, they were nestled beneath the sheets again. C. J. placed a series of butterfly kisses on his neck and his chin before she burrowed into the crook of his arm, resting her head on his shoulder.

"'Night, Terry," she said before closing her eyes.

"Good night," he replied, extinguishing his night table light and dropping the bedroom into darkness. He told himself that his doubts would disappear and he would feel better when he woke up in the morning, but he knew in his heart that probably wasn't true.

Chapter 4

C. J.

"Good afternoon," C. J. said to the receptionist who sat behind the lacquer desk. On a wall behind the desk was a thirty-six-inch flat-screen television that displayed C. J.'s father's sermon from that morning. The camera briefly panned across the auditorium filled by more than nine thousand parishioners before zeroing in on her father's face doused with perspiration as he raced across the stage to the pulpit, leaving his audience captivated.

"Afternoon, Miss Aston," the young woman answered.

C. J. walked past the desk and headed down the plush carpeted corridor of Aston Ministries, listening to the mellow sound track of gospel music playing on hidden speakers overhead. Her high-heeled feet felt heavy with trepidation as she walked, and not just because she was headed to her brother Victor's office, a place she usually tried to avoid. She also was wary because she couldn't keep from replaying in her head her night and morning with Terrence. Every time she thought about it, it filled her with unease.

Even after they had taken a shower and made love yet again against the shower stall's mosaic tiles, even after she had dressed and done her hair, even after he had made them a breakfast of bacon and eggs that they had eaten standing at his kitchen counter, C. J. had still felt like something was off between them. Before heading out the door, she had given him a kiss good-bye, putting all her love and lust for him into her kiss, but she hadn't gotten the same in return. Something had held him back.

It was no secret Terrence was frustrated with her because she was gone so much. In the beginning she had found it flattering that Terrence wanted her around all the time, that he seemed to need her to be there at his side. She never thought that in their relationship *she* would be the one reassuring *him*; she thought it would be the other way around. After all, Terrence was the more experienced one in their relationship, having had a long list of past girlfriends, whereas C. J. could count all her boyfriends with two sad little fingers. He knew how relationships went much better than she did and could take the highs and lows in stride.

Terrence also knew that she was reluctant to play the role of prim and proper Courtney Jocelyn Aston again, but she had made a promise to her father that she would do so for the next few months, until he didn't need her to do it anymore. She had explained her reasons to Terrence, and he had seemed to accept those reasons—grudgingly.

So why is Terry still acting so weird? she wondered as she drew near Victor's office door.

He wasn't trying to push her away, was he? Rather than say aloud that things weren't working out anymore or that he was ready to move on to someone else, he was using some reverse psychology and forcing conflict, forcing her to break up with him.

No, he wouldn't do that, she thought. That was ridiculous and immature and totally unlike him. Terrence knew he could be honest with her. If he wanted to end it between them, all he had to do was say the words. It would break her heart, but she'd get over it. No, his sullenness and outright anger was due to something else—she could feel it. He just wasn't telling her what it was.

C. J. leaned her head through the opened doorway and gently rapped her knuckles on the door frame.

"Hey, Brian, is Victor in?" she called out, peering into the reception area, which featured a large desk, glass bookshelves, and several photos of her brother posing with his wife and son, Victor Jr. An adjacent wall featured photos of Victor with their father and a few celebrities who had appeared on Rev. Pete Aston's Sunday worship broadcast. A zebra-print rug took up the center of the floor. An oversize gold cross hung on the back wall.

Victor's assistant, Brian, looked up from a notepad he was holding, and he quickly set it aside along with his pencil. Seeing her enter the office, his strikingly handsome face broke into a smile.

"Mr. Aston is just finishing up a meeting, Courtney. It ran a little over, I think," Brian said.

She nodded and strolled into the room, glancing at his notepad as she neared his desk. She narrowed her eyes when she saw what he had been doing, sketching a child sitting on a sofa, backlit, holding a toy dump truck.

"Who's the little cutie?" she asked, pointing down at the drawing.

"My little brother, Sydney. He turned three last week."

"Well, he's adorable!"

"Thanks. He's a little terror, too. Mom caught him trying to finger paint on our collie."

C. J. laughed. "That drawing is really good. Where'd you learn to draw like that?"

Brian's olive-toned cheeks flushed crimson, and he bashfully lowered his dark eyes. "I didn't learn it. I've just . . . kind of done it all my life. I like to sketch. I do it mostly when I'm bored." He gazed around the cavernous office and sighed. "There isn't much to do here all day but answer phones and fetch coffee. It helps to pass the time, I guess."

"Maybe you could make a career out of it. Go to an art school and refine your talent," she said, sitting on the edge of his desk near a gold paperweight that, like everything else in the building, sported the emblem of Aston Ministries. "It might be worth trying. I'd hate to see all that," she said, gesturing down to the drawing again, "go to waste."

He shrugged and closed his notepad. "I thought

about it. There's this art college in Charlotte. I thought I might take a few classes, but . . ." His words drifted off.

"But . . . *what?*" she asked, raising her brows.

"Well, Victor . . ." He paused and seemed to catch himself. "I-I mean *Mr. Aston* said it would be a waste of time. He said the only guys who make money drawing pictures are the ones who do those caricatures at amusement parks, and you couldn't live on that."

C. J. fought the urge to roll her eyes. She wasn't surprised that her brother had tried to deter Brian from entering art college or pursuing his own dreams. He wouldn't want his boy toy to get too far away from him.

Brian was one of many pretty, young things that Victor kept on the side, despite the fact that he had a wife and son and projected the image of a straight, upstanding Christian who was the executive director of Aston Ministries. Her brother was an even worse hypocrite than her father had been before the old man learned better and changed his ways.

"Look," she said, leaning toward Brian and dropping her voice down to a whisper, "I know you think my brother has your best interest at heart, but I don't think he's the best person to give you advice on something like this."

Brian furrowed his brows. "What do you mean?"

"I mean, if you really want to do it, then *do it*! Don't let anyone, including my brother, tell you—"

She paused and looked up when Victor's office door opened. Her brother stood in the doorway, smiling—a rare sight. Beside him was another young man, just as tall, tan, lithe, and attractive as Brian.

Victor patted the young man on the shoulder as he exited his office and C. J. watched as Brian flinched. He then turned away from her and stared at his computer screen, like they hadn't been talking just seconds ago. He began to type on his keyboard.

"Thank you for stopping by, Diego," Victor said, his voice oozing with honey.

"Anytime, Mr. Aston," the young man answered with a grin before strolling across the office and passing Brian's desk. As he passed, C. J. rose to her feet and Brian glared up at Diego.

"Brian, I want you to schedule another appointment on my calendar with Diego next week," Victor said. "He'll tell you what time works best for him."

"Yes, Mr. Aston," Brian answered tightly.

"Courtney," Victor said, finally acknowledging his sister. His saccharine smile disappeared.

"Victor," she replied just as flatly before strolling across the reception area and into his office. She then took one of the armchairs facing his desk, adjusting her knee-length skirt as she sat.

"We missed you in church this morning," he said.

"I had something to do back in Chesterton. I couldn't make it back here in time for the service."

"Is that right?" he murmured as he shut his office door. "I noticed that you and Brian were talking just now."

"Spying, are we?"

"Not spying. Just observing what goes on in my office. What were you two talking about?"

"Oh, nothing! He mentioned that he had thought

about going to art school and getting a job as an artist—and that you told him it was a bad idea. I said I disagreed and that he should follow his heart."

"And why should he listen to you?" Victor gave a cold chuckle. "You followed your heart. How well did *that* turn out?"

She tensed in her chair. "I happen to like my life, Victor."

"I bet you do." He sneered as he walked behind his desk. "Look, I'm going to ask you to refrain from giving employment advice to my staff. He's my office assistant and I'd like it to stay that way."

"*Why?* Judging from who just walked out of your office, it looks like you've already lined up a new assistant," she taunted. "A fresh, young, pretty face to type your memos and give you coffee and . . . well . . . do *whatever else* Mr. Aston needs done around the office."

Victor paused halfway from pulling out his desk swivel chair and glared at her. "Watch it, Courtney."

"What?" she asked, feigning innocence. "I don't know what you mean."

"Cut the shit!" he snarled. "I know what you're insinuating. I'm not up to dealing with your bullshit today. That," he said, pointing to his office door, "was a business meeting. That's all it was!"

"*Oh, really?*" She crossed her arms over her chest. "Then why is your fly still open?"

He glanced down at his crotch and saw that the zipper of his slacks was, indeed, open and a bit of his shirttail was hanging out. His gritted his teeth and raised his zipper. He sat down behind his desk

as she bit the inside of her cheek, trying not to
laugh.

She suspected if she peeked behind her
brother's desk, she'd probably see two indenta-
tions in the carpet where Diego had been kneeling
minutes earlier—and not in prayer.

Victor shook his head. "You just *can't* help yourself, can you, Court?" he asked, reclining in his
chair. "You've always gotta poke and prod . . .
you've gotta be that squeaky wheel making all the
noise. I have no damn clue why Dad wanted you
back here so badly. He thinks having you here will
help him, but I knew you'd never toe the line."

"Oh, but I can! I can pretend just as well as you,
Victor. Except I'm willing to admit that it's an illu-
sion, and you insist on pretending that it isn't, like
I don't know who and what you really are."

"And what am I?" he asked, cocking an eyebrow.

She pursed her lips. "Something that I'm too
polite to say in a church."

At that, he did let out a genuine chuckle. He
grabbed a file folder on his desk and tossed it toward her. "Here's the dossier on the women's
group you'll be meeting tomorrow on Dad's be-
half. It gives a background on the chairwoman
and its members, and what you should focus on
during the meeting so that they'll endorse Dad
for his congressional run."

"You called me in here for this?" She reached
for the yellow folder and flipped it open, shuffling
through pages before staring at him. "You could've
just emailed this to me."

"Not really." He adjusted one of his gold cufflinks. "Now that Dad's running for office, we're getting a little more selective about what we discuss by email. Wouldn't want any sensitive exchanges to accidentally or intentionally get in the hands of your little reporter friends if they decided to start sniffing around here." He pointed at the folder. "That'll have to be shredded and bagged tomorrow, by the way. No paper trails."

C. J. let out a deep breath in frustration. Did her brother have a devious reason for doing *everything*?

"Got it. It will be shredded. Is that it?"

He nodded and she rose from her chair.

"Oh, and Court," he called out as she walked across the room to his door, making her pause again.

"What?"

"Don't fuck up and disappoint Dad tomorrow. He has enough on his plate with the congressional run and that bitch filing her bullshit fake paternity suit against him. Do what you're here for. *Stay* on message."

She didn't respond. Instead she walked out of Victor's office, slamming the door behind her.

Five minutes later, C. J. slumped back into the chair at her desk, kicked off her high heels, and flexed her painted toes. She had been given an office toward the end of the long corridor, one of the forgotten rooms that was usually used by interns and teleworkers, but it had become a refuge for her. It was a little oasis in the battleground that was now Aston Ministries with her brother at the helm, doing all his dastardly plans.

She'd had the facilities staff move out the battered boxes and empty file cabinets, the old fax machine and the discarded phones, and set up the room the way she wanted it. It was decorated in simple tones of cream, beige, and pale blue, with one desk, a bookshelf, and a love seat. Silver vases filled with fresh roses, hydrangeas, and dahlias were on the coffee table and windowsill, filling the room with their fragrance. There weren't many photos on her desk or shelves with the exception of one she had taken of Terrence not too long ago when he wasn't aware she was snapping the photo.

She now picked up the picture frame and ran her hand over the cool glass, tracing her fingers along his jaw line and brow, thinking again about him and wondering if she should call him to find out what was really going on between them.

She hesitated before she reached for her cell phone perched on her desk, but then she heard a knock at her office door. C. J. reluctantly set down the picture frame. She sat upright in her chair, forcing herself to put thoughts of Terrence aside for the time being.

"Come in!" she said.

Her door eased open with a loud creak and she stared in surprise when she saw Pastor Shaun Clancy standing in her doorway with his knuckle raised. He was wearing one of his impeccably tailored suits with the Aston Ministries pin prominently displayed on the lapel.

"Hey, Court," he said.

"H-hi, Shaun! How . . . how are you?" she asked nervously.

C. J. still didn't quite know how to behave around Shaun. How exactly was a woman supposed to talk to a man whom she'd left standing at the altar in front of three hundred–plus people?

At least things weren't as on edge between them anymore. A month ago, Shaun would have looked at her like he was trying to murder her with his eyes. Now he seemed a lot less hostile, though all conversations between them were still stilted. It was hard to believe they had once sat in movie theaters holding hands and sharing popcorn between them, that they had once planned to spend their lives together.

"Are you busy?" he asked, taking a step into her office. He scratched the back of his clean-shaven head, a gesture she knew from the past meant that he was also nervous. "Did I catch you at a bad time?"

"No. No, I'm not busy! It's . . . uh . . . a-a great time! H-how can I help you?"

He shoved his hand into his pockets. "I was just wondering if you've eaten yet. Would you like to grab some lunch?"

Her mouth fell open in shock. When she realized it had, she clamped it shut. "Lunch? You want to eat lunch with . . . with *me*?"

He nodded and gave a small smile. "Sure. Why not? There's this new place that opened up downtown that I've wanted to try. I heard they sell a mean chicken and waffles. I know that used to be your favorite."

"It still is," she answered softly, still stunned that he wanted to sit at a table and have a meal—with her.

"All right. I'll meet you in the lobby in . . . say, ten minutes then?"

Part of her wanted to say no. If having a conversation with him standing in her office doorway was awkward, she could only imagine how awkward it would be if she had to sit at a table for an hour or two. But then she reminded herself that she had walked out on him, that she had broken his heart. The very least he deserved was for her to agree to have lunch with him.

After some time, C. J. numbly nodded. "O-okay. Sure."

C. J. still felt a little numb thirty minutes later as they walked into a small restaurant in trendy Glenwood South. The restaurant, which was already crowded with lunchtime patrons, was designed to look like a packrat's dining room. It was filled with mismatched chairs, distressed wooden tables, hanging potted plants, and the walls were covered with kitschy collectable plates like you might find in a cat-owning grandma's curio cabinet. The hostess smiled as she showed C. J. and Shaun to their table, a small two-seater toward the back. Shaun pulled a chair out for C. J. and she thanked him before sitting down. He took the chair facing her.

"Your server will be with you shortly," the hostess said after handing them their menus.

The young woman turned to leave and head back to the front of the restaurant; C. J. had the irrational urge to ask the hostess—a total stranger—to stay. With the hostess around, C. J. and Shaun would have more to do than just glance clumsily at each other over the tops of their menus, which was exactly what they were doing right now.

C. J. studied Shaun as he read. He was an attractive man, though not like Brian, whose face was so flawlessly crafted it was almost beautiful, and he didn't have the rugged good looks, like Terrence, that made women do double takes.

No, Shaun had a noble face, one that projected authority and respect. It was the face that looked like it belonged on the back of a coin with some Latin phrase beneath it.

"Everything looks good," she said, scanning the list of entrees.

"It does," he murmured politely. "A lot of people at Aston Ministries have eaten here. It came highly recommended."

"*Oh?*"

He nodded.

The table then fell silent again.

"So how does it feel to be back home?" Shaun asked, mercifully ending the awkward silence between them. "How are you settling in?"

"Fine, but I'm not really back home. I mean . . . I stay at my parents' house during the week now, but I still live in Virginia. My apartment is there."

He frowned as he squeezed his lemon wedge into his water glass and took a sip. "That seems like an awfully long commute to have to make every week. Why not just move back here to Raleigh?"

"Well, this is only temporary. I still have a life back there. I have my job and . . . and friends," she said cryptically, staring at her menu again.

"Friends of the male variety, I'm guessin'," he

said, making her eyes jump up to look at him
again. She gazed at him quizzically.

"I noticed the picture on your desk when I
stopped by earlier," he explained as he opened the
linen napkin at his place setting and tossed it onto
his lap. "The guy with the eye patch . . . Is *he* the
friend you're talking about?"

C. J. could be mistaken, but she could have
sworn she'd detected a note of jealousy in Shaun's
question, maybe even a little hostility. But she had
heard he had a girlfriend now. Word was that he
had been dating her for almost three years—a nice
Christian girl with a pretty smile and a warm demeanor who was a suitable fit for him, a much better fit than C. J. ever would have been.

Why would Shaun care about her being with
Terrence?

"Yes, he's one of my friends. He's my . . . my
boyfriend, actually."

"Oh, really? What church does he go to?"

She cleared her throat and lowered her menu.
"He and his family are members of a Baptist
church in Chesterton, but . . . he doesn't really go
regularly. It's not his . . . his thing."

"It's not 'his thing'?" he repeated back, his
voice oozing with sarcasm. "Is he a Christian?"

"Yes, he believes in God."

I think, she wanted to say but didn't add that
part.

"You know what they say, Court. Be careful of
the company you keep. If you want to stay on the
righteous path, you have to associate with like-
minded people."

At that, she wanted to laugh. Considering that

she had spent so many years in close proximity to her brother and her father, who were top-level sinners, if what Shaun was saying were true, then she was already damned to hell.

"Terry is a good man, Shaun. I have no worries about him. When I'm around him, I'm in good hands."

He leaned back in his chair and fixed her with his dark eyes. "You sound like you're in love with him."

"I guess because . . . because I am," she admitted.

The look on Shaun's face at those words told her the truth better than if he had said the words aloud: He hadn't moved on and gotten over her like she'd thought. The emotions that flashed across his features were a mix of anger and a sad, wounded look that made her want to turn away. He allowed it to pass briefly before getting his features back under control.

"Well, I'm happy for you." He sipped from his glass again. "Hope this one works out for you better than your *last* boyfriend did."

She winced. That was a low blow.

"I'm just kidding, Court," he said with a laugh.

She wasn't sure she believed that.

"Good afternoon, folks," a chipper voice suddenly called out. C. J. looked up to find their waitress striding to the table. "What can I get for you today?"

They gave their orders and the waitress disappeared soon after. Another uncomfortable silence swept over their table while a family of four talked loudly beside them and a table of women giggled and squawked about some movie. C. J. began to fiddle with her glass, her fork, and her table mat. Finally, she couldn't take it anymore.

"Look, Shaun," she began, leaning forward in her chair, "I've gotta be honest with you."

"What do you mean?"

"I mean I know you're still angry at me for running out of our wedding."

He opened his mouth to respond, and she held up her hand to stop him.

"Which I can perfectly understand," she continued. "I would've been angry, too. No . . . I would have been *furious* if someone had the audacity to do that to me, especially someone I thought loved me. I hadn't planned to do that to you, Shaun. Of all the people I disappointed that day, you were the one I felt the worst about. I still do!"

"So why did you do it?" he asked. He didn't sound angry now but genuinely curious. "Why did you walk out on me?"

"Because I was a coward. Because I couldn't stand up to my father, and, rather than refuse to get married and say it to his face, I ran away."

He lowered his eyes to the tabletop and swallowed. "Being married to me would have been so horrible that you had to run away?"

"No! *No,* of course not!" she said, reaching across the table and grabbing his hand.

He stared down at her hand, and she instantly drew it back, like she had touched a live wire. She placed her hands in her lap to keep from accidentally touching him again.

"Being married to you is what most women would *dream* about! But the woman you would've been marrying didn't exist. I wasn't really that girl you thought I was, and . . . and it would've been unfair to you *and* me to walk down that aisle knowing that I was pretending. That's not a foundation to build a marriage on."

"So who's the real you? What is there about you I don't know?"

"Well . . ." She took a deep breath, wondering where she should begin. "I go by C. J. now, not Courtney. I've always hated the name Courtney. Oh, and I cuss—a lot. I like a glass of red wine every now and then, and I got really, *really* drunk on Long Island iced teas two years ago." She chuckled. "I'll never do that again! I don't go to church that much. Maybe four times a year."

He raised his brows. "Does your daddy know that?"

She shook her head.

"All right," Shaun said, beckoning her with a wave of his dark hand, "keep going. What else?"

She took another deep breath, bracing herself for the hardest revelation. "I'm . . . I'm not a virgin anymore."

His eyes widened. His shoulders fell.

"So you see, I'm not Snow White. I'm not perfect. I'm just"—she shrugged helplessly—". . . me. I'm just me, Shaun."

"Well," he said in one slow exhalation, "thank you for telling me all that."

"No, thank you for letting me finally get it off my chest."

"Now can I tell you something?"

"Of course!"

"I never thought you were perfect, Court, I

mean, C. J. I had no illusions that you were some
Snow White. I realized you had flaws—just like we
all do, but I loved you anyway."

She stilled.

"I wanted to marry *you*, flaws and all. I just wish
you would have trusted me enough, that you
would have known me better to understand that. I
loved you, C. J." He pursed his full lips. "And I
think in some way . . . I still do, even after all this
time . . . even after you running out on me. I can't
get you out of my head—or my heart."

Oh, God, C. J. thought with alarm. Had he just
professed his love for her?

"Okay! That's chicken and waffles for the lady,"
their waitress said with a smile as she sat a steaming
hot plate in front of C. J. "And fried catfish, slaw,
and a side of cornbread for the gentleman!"

After she handed Shaun his dish, the waitress
smiled down at the couple and placed two straws
between them. "So, do we need anything else?
Napkins? Ketchup?"

"No," Shaun said, still staring at C. J. "We're
good."

C. J.'s throat tightened. But they weren't good.
They weren't good at all.

Chapter 5

Evan

Evan rushed up the staircase, glancing at his wristwatch and cursing under his breath as he did. He was late—*very* late. He had told Leila he would be back home nearly an hour ago to head to the obstetrician with her for her ultrasound appointment. He had missed the two previous appointments because he had had important business meetings—one with a Murdoch Conglomerated distributor and the other had required him to travel overseas at the last minute. But he refused to miss this appointment, not after they had already rescheduled it twice. Work obligations be damned! They were going to find out whether they were having a baby boy or girl, and he had to be there. Too bad rush-hour traffic hadn't cooperated.

"Lee!" he called out almost out of breath as he

headed down the west wing corridor leading to their bedroom. He was at a near run. "Lee," he said as he drew near the door and shoved it open. "Shit, baby, I'm sorry I'm so late. I—"

His words drifted off when he saw who was in their darkened bedroom. It wasn't Leila, but her daughter. The little girl was standing on the balls of her feet in front of her mother's mahogany dresser holding a pair of diamond earrings. Evan watched as she quickly shoved the earrings into the pocket of her plaid jumper. He flicked a switch to turn on one of the overhead lights. Isabel turned around to face him.

"What were you doing?" he asked.

Isabel shook her head, sending her braids whipping around her shoulders. "N-nothing," she stuttered.

"It wasn't nothing." He walked toward her across the bedroom. "I saw you put your mother's earrings into your pocket."

Her big, dark eyes went wide. She clamped her lips shut and began to fidget, pivoting from one foot to the other. One of her red knee-high socks slid down her skinny calf and slumped to her ankle.

"Were you stealing your mother's earrings, Izzy?"

She furiously shook her head again. "No, I-I was just . . . just b-b-borrowing them. I was . . . I was going to wear them . . . to . . . to school!"

"If you're going to do something like that, you should probably *ask* first." He held out his hand to her as he drew close. "Give them to me."

She hesitated before reaching into her pocket

and pulling out the earrings. She dropped them into his open palm before lowering her gaze to her penny loafers in shame.

Evan stared down at the earrings that he had purchased Leila for Christmas, four-carat diamond cluster teardrops. Leila had mentioned that other jewelry had gone missing in the past few weeks: a Tiffany bracelet and diamond studs. Evan had thought that maybe they had fallen behind her bureau, or one of the new maids had a case of sticky fingers and slipped them into her apron. He had told his housekeeper to keep an eye out for any suspicious behavior among the staff. But he'd had no clue that little Isabel might be the real culprit, the one they should have been watching.

"I don't think these will go very well with your school uniform," he said dryly. "And your ears aren't pierced. You wouldn't be able to wear them anyway." He set the diamonds back on the dresser top and scrutinized her more closely. "Now why did you really take them? Tell me the truth."

Isabel's eyes began to fill with tears. "Daddy . . . Daddy asked me to," she whispered.

"Your *father* told you to take them?"

She nodded.

Brad, you asshole, he thought angrily. *I should've known.*

Even though he had been sentenced to seven years for his embezzlement and fraud conviction, it seemed that Brad wasn't going down without a fight. He was still trying to make Leila's life miserable from a distance.

"Daddy said Mommy wouldn't care," Isabel explained, sniffing. "He said she didn't need that stuff, b-but . . . but he did! He said—"

"Wait. You've been sending your mother's jewelry to your father?" Evan asked in disbelief.

"Daddy told me to put it in the box that we're mailing to him for his birthday next week. He said it can be another one of his gifts. I'm . . . I'm supposed to stuff it with the . . . the teddy bear I got him."

"Jesus Christ," Evan exhaled, feeling his stomach turn.

Brad was getting his eight-year-old daughter to funnel stolen jewelry to him! That man was beyond evil. Evan inclined his head, considering the situation. Actually, Brad reminded Evan a lot of his own old man, which made Evan even more sympathetic to Isabel. He remembered being a kid powerless against his father's lies and manipulations. No matter how angry Evan wanted to be right now, he couldn't direct that anger at her.

He sighed, dropped to his knee in front of Isabel, and placed a consoling hand on her thin shoulder. "Izzy, sweetheart, we talked about this, didn't we? Remember when I told you—"

"Talked about what?" Leila called out.

Evan turned and Isabel looked up. Their eyes settled on Leila, who was standing in the doorway in an orange sundress and white cardigan with her purse draped on her shoulder. She was staring at them.

"What did you guys talk about?" she repeated.

Evan forced a smile and rose to his feet. "Oh, nothing! Nothing! I was . . . uh . . . just reminding Isabel that when she's playing with things in here to put it back. She was doing a bit of dress-up with some of your jewelry." He gestured to Leila's dresser. "And dropped a pair of earrings. No big deal."

Leila squinted at them and crossed her arms over her chest. "Oh, really?" She didn't look remotely convinced.

"I forgot to put it back," Isabel echoed, wiping her runny nose with the back of her hand. "I'm sorry."

Evan clapped his hands. "Well, now that that's handled, we should get going, Lee. We're going to be late for your appointment if we don't hit the road soon, right?"

"Yeah," she said vaguely. "We should get going."

"You're lying," Leila announced unceremoniously as they sat in the backseat of the Lincoln Town Car minutes later as the car pulled away from the curb and sailed down the driveway.

Evan stared at her, startled. "Huh?"

"You're lying to me, Evan Murdoch." She rubbed her belly in slow, circular motions. Her body was rigid. "You weren't talking to Izzy about putting jewelry back where she found it. You think I'm stupid?"

"No, of course not, baby! Where the hell is this coming from?"

"You keep doing this. You keep . . . you keep lying to me, Ev. And it's really pissing me off!"

"What are you talking about? When did I lie to you?"

"You didn't tell me that Charisse refused to grant you a divorce. She told me that she told you *a month* ago."

He squinted. "When the hell did you talk to Charisse?"

"At the lovely fund-raising committee meeting that I went to a couple of days ago. The one Paulette invited me to. Your wife ambushed me there! She made this big deal in front of everyone about how I shouldn't be there because I wasn't your wife, I was your *whore*! Charisse said she told you that she's going to drag out your divorce until either you give up on the idea of us getting married or I give up. *Why* didn't you tell me that, Ev?"

Evan tiredly closed his eyes. He had wondered why Leila had been acting so strange since that day at the country club. She had been tight-lipped, almost aloof. This explained it.

He didn't know why Charisse had said those things to Leila. No, actually he *did* know why she had said it. She did it because she hated Leila with a passion. Unfortunately, he couldn't work up too much rage against his wife, knowing what he knew about her—about her screwed-up childhood and the sexual abuse she had suffered at her father's hands. Charisse had come to terms with her dark past in rehab and had revealed the truth to Evan soon after. He now saw Charisse as a wounded animal, and wounded animals fought the hardest when cornered.

"I'm sorry, baby," he said softly, opening his eyes and reaching out for Leila. He squeezed her hand reassuringly. "I'm sorry Charisse upset you. I wasn't trying to lie to you. I just . . . I just knew that you've been looking forward to getting married. You've been looking at reception spaces, for Chrissake! You were designing our invitations. I didn't want to burst your bubble."

"Yeah, well, it's been burst," she muttered, yanking her hand out of his grasp and glaring out the car's tinted window. "So are you going to tell me the truth about your little conversation with Izzy, or are you going to make me pry the secret out of an eight-year-old girl instead?"

He slouched back into the leather seat. "She was stealing your jewelry . . . a pair of your diamond earrings."

Leila's brows furrowed. "Why would she steal from me? Izzy's never stolen from me before in her life! She wouldn't do—"

"Because she was going to mail it to Brad. She was going to put it in the birthday gift you guys were going to send him. He asked her to mail it to him. I guess he planned to pawn it. Maybe he's desperate for money."

"*What?* He really told her to steal from me? That . . . that son of a bitch!"

"He's done something like this before," Evan continued, figuring if he was going to tell the truth, he might as well say everything. "Izzy told me when she ran away a month ago, he had talked her into it. He bought the ticket to L.A. for her. He arranged for a driver to pick her up near her school. He told her to come to him and not to tell us what she was doing." He chuckled ruefully. "He told her he'd take her to Disneyland."

"I don't find any of this funny, Ev," she snapped.

"Neither do I!"

"Then why the hell are you laughing?" she shouted.

He stared at her, thunderstruck. This whole conversation was going wrong, horribly wrong. They were heading to the doctor to learn the sex of their baby. This was supposed to be a joyous moment. They shouldn't be arguing.

"You knew that my daughter was coerced by *her own* father into running away and you didn't mention it. You knew this whole damn time and didn't breathe a word . . . not one *single* word to me! Do you know what level of betrayal that is?"

"Lee," he pleaded. "Baby, I was trying to *protect* you, not betray you! I knew how upset it would make you. You're pregnant. It's a delicate condition. You didn't need the stress. Besides, Izzy was home—safe and sound. I talked to her and I took care of it. I didn't think it was necessary to—"

"But you don't get to make those decisions! Not without consulting me!" she bellowed, pointing at her chest. "Brad used to do that shit to me *all* the time, Ev, and I'm not putting up with that again."

"You know damn well I'm not Brad. I won't treat you the way he did. You know that!"

"I want you to . . . no, I *need* you to respect me, Ev!" she continued, undaunted like she hadn't heard him. Her chest heaved up and down as she spoke. "I'm not 'delicate.' I'm not some china doll you might break or . . . or some helpless child, goddammit! I'm a grown woman! If our relationship is really going to work, you have to treat me like an adult, like an equal partner. You have to be straight with me. Okay?"

At her words and her tone, Evan could feel his

wrath awaken. It was a spark that ignited without him even trying. How could Leila be so furious at something he had done out of love? Leila couldn't remember what she had been like the day Isabel had disappeared or the days after. She went from a complete sobbing basket case to a hovering mother who was loath to let Isabel out of her sight. She had only started to act relatively normal again recently, and he had worried that the stress might make her miscarry. Was he really supposed to tell her what Brad had done, to dump even more emotional turmoil onto her?

And though she insisted he always be honest with her, she hadn't done the same for him. Leila had known about Paulette's affair and how Paulette's lover was blackmailing her. She had known that Paulette was pregnant even before Paulette's husband, Antonio, had discovered the truth. Had she told any of that to Evan? *No!* And he hadn't raked her over the coals for it, so why the hell was she doing that to him now?

He opened his mouth to say just that, then abruptly closed it.

Evan decided to put a lid on his indignation and fury, opting to let them both simmer rather than boil over. Yelling back at her would serve no purpose. Besides, Leila wasn't normally like this. Maybe it was just the pregnancy hormones taking her over again, making her normal good nature go haywire. He would just have to let this go—for now. Evan released a deep breath and nodded.

"Okay," he said, almost choking on the word. "I'm . . . I'm sorry I hurt you. That's the last thing I wanted to do."

"I know you didn't." She lowered her eyes and nodded. "And I accept your apology. Just . . . just please don't do it anymore, Ev."

"I won't," he said.

Twenty minutes later they sat in a dimly lit doctor's office with the shades drawn while a technician in white scrubs covered in Peanuts characters squeezed clear gel on Leila's belly.

"It's a little cold, I know," she said with a smile as she grabbed the ultrasound wand and Leila shuddered slightly. "But you know the drill, right?"

"I know the drill," Leila said with a resigned nod as she lay back on the examination table. The white paper crinkled underneath her as she shifted to get more comfortable.

"All righty then," the technician said as she climbed on top of her stool and lowered her ultrasound wand to Leila's protruding belly. "Let's start the show, shall we?"

And that's when he heard it—a heartbeat. It was loud, strong, and clear. It played over speakers, filling up the room with its reverberation. Evan blinked in surprise and breathed in audibly. Was that really their baby he was hearing?

"Let's see what we've got here," the technician whispered, pushing aside her fluffy blonde bangs as she looked over her shoulder at the black-and-white screen.

Evan stared, transfixed, at a TV screen on the other side of the room that simultaneously showed the ultrasound. He had missed the other appointments, so all he had seen in the past were the printouts Leila had brought home. Each one had shown amorphous blobs that could be anything from a baby to a chicken to those little peeps you got in Easter egg baskets when you were a little kid. But this was different. This looked like a real baby that would one day cry, crawl, and take its first toddling steps. This was *his* son or daughter.

"There's the head," the technician said, speaking more loudly to be heard over the thud and whoosh of the baby's heartbeat. "And there's the heart. Oh, there's the hand! Look, the baby's waving. 'Hi, Mommy and Daddy!'"

Evan felt overwhelmed with a flood of emotion as he watched his child's image on the monitor, as he watched it wave then shift to the side.

He flashed back to the days long ago when Charisse was going through IVF treatments and she'd rushed into their bedroom with a positive pregnancy test. They had been so happy, musing about baby names and whether the baby would look more like him or her. And then a few weeks later she had miscarried. Charisse had become quiet and withdrawn, and because he hadn't wanted to burden her with his feelings, he'd quietly mourned the loss alone. And he hadn't just mourned the loss of the baby, but the chance to make things right, to be a better father than his father ever had been, to raise a child who felt wanted and loved.

Evan and Charisse had played out that scenario over and over again, and each time he became less jubilant when he saw the positive pregnancy test. Instead, his stomach would clench with a sense of foreboding and he would have to tell himself not to lose hope, that one day Charisse would hold a baby in her arms. But finding that balance be-

tween hope and resigned acceptance of disappointment had been a challenge that Evan had
never quite mastered. And with each miscarriage,
Charisse fared even worse than Evan. She became
moodier and more sullen, shutting herself away in
one of the mansion's rooms for hours at a time,
drinking and watching television. Finally, they had
decided to stop trying—it wasn't worth it anymore. Of course, by then the damage to their marriage had been done, so maybe having a baby in that
environment wouldn't have been the best idea anyway.

But now, here he was, looking at a baby with a
heartbeat, a baby that moved and shifted. He
blinked furiously when he realized he was actually
getting teary-eyed.

Goddamn, he thought with amazement. *Am I
about to break down in tears in the damn doctor's office?*

He reached for Leila's hand, grabbed it, and
squeezed it tight. She turned slightly to look at
him, frowning. But when she saw the expression
on his face, she smiled.

"Okay, it looks like the little one has decided to
moon us," the tech said with a laugh. "But that
makes my job a lot easier. You guys ready to hear
what you're having?"

"Of course!" Leila said.

Evan's throat tightened. He couldn't utter a
word so he only nodded.

"You are having a girl!" the tech said. "Congratulations, Mom and Dad."

A girl, Evan thought.

And that's when he knew he would have to
break the promise that he had made to Leila only

twenty minutes ago during their car ride. He would do whatever he had to do—lie, cheat, steal, and kill if it came to it—to protect their daughter, and for her, Leila. Leila might be angry about it, might even resent him for it, but she would have to deal with it. There was no going back now.

That night, Evan stared at the bedroom ceiling, remembering the sound of their daughter's . . . his *little girl's* heartbeat and the silhouette of her little face in the black-and-white image on the screen. He felt the protectiveness swell inside of him again. He turned to Leila, who was slumbering softly beside him in the faint moonlight.

Despite holding hands during their appointment, they hadn't talked much after. They shared stilted conversation during the ride back and went their separate ways once they arrived home. He sought out his study and unfinished work, and she went looking for Isabel and her mother. He had eaten dinner alone, feeling uneasy, like he had a fishbone from the salmon he was eating caught in his molars. He couldn't figure out what it was until he realized that he missed her, he physically and emotionally missed Leila. Despite them moving in and having a baby together, she felt further away from him now than she had before. But he couldn't let that happen. There was too much at stake now. *This* was his family.

As Leila slept, Evan literally closed the distance between them, easing across the bed in the dark. He cradled her from behind and reached around her, gently placing his hand on top of her belly, splaying his fingers across the pale pink charmeuse. She stirred against him but only slightly. To

his relief, she drew closer instead of easing away,
seeking his warmth. He lowered his nose to her
shoulder, inhaling her scent—milk, honey, and the
faint smell of the cocoa butter cream she now rubbed
on her stomach constantly. He languished in the
feel of her silken skin against his rough cheek. He
placed a kiss on the nape of her neck, just below
the hairline. Then he kissed her shoulder lightly.
She stirred again. He watched as she yawned and
turned to face him. Her dark eyes fluttered open
and she stared at him quizzically.

"What are you doing, Ev?" she whispered groggily, smacking her lips. "What's wrong?"

In response, he lowered his mouth to hers, swal-
lowing any arguments she could make against them
making love tonight.

They hadn't made love in more than two weeks.
Leila seemed hesitant to get naked in front of him
these days, loving the idea of having a baby, but
hating what it did to her body. Though Evan swore
to her he found her just as beautiful and alluring
now as he had before she had gotten pregnant, he
could sense she didn't believe him. She'd mutter
ruefully about her wide hips and thighs and heavy
breasts, about her distended belly and budding
stretch marks. She'd shut the door when she took
showers and would always wear a robe in front of
him.

But tonight she didn't seem hesitant or demure.
She didn't argue or resist his kiss, to his surprise. She
wrapped her arms around his neck and drew him
close, kissing him back with just as much fervor as
he did, just as hungrily.

He shifted his hand from her stomach to one of

her breasts, kneading the brown nipple through the silk fabric of her nightgown. With the other hand he eased the long gown she wore up her calves and then her thighs. Evan reluctantly tugged his mouth away from hers and climbed to the end of the bed. He braced his hands on her knees and slowly eased her legs apart before climbing between them. By the time he eased her peach silk panties over her hips and down her legs, she was panting for him.

He lowered his hand to her parted legs first, coaxing forth the wetness there, making her fist the bedsheets in her hands and let her legs open as she moaned. He then knelt and placed a winding trail of kisses along the inside of her honey-colored thighs, intermingling a few licks and nips that left her squirming. He finally kissed her between her legs and licked, making her yell out. He kept licking her there, flicking his warm tongue over her clit until she screamed out his name, until the tremors assailed her entire body, until her toes curled and her muscles tightened, then unspooled like woven yarn.

After she came, he climbed on top of her, prepared to enter her.

"I can't . . . I can't stay on my back," she panted. "The baby . . . the weight . . . I'm gonna . . . I'm gonna black out."

That was a cold bucket of water on their hot moment. "Shit! I'm sorry, baby!"

He immediately climbed off of her and eased back onto his elbows. He helped shift her onto her side.

"Is that better? Are you all right now?" he asked while worriedly gazing down at her.

She nodded and smiled. "I'm ready, if that's what you mean," she whispered before reaching out to him. "Come on, Ev."

He did as she ordered, crouching behind her, kissing her shoulder and cupping her breast as he entered her with one swift thrust that made her cry out again. His pace was tempered at first, but she spurred him on, arching her back and moving her hips against him, commanding him to make love to her harder, faster. The pace increased, and he became lost in sensations of the moment—the sound of her cries, his grunts, and the bed squeaking rhythmically beneath him, of her warm wetness enveloping him and the slick sweat dripping down her back and his stomach, and of the salty taste of her skin against his tongue.

When the orgasm hit, Evan closed his eyes and let the sensation overtake him. His breath caught in his throat and he released it with a shudder that made all of his limbs shake. He then went limp beside her. She sighed contentedly as he pulled out of her, but still held her close, cradling her stomach again.

"You're mine," he said in her ear just as she started to drift back to sleep, whispering it to her and to their baby.

She turned her head to look at him and squinted. "Huh?"

"I said you're mine . . . and you'll *always* be mine." His voice hardened with possessiveness, making her frown.

"No, we're *each other's*, Ev." She then kissed him and turned away again. "Good night, baby," she said before closing her eyes and finally falling asleep.

But they weren't "each other's." What he felt was different than just kinship or love. It was unlike what he felt for his brother and sister, what he had always considered family loyalty. It was unlike the desire and adoration that swelled inside him when he looked at Leila. This was . . . deeper, like a lion protecting its pride. It was the primordial surge of testosterone that urged him to claim and defend what was rightfully his—and he wouldn't resist its call.

Chapter 6

Leila

Leila strode into her home office, basking in the cheerful warmth from the light coming through the two bay windows on the opposite side of the room. She bit into a slice of toast smothered with as much strawberry jam as it could hold as she rushed toward her desk. She hadn't had time to eat the larger breakfast that her mother and daughter were now enjoying—link sausages, scrambled eggs, hash browns, and pecan waffles, which were supposed to be Evan's cook's specialty. She hadn't wanted to miss her appointment with a new client, a woman who was holding a winter soiree next year and wanted custom-made invitations. She would be one of many new clients in Chesterton that Leila had brought on board in the past seven months since she had opened her graphic arts studio in the guesthouse.

As Leila finished the rest of her toast, she dropped the high heels she had been carrying to the hardwood floor and quickly put them on her stockinged feet. She wiped the remaining bread crumbs from her hands, adjusted the elastic waistband of her linen skirt, and glanced around the room, making sure it was presentable.

At least she kept her office relatively neat. But the adjacent room and studio where she did most of her actual work was a disaster area, covered with spools of ribbons and acrylic accents, open sample binders and reams of parchment. Only a two-foot area directly around her Mac was clutter-free. But she liked the space that way. She seemed to be most creative in utter chaos, something that Evan couldn't understand. He had stumbled into her studio almost a month ago and had nearly had a heart attack when he saw all the disarray. The borderline OCD in him wanted to charge into the room and start cleaning, to give the space some semblance of order. She had to physically pull him away and shut and lock the door to keep him from doing so.

But Evan needs *order,* she thought as she paused to remove a sample binder from one of the wall shelves. *He needs to feel like he's in control.*

It was one of the few unfortunate traits he had inherited from his father, George, and something that she had known about him for years, ever since they were little kids. When they played board games together or kickball or tag, he was the one who always had to dictate the rules of play and chastise whoever broke those rules.

Leila could let his bossiness slide back then and just roll her eyes at the little dictator. But she couldn't let it slide anymore, not when they were adults in a serious romantic relationship and talking about spending their lives together. She had relinquished control in her previous marriage, placing all her trust and hopes in Brad, and look where it had gotten her! She knew Evan was a very different man than her ex-husband, a loving and kind man who had no nefarious intent behind what he did, but she couldn't . . . she *wouldn't* relinquish that type of control again. She was no one's puppet, including the man she loved. Evan had to understand that.

Just as Leila rounded her desk, her phone began to ring. She reached for the receiver and raised it to her ear while shifting a stack of folders aside on her desk. "Leila Designs," she answered. "How may I help you?"

"Hello, Ms. Hawkins?" a voice answered. "This is Maggie Sutter."

"Hey!" Leila said with a smile as she sat down in her rolling chair. "I was just getting ready for you." She glanced at her wall clock and saw it was the scheduled time for their appointment. Her smile disappeared. "Are you running a little late? Is that why you called?"

"No, actually . . . uh, I . . . I wanted to tell you that I won't be able to make today's appointment."

"Oh," Leila said, feeling a little crestfallen. She had been excited to show Sutter her ideas, which mostly involved a winter wonderland theme. "Well, when would you like to reschedule? I have a few slots open later this week and next week if—"

"Actually, I . . . I don't know when I would be able to reschedule. At least, not . . . not now."

"But I thought you wanted to get started on this soon. You said you were interested in save-the-dates, invitations, and maybe menus, correct?" She glanced down at her notepad where she had scribbled relevant information about Sutter's event. "If it's taking place in early January, I would have to start ordering—"

"Perhaps I don't need as elaborate invitations as I thought. My husband is already complaining about the budget for this," she said with an awkward laugh. "I thought I might save money by scaling back in some areas, like the . . . the stationery."

Leila leaned forward in her chair, bracing her elbows on her wooden desk, feeling her baby shift. "Mrs. Sutter, if you want a simpler, more economical design, I can do that. Just let me know what your new budget for invitations is and I can—"

"I'm sorry but no. No, that won't be necessary," Mrs. Sutter rushed. "I apologize for wasting your time, Ms. Hawkins. Good-bye."

She then hung up, leaving Leila staring at the phone receiver, dumbfounded.

That was weird, she thought with furrowed brows. She hung up the phone and shrugged off her bewilderment and disappointment and booted up her computer. Now that Sutter had canceled, she had time this morning to check and respond to her emails. But as Leila read through her emails, the furrow in her brows deepened.

She had received messages overnight from at

least three other clients who were canceling scheduled appointments, including one scheduled for later that day. Another client was even canceling invitations she had already contracted, despite the fact that Leila had already ordered the supplies and the woman would have to pay a hefty cancellation fee.

"I've found services elsewhere," the woman had written in her terse email.

"What the hell is going on?" Leila muttered as she stared at her computer screen.

If the trend of cancellations continued, she didn't know what she would do. She needed clients to keep her new business afloat.

Still frowning, Leila powered down her computer. With a grunt and bracing her tummy, she rose from her desk and opened the door that led to her studio. Now that her morning was open, she had some time to work on her other projects. She kicked off her heels and headed to her crafting table. She sat down on her swivel stool after adjusting its height, reached for the place cards she had been finishing up yesterday, and got to work.

As she toiled with ribbons and a hot glue gun, her mind wandered. She thought again about the cancellations and why they had just started happening now. Was there some bad buzz about her studio? Was someone spreading it around town?

All of a sudden, she remembered Charisse's words at the country club.

"I will make your life a living hell—and I'm only getting started," Charisse had said.

Leila paused from her work and lowered the scalpel she was holding to the crafting table.

Charisse wasn't sabotaging her, was she? Was that woman spreading lies about her around Chesterton?

No, I'm just being paranoid, Leila told herself.

It was purely a coincidence. A few cancellations did not mean bad buzz. She had never owned her own business before. Maybe trends like this were normal and she was just hitting a brief rough patch.

But still she couldn't shake her unease, making it hard to concentrate on what she was doing. She pushed her stool away from the table in defeat.

"To hell with this," she whispered. She wouldn't spend all morning and possibly her afternoon with her brain stuck in a loop of the same thoughts and worries. She released a gust of air, pushed herself to her feet, and walked back into her office. She reached for her desk phone and dialed a number. The line picked up after the third ring.

"Hello!" Paulette shouted over the sound of a wailing infant.

"Hey, girl," Leila said, smiling again. "It sounds crazy over there. Need reinforcements?"

"Oh, dear God! Yes, please!" Paulette yelled, making Leila laugh.

"Okay, I'll be over in thirty minutes."

"Lee, it is *so* good to get out of that house," Paulette said as she adjusted the visor top of little Nate's carriage.

"And good to get out of the office," Leila concurred.

The two women were strolling along one of the

asphalt trails of Macon Park, enjoying the warm sunshine and all the lovely scenery nature had to offer. Summer was drawing to an end and the first signs of fall were emerging in Chesterton. The canopy of leaves overhead showed a tableau of reds, yellows, oranges, and even shades of purple. The scorching heat was starting to wane and give way to balmy weather with a light breeze. It was a perfect day for a walk.

"Thanks so much for saving me!" Paulette said.

"I didn't *save* you," Leila insisted with a grin as she adjusted her sunglasses and smiled at a group of children who were squealing and playing on a nearby playground. "I just stopped by."

"No, you saved me. Nate was losing it and I was on the verge of losing it, too. He's been crying constantly for the past few days. I thought something was wrong with . . . you know . . . him being a preemie. I thought maybe he was suffering some complication, but then I took him to the doctor and she said it was just—"

"Colic," Leila said with a resigned nod. "Yeah, I know. Izzy went through the same thing when she was an infant. She wasn't premature, but she cried *constantly* the first two and a half months. It almost broke me." She sighed. "Of course, I was all alone. Brad was of no help and Mama was on the other side of the country. I had to figure it out myself. Eventually, I figured out that sometimes sun and fresh air helps. I don't know why, but it does."

"Well, thanks for letting me know!" Paulette gushed with relief, gazing down at her slumbering baby's now perfectly angelic face. They approached a wooden bench perched underneath the shade of hundred-year-old oak trees. "But enough about my agony . . . how are things back home at *casa de* Murdoch? How are you and Evan doing? What's he been up to?"

"Oh, you know your brother!" Leila said as she carefully lowered herself onto the bench, landing with a grunt. Paulette, who was no longer hindered by a bulging belly, gracefully sat down beside her. "Ev is pretty much the same as always: kind, giving, protective . . . and mildly manipulative and addicted to micromanaging," Leila said with a droll roll of her dark eyes.

Paulette laughed. "That's just how he is! You've known him for forever, Lee. You knew what you were getting into when you two hooked up."

Leila sighed, rubbed her belly, and nodded.

"But the good outweighs the bad though, right? You two are still happy?"

"Of course we are!" she said a little too eagerly.

But the truth was that some days . . . *some days* she wasn't so sure. She wasn't sure if she should start to rebel against the dynamic she and Evan had created. Charisse may have been happy to be *Mrs. Murdoch*, the pampered housewife of a very rich husband. She believed that it had been Leila's goal all along to become the same, but that was far from the truth. Leila hated that Evan had all the money, property, and power in their relationship.

"*You're mine . . . and you'll* always *be mine,*" he had said just last night, giving her that intense gaze that let her know what he said wasn't open to debate. She still chafed at the memory of those domineering words.

"You don't *own* me, Evan!" she had wanted to scream at him.

But she knew in her heart that he loved her and she loved him. She wasn't going to give up on them.

"So how are things between you and Tony?" she asked, changing the subject. "Is he adjusting to fatherhood well?"

"Oh, he loves it!" Paulette said, gently rocking the carriage back and forth, easing it with the toe of her Tory Burch slipper. "Ever since Nate came home from the hospital he's been holding him and cooing over him. It's so adorable."

Leila gazed at the children on the playground, keeping her focus on a set of girls who were playing on the ladybug-themed seesaw, squealing as they went up and down. She didn't think she could look at Paulette directly while she asked her next question.

"So Tony's okay with . . . with everything? He isn't . . . he isn't angry about everything that happened?"

Paulette stopped rocking the stroller. She lowered her foot to engage one of the stroller brakes. "You mean is he okay with not knowing who Nate's real father is?"

Leila's eyes snapped toward Paulette's. "I'm sorry for being so nosy. You don't have to answer that. I just—"

"No, it's okay. I've told you everything else, haven't I? I could see why you're wondering." She took a deep breath. "Yes, Tony seems okay with it—shockingly so. He said he accepted Nate as his son no matter what, and it definitely seems like he means it."

"Why do you keep saying 'seems'?" Leila asked, narrowing her eyes at her friend. "Are you saying that you don't believe him?"

Paulette shook her head. "It's not that I don't believe him. I think he really *is* trying to move on with our lives and wants to be a good father to Nate and a good husband to me. We're happy together. We're happier than we've been for a long while! He even moved out of the guestroom back into our bedroom. He finally got his mom to give back her key to our home and told her no when she tried to move in so she can come and help me out with Nate. 'If she wants help, she'll ask for it, Ma,' he told her." She chuckled. "I was so shocked, Lee. He hardly *ever* stands up to his mama! We're better than we've been in almost a year, since we came back from our honeymoon in Cabo, but something . . . something still doesn't feel . . . I don't know . . . right, I guess."

"What do you mean?"

"I mean he won't talk about what happened! He doesn't want to talk about the affair, about me keeping my pregnancy a secret the whole time. He won't let me utter the name Marques." She sighed. "I guess some women would be happy that he doesn't want to bring it up, that he wants to forget. But to me, it doesn't seem . . . healthy." She turned slightly on the bench to face Leila. "You know I suggested to him that we go to a therapist or a marriage counselor to make sure that we're really okay since we've been through so much. And he told me no! He said we didn't need it."

Leila frowned. "You didn't need it?"

Of all the couples who needed counseling, Paulette and Antonio needed it the most, in Leila's humble opinion. She didn't see how they could have a healthy future if they couldn't unravel everything that had happened in their tangled past.

Paulette shook her head again. "No, he said we were fine and that we should just . . . just move on. He said that he didn't know what other secrets might come out if we started babbling to a counselor."

"*What other secrets?* But you told him everything, right?"

"Yes! I don't *have* anything else to hide! He knows just as much as I know! But he still refuses to talk to someone for . . . for whatever reason."

Leila pursed her lips. "That's so strange."

"I know. But I don't want to push him. I've already put him through so much. I told myself that people heal in their own way and in their own time. This is just *his* way. I guess I should respect that, right?"

"I . . . I guess."

Just then, little Nate began to stir, whimpering softly underneath his blanket, curling his tiny hands into tight fists.

"Oh, I think we better get moving," Paulette said, rising to her feet and leaning toward the carriage. "I don't want him to start up again."

"All right," Leila said, pushing herself upright. It was starting to take more and more effort the further along she got in her pregnancy. "Let's walk another half mile and then call it a day."

"Don't overexert yourself, lady," Paulette said.

Leila waved off her warning. "Pssh, don't worry about me!" She dropped her hand to her lower back as they stepped back onto the asphalt. "I can waddle with the best of them."

Paulette broke down into giggles as Leila started to do an exaggerated waddle like one of the ducks in the nearby pond. "Girl, come on!" She swatted Leila's shoulder, making her laugh too. "You and your crazy self!"

Chapter 7

C. J.

"So," Terrence said on the phone, "I'm making reservations online, as we speak, for tomorrow seven thirty p.m. My cursor is hovering over the submit button," he continued, making her laugh as she leaned back in her office chair and gazed at the grounds of Aston Ministries outside her window. "If you think something might come up . . . if you think your car might break down . . . if you think a tornado might hit and you won't be able to make it to dinner, speak now or forever hold your peace, Miss Aston."

"I *will* make it, Mr. Murdoch! I told you we were going to celebrate your recovery and I meant it!"

"Uh-huh," he murmured, oozing with incredulity. She had canceled on him the last time he had made reservations for their dinner. This was their second try. "Promises, promises. I know you have a busy social calendar these days."

"*Social calendar*? It's not like I'm going to cotillions and tea parties! I'm going to boring meet-and-greets and sitting in the background while Dad makes speeches."

"Still . . . doesn't leave us with much time to do anything together. I feel like a housewife sitting alone at home, staring out the window waiting for hubby to come home from the office."

C. J. reached for a ballpoint pen sitting on her desk and tapped it restlessly against a notepad. "Well, maybe you could find something to do that could occupy your time while I'm down here . . . something to keep you busy."

"*What*? You mean like a hobby? You want me to take up stamp collecting?"

"No! Maybe you could get . . . I don't know . . . a job, maybe," she ventured, making him fall silent on the other end of the line.

She knew this was a touchy subject with Terrence. For the past few years, he had been happy to live the life of a wandering playboy, waking up at noon, coming home at dawn, and living the fast life in between while paying his bills solely with the proceeds from the trust fund his father had set up for him. But he was nearing thirty. Shouldn't he have a bit more ambition, a better sense of direction? His brother Evan was the CEO of a major corporation, for Chrissake! Meanwhile, Terrence spent his days going to the gym, watching TV, playing video games, and lying around in bed with her.

C. J. loved him and wouldn't change him for the world, but is this what their future would be like if they stayed together, if, hopefully, they got married one day? Would it be her going to a newsroom to pull ten- to twelve-hour days as a reporter only to return home to find him sitting on the couch watching marathon rounds of ESPN? Sure, he still would make ten times more money sitting around on his butt all day than she would from hustling at her newspaper, but it was the principle of the thing.

"I don't *need* a job," he said tightly.

"I know you don't, honey," she replied, softening her voice, hoping to placate him. "It's just—"

"I had a job six years ago, where I would walk around New York all day to show up at casting calls only to get rejected by stuck-up designers who didn't like my shoulders or my skin tone or the bridge of my nose or some random shit! And when I did get a job, I'd sit around bored for hours in makeup chairs and through fittings. I've done that shit, C. J. I don't wanna do it again!"

"Terry, sweetheart, I'm not saying that you have to. There are other places you can work, like . . . uh . . . uh . . ."

"*What?* An office? Starbucks? There are people who *dream* of quitting those jobs! Why the hell would I purposely seek out a nine-to-five to make myself miserable?"

"But you said you have plenty of time on your hands and you need something to keep you busy, right? Maybe Evan could hook you up with something at the company, something that wouldn't bore you."

The phone line went silent again, and she started

to shift anxiously in her chair. She was pissing him off. She could tell.

"Okay," she said, setting down her pen, "never mind. Forget I even mentioned it. I was just—"

"What the hell is this?" her brother shouted as he threw open her office door, making her jump in her chair and almost drop her cell phone.

C. J. spun away from the window and the tranquil views of water fountains and lush gardens to find Victor's scowling face drawing closer and closer as he strode toward her desk. She watched as he tossed a folded broadsheet in front of her, slapping it on her desktop, sending her pen holder and stapler crashing to the floor.

"Why the hell would you say this shit to the newspaper?" Victor yelled, glaring at her, his face ablaze with fury.

"C. J., what's wrong? Who the fuck is yelling at you like that?" Terrence asked angrily on the other end of the line.

"N-no one. I mean . . . I'll call you back," she stuttered before hanging up, cutting Terrence off mid-protest.

She set her phone down on her desk and stared up at her brother. "Keep your voice down. The door is still—"

"What was this shit that you pulled in the interview with the *Winston-Salem Journal*?" he shouted, ignoring her words of warning. He jabbed his finger down at the newspaper in front of her. "If I had known you were gonna say this shit, I never would have sent the reporter to talk to you!"

She shook her head in bafflement. "I . . . I have

no idea what you're talking about, Victor. I didn't do or say anything wrong. I stayed on message!"

She watched as he snatched up the copy of the newspaper and zeroed in on one of the news stories below the fold. "When asked about the controversy surrounding the paternity of former Aston Ministries employee Rochelle Martin's baby and whether Rev. Pete Aston is the father, Courtney Aston said she did not 'feel comfortable speaking on the issue,'" Victor read aloud. "'The baby is supposed to be born any day now, Courtney Aston said. I guess the truth will come out then.'"

He then tossed the newspaper back on her desk.

"Okay?" C. J. raised her hands and her eyebrows. "What was wrong with that?"

"What was wrong with that? *What was wrong with that?*" he shouted. "You were a reporter, right? You wrote for a living! You understand how words and sentences work, correct?"

C. J.'s lips tightened at her brother's sarcasm. "*Yes*, Victor, I understand how they work. But I didn't know what else to say! I didn't say the baby was Dad's! I just said—"

"I read what you said and that's not the fucking answer you give when someone asks you if our father knocked up his twenty-year-old assistant, you . . . you dumb bitch!" he sputtered, looking like his head was about to explode. "You tell them that it's a lie . . . that it *has* to be a lie because the Honorable Reverend Pete Aston would never do such a thing! You swear to it! You—"

"Victor," a calm voice interjected from the doorway.

They looked in that direction only to find Shaun standing there, leaning inside her office, and fixing them both with a worried gaze.

"Victor," he continued, "I get that you're upset. But is all this yelling really necessary?"

"Yes, it's fucking necessary to get through her thick head! She could've—"

"She made an innocent mistake," Shaun said, surprising her by coming to her defense. "That's all it was. Cut her a break."

She watched as her brother ground his teeth so hard she thought sparks might shoot out of his mouth. He closed his eyes and took several deep breaths through his flared nostrils. Miraculously, when he opened his eyes again seconds later, he didn't look quite as furious or terrifying.

"The next time," he began in a harsh whisper, returning his glower to C. J. and pointing a finger at her, "a reporter asks you a question and you aren't sure the best way to answer it, you tell them, 'No comment.' Understood?"

She nodded. "Understood."

Victor abruptly turned on his heel to leave her office, and Shaun stepped aside to let him pass. Her brother stalked back down the hall, likely to his own office, where he would unleash his unspent fury on poor Brian, his lover and assistant.

As soon as he left, C. J. slowly exhaled and gave a pained smile at Shaun. "Thank you. Thank you so much for doing that."

He shook his head. "No problem."

"It was brave of you. Whenever Victor gets like that, most people want to run for cover."

"Well," he said with a shrug, "you forget . . . I've

known your family for quite a while, C. J. I don't find them as intimidating as everyone else."

She laughed halfheartedly as he took a few more steps into her office.

"You seem to be intimidated by *me*, though," he said. "I see you in the hallway and you walk the other direction. Ever since we had that lunch together, I've gotten the distinct feeling that you're avoiding me."

She lowered her eyes and cleared her throat loudly. In all honesty, she *had* been avoiding him. Ever since he had confessed that he still had feelings for her, she didn't know how to behave around him. It left her confused because she thought he had moved on, that he was in a serious relationship now. C. J. had even made inquiries to the church's biggest gossip to confirm that information.

"Oh, honey," Sister MacIntosh had told her in the church lobby while patting her hand, "Pastor Clancy and that girl, Monica, done broke up more than a month ago! You didn't know?"

C. J. had shaken her head, making Sister MacIntosh's eyes widen eagerly when she realized this was a chance to do her favorite pastime: share more gossip.

"Well," she had said in a breathy whisper, leaning toward C. J.'s ear, "I heard she was ready to get married but he wasn't ready, on account of . . . well, you know . . . how bad it went between him and you. You know . . . with you leaving him standing at the altar like some poor fool! That girl done gave him an ultimatum and he told her no. He couldn't do it! Broke her heart, chile! I heard she even left North Carolina and moved on up to Chicago to live with her sister."

So Shaun had turned down the chance to marry a woman that was right for him only to continue to pine after C. J., whom he had no chance in hell of ever marrying. It made C. J. feel horrible. It made her feel guilty that she couldn't return his feelings.

She had wanted to tell Terrence about her guilt and ask him how she should approach Shaun, but she had been hesitant to do it. Terrence still acted odd whenever she mentioned Shaun, even though she had told him repeatedly she felt nothing for her ex. She had no idea what he might say if she told him about Shaun's admitted feelings for her.

"I just . . . I just don't know how to respond to what you told me that day, Shaun," she now confessed to him.

"You don't *have* to respond!" He leaned down and picked up her stapler and pen holder from the floor, placing both back on her desk. "You told the truth and I told the truth. We put everything on the table. It's as simple as that."

"But I . . . I don't—"

He held up his hand. "I'm not asking for you to declare your love to me. I just told you how I felt. I *still* think about you. I *still* care about you and . . . and I'll always have your back, even when it means taking sides against Victor."

She sighed. This man was too sweet, too good. He was practically a saint. She wondered why he hadn't been canonized yet.

"That's it!" she said with a grin, slapping a hand

on her desk. "I'm going to find a nice Christian girl who's perfect for you. She will make you the happiest man ever, Shaun! I'll make it my mission to seek her out."

He nodded and gave her a forlorn smile, not looking remotely like he believed her, and he walked out of her office.

Chapter 8

Terrence

"Terry, you got this, man," his trainer, Raheem, said while peering down at him from behind the workout bench, his face cloaked by a nest of dreadlocks that looked like tangled vines from this angle. "One more. One more! You can do it."

Terrence closed his eyes, gritted his teeth, tightened his hold around the steel bar, and pushed upward, lifting the three-hundred-ten-pound bench press bar. His arms shook as he did it. He reminded himself to breathe, to not dare hold his breath or he might pass out.

"You're doin' it, man!" Raheem exclaimed. "You're doin' it!"

Terrence held the weight for a few seconds longer before lowering the bar and shifting it back. The weight landed with a loud clang, and Terrence breathed in and out, almost gasping. He opened his eyes, slowly sat up from the weight bench, and wiped at his sweaty brow with the back of his trembling hand. He reached down for his water bottle and squeezed a stream into his mouth. When he looked up, Raheem was grinning ear-to-ear.

"That's what I'm talkin' about, nigga!" Raheem slapped him on the back. "You couldn't even do that before the accident! You kickin' ass and takin' names!"

Terrence slowly nodded, then smiled, too exhausted to join Raheem in his elation.

The truth was that getting his body back to the state it was now had been hard fought and hard won. He could remember the days when doing three reps of a three-hundred-pound bench press had been routine, when he could do an eight-minute-per-mile run for five miles on the treadmill and barely break a sweat. He would hang around with the other guys in the gym, comparing workout routines and talking shit, but he couldn't do that anymore.

"All right," Raheem said. "Good work! I'mma see your ass Saturday, right?"

Terrence nodded again and shakily rose to his feet. "Saturday," he repeated breathlessly before they bumped fists and Raheem slapped his back again.

Terrence slowly made his way out of the weight room and across the gym toward the locker room to seek the hot embrace of the sauna and then take a long, hot shower. As he entered the locker room and neared his locker, he set his water bottle down on one of the wooden benches and yanked his sweat-soaked T-shirt over his head. He raised his water bottle to his lips and squirted another stream into his mouth, letting some of the water dribble down his goateed chin, throat, and chest—too exhausted to care about the mess he was making.

"Good Lord!" someone shouted, making Terrence lower the water bottle from his mouth. "Do that again!"

He turned to find a short, dark-skinned man in a tank top and gym shorts staring at him in awe.

Terrence frowned. "Huh?"

"I said do it again, honey," the man repeated, tugging the towel from around his neck. His dark eyes were wide, like he was totally enraptured. "The thing with the shirt and the water . . . It was absolutely beautiful!"

Terrence cocked an eyebrow.

He had been approached by men before, though this was the first time it had happened in a locker room. In the old days, when he was still modeling, it had happened quite a lot. For some reason, people assumed that just because you were willing to wear lipstick and eyeliner on the runway or for photo shoots, you also wouldn't mind sucking a dick every now and then. He'd had to disappoint a few admirers and let them know that though he appreciated the adoration, he didn't swerve that way. It looked like he would have to do it again today.

"Sorry," he said, "not interested."

"*Not interested?*" The man laughed. "But you don't even know what I'm offering!"

"I *know* what you're offering, and trust me, I'm not interested."

The man took another step toward him. "How about I offer you the cover of a magazine like *Men's Health* or a soda ad on TV that will have every woman in America wondering who was that fine-ass brotha in the leather jacket?" The man inclined his head. "Ever thought of modeling professionally?"

Terrence laughed. Here he was, thinking he was getting hit on, but instead he had been spotted by a recruiter for a modeling agency.

"What's so funny?" the man asked, his smile disappearing. "You don't believe me?"

"No, I believe you! It's just . . . I used to be a model, but I'm five years older, fifteen pounds heavier, and not up to that shit again."

The man narrowed his eyes. "I thought you looked familiar! Were you . . . were you in a few Gucci . . . *no*! Valentino ads, right?"

Terrence nodded. "You've got a good memory."

"Oh, honey, it's not the only thing I've got!" He reached into the gym bag slung over his shoulder and pulled out a business card and held it out to Terrence. "My name is Andre Lewis and I'm with the Sigmund Agency based out of New York. I'm just here in Chesterton visiting family, not even worried about business, and I ran across your beautiful face. It has to be kismet! What's your name?"

"Terrence . . . Terrence Murdoch."

"Oh, and such a *manly* name! I love it!" Andre

exclaimed. "Well, Terrence Murdoch, why don't you give me a call later this week? I can see if I can set you up with a photographer who can take some more recent headshots of you. We can build up your portfolio and get you working again."

Terrence shook his head. "I told you, I'm not up to that shit. And I'm too damn old!"

"*Too old?* What are you, twenty-eight?

"Twenty-nine."

"Humph!" Andre breathed through his nose, waving him off. "Ever heard of Lars Burmeister? Jamie Strachan? Armando Cabral? They were modeling past thirty! And, sweetheart, you can't put an expiration date on those cheekbones, those lips, and those *eyes!*"

At the mention of his eyes, Terrence winced. The prosthetic shell he had gotten was good, but he wondered if some photographer would notice the difference between the real eye and the fake one and play on Terrence's lingering insecurities. It had taken intensive therapy to drag him out of his depression and regain most of his confidence. There was no way he would put himself through that again.

"Sorry, Andre, but, like I said, I'm not interested."

Andre sighed gruffly. "Just take the card and think about it! There's no harm in that, right?"

Terrence hesitated for a few seconds before finally reaching out and taking the business card from him.

"Think about it and let me know," Andre repeated before winking and walking off, leaving Terrence alone in the locker room.

* * *

Several hours later, Terrence was once again gazing down at Andre's business card as he sat at a restaurant table waiting for C. J. to arrive. He hadn't had the chance to talk to her about his encounter at the gym, but he wanted to get her opinion on what he should do. He didn't know if he really wanted to go back to modeling, but C. J. might have had a point when she said yesterday that it was time for him to start working again. Unfortunately, he couldn't see himself at an office job. The prospect of having to wear a tie every day and sit behind a desk practically made him break out in hives. Modeling had been his first job and his only job since a talent scout had spotted him on his college campus when he was nineteen years old. While it hadn't been perfect, it did have its good side—the parties, the hobnobbing with celebrities, and the beautiful women. Of course, that fast lifestyle and the women didn't hold quite the appeal that they had six years ago, but it would still give him something to do all day, especially now that C. J. was away so much. But if he was really going to do this, he'd probably have to move back to New York. If he thought he and C. J. rarely got to see each other now, he could only imagine how often they would be together if he moved up there.

Terrence took a deep breath and tapped Andre's business card on the linen tablecloth, still deep in thought. He really needed to talk to C. J. about this.

Suddenly, his phone buzzed. He looked down to see the text on the screen.

"*So sorry, baby* ☹ " C. J. wrote. "*I'm JUST heading*

out from a last-minute event I got pulled into. Not gonna make dinner. I'll meet you at your place later tonight!"

He closed his eyes and grumbled. So much for their romantic, celebratory dinner, and so much for talking to her!

He glanced at the business card again. Maybe he should just give Andre a call after all; it looked like him moving to New York wouldn't make much of a difference, considering how much time C. J. seemed to have for their relationship.

Terrence angrily shoved himself up from the restaurant table before stalking toward the restaurant's front door. He swung the door open and headed to his Porsche to make the long drive home.

It was around midnight, and he had just stepped out of the bathroom, about to climb into bed, when his doorbell rang. Before even answering the door, he knew it was C. J.—finally.

He groused as he put on his eye patch and headed out of his bedroom to answer the door. Frankly, he wasn't in the mood to see C. J. right now. She had canceled on him *yet again*. Whatever excitement he'd had at the prospect of seeing her had evaporated hours ago while he sat alone on his sofa, flipping channels on his television as he waited for her to arrive. He was pissed and tired and just wanted to go to sleep.

Terrence swung open the door, still scowling. She stood in the hallway with an awkward smile, cradling an overflowing bouquet of yellow roses. She held them out to him.

"A peace offering?" she said.

He glared down at the flowers.

Being in a serious relationship had definitely put him off his game. In the past, *he* had been the one offering flowers and apologies to some chick he had pissed off. Now it was the other way around. He tugged the flowers out of her hand and turned to head back to his bedroom to finally get some shut-eye.

"Please don't be mad, baby," she pleaded from behind him, unbuttoning her coat.

He tossed the roses onto his glass coffee table and kept walking.

"I had no idea that event was scheduled for today. My brother threw it at me at the last minute and I couldn't—"

"You couldn't say no. Right," he muttered, stepping back into his bedroom. "Same ol', same ol'."

"Come on, Terry. I said I was sorry, honey. Don't be this way!"

"Don't be *what* way?" he snapped, yanking his T-shirt over his head and tossing it aside. "Don't be pissed that you canceled on me a second time? That you came here thinking you could show up almost *five* hours late and all you have to do is give me flowers and an apology and I'm supposed to be all . . ."

His words drifted off when he turned just in time to watch her strip off her skirt and let it fall to the floor and pool around her ankles. She strolled toward him, wearing only a red lace bra and thong, gnawing her bottom lip.

"No, I don't think that's all I can do," she whispered as she braced her hands on his shoulders and eased him back onto his bed.

He gazed up at her, turned on despite himself.

"I can do a lot more," she said as she dropped to her knees on the hardwood floor, pushed his legs wide so she could kneel between his thighs, and then pulled back the waistband of his sweat-pants.

"So you think sexual favors are gonna work? That sex is . . . is supposed to make it all . . . all better? You think . . . Oh, shit!"

The last part was barely audible. She had already wrapped her hand around his dick and started to slowly stroke him, making him gulp for air and grip the edge of the bed.

"Of course not," she said, meeting his gaze, licking her lips. "But it's a start, right?"

She then lowered her head and took him whole into her mouth. As she suckled him he fisted one hand in her hair and the other held on tight to the bed to steady himself.

"Shit," he groaned again.

After that, Terrence forgot what he was so mad about. In fact, he didn't do much thinking at all.

Chapter 9

Dante

Dante floated back to consciousness gradually, like a boat set adrift that was finally making its way back to shore. He heard beeping and the drone of voices he didn't recognize. He slowly opened his eyes and squinted reflexively at the bright aura of light around him. He tried to raise his hand to shield his eyes but realized, belatedly, that he couldn't raise his arm. It was limp with fatigue, as if he had done two hundred curls at the gym. It was also weighed down. He would later realize it was weighed down by electrodes, an IV, and a series of wires. Unable to shield his eyes, he closed them instead.

"The sedative should be wearing off now," a female voice murmured. "Dr. Basak said to keep a careful eye on Mr. Turner for the next few hours."

Dr. Basak?

"Like we wouldn't," another female voice countered with a snort. This voice was throatier. It sounded older. "That's our job, ain't it?"

"Yeah, but I think Dr. Basak is a little more worried about this guy. His recovery took longer than expected on account of . . . well . . . what happened. You know what I mean!"

"Yeah, I know," the other voice answered. "Kelly's still on suspension for that one."

Wait, he thought. *What happened?*

He didn't know what they were talking about. Nor did he know who the doctor was or who these women were, for that matter. Why was he here in this bright room, more than likely a hospital room? His last memory was of being in a very dark, quiet place. He struggled now to remember what place that was.

An office building? A parking lot? No, that's not right.

His mind felt sluggish. His head felt like it was filled with cotton, not brain tissue, and was operating accordingly. Maybe it was the effects of the sedative one of the women had mentioned.

No, I wasn't in a parking lot, he realized. *It was a . . . a garage!*

It was the multi-level parking garage near his law office.

He could see the parking garage now and where he had fallen on the second floor. He remembered cold, wet asphalt against his forehead and cheek and the smell of gasoline and car exhaust. He remembered the searing pain spreading across his abdomen and seeing the tread of his back tire only inches from his face after he had fallen to the ground.

But why had he fallen?

Before Dante fell, he remembered bringing up his briefcase to shield himself and shutting his eyes when he heard a booming sound.

Even now, Dante recoiled from the reverberation that had bounced around the concrete garage. After the boom, he had opened his eyes.

"What the hell?" he had mumbled.

And then a minute later, he had noticed the red spot bloom on his dress shirt and spread across his torso. He remembered touching the spot and marveling at the bright red blood on his fingertips.

He remembered now what had happened that night.

I was shot, Dante thought, letting the full comprehension slam into him like the bullet that had torn into the flesh and muscle of his torso. *I was shot! And now I'm in a hospital.*

His mind struggled to remember who shot him. He could see a shadowy silhouette under the dim light of the garage. The face . . . that face! He was on the cusp of remembering who it was, but his mind felt so listless. The face was like an inkblot he was trying to form into a recognizable shape.

"So what did you bring to lunch today?" Dante heard one of the women in the hospital room ask.

"Fettuccine alfredo. My boyfriend made it. It's pretty good," the other answered. "He even used wheat pasta, which isn't something I usually go for."

"*Wheat pasta?* Please, girl, I bet it isn't as good as the pork chops and greens I'm having!"

Shut up! Shut up, you stupid bitches, Dante thought, annoyed by their mundane prattle, which only distracted him. He fought again to remember who the shooter was.

The image began to coalesce into someone he recognized, someone he had known well. When he realized who it was, he tried to clench his hands into fists on the hospital bed but only managed to twitch his fingers.

He wanted vengeance. He wanted to kick some ass! Dante tried to rise out of the bed he was lying on to do just that, but he couldn't. His body wouldn't follow his command. He opened his eyes again. This time the bright light wasn't quite as painful. His vision was a bit blurred, but he could now vaguely see the two women standing near his hospital bed. One was adjusting his bedsheets at the foot of his bed, and the other was examining his IV bag. His fluttering movements drew their attention simultaneously, and they both turned to look at him.

The large black one smiled and dropped her hand to her hip. "Well, look who's awake!"

"We better tell Dr. Basak," the one with the red hair and freckles whispered, leaning toward him.

"Uh-huh," the other echoed. "We better tell those cops, too."

Chapter 10

Evan

Evan was interrupted from his work by knocking at his office door. "Mr. Murdoch," a voice called out to him. "Mr. Murdoch, sir?"

He looked up from his computer screen, squinting with irritation, to find his assistant gazing timidly at him from a crack in the doorway.

"Yes, what is it, Adrienne? I was in the middle of something."

He hated when his thoughts were cut off midstream.

"I'm sorry, sir, but you have a Detective Morris waiting for you out here," Adrienne said, pushing the door open a little wider. She stepped inside and shut the door behind her. "He said he wants to speak with you."

At the sound of that name, Evan's stomach

plummeted. Why was the detective sniffing around him again? Why couldn't that man leave him the hell alone?

"Because he can sense you know something," a voice in his head answered. *"And he's going to keep sniffing until he finds out what that something is."*

"Did he say what he wanted to speak with me about?" Evan asked.

The petite young woman shook her head, sending her curls flying. "I'm afraid not, sir."

Evan leaned back in his chair. "Well, then tell him I'm busy. If he really wants to speak with me, he can make an appointment."

Adrienne frowned, then glanced anxiously over her shoulder at the closed door.

"Is there a problem?" Evan asked.

"N-n-no, sir. It's just . . ." Her words drifted off. She shook her head again. "I'll tell him, Mr. Murdoch."

He then watched as she fled from the room, shutting the door behind her.

A couple of hours later, Evan powered down his computer. He glanced at his watch. He would have to head out soon if he didn't want to be late. He was supposed to have lunch with Terrence today, but, prior to that, the two were meeting at a jewelry store where Evan wanted to buy Leila a "push gift"—an expensive piece of jewelry that he was supposed to bestow upon her after she delivered their daughter.

"You want to buy her *more* stuff?" Terrence had exclaimed over the phone when Evan had asked him to come with him to the jeweler. "Does Lee really want more jewelry, Ev?"

Probably not, Evan had thought.

Leila now had several chests full of jewelry he had purchased for her in the past year or so. It was more than she could ever realistically wear, and she never had been a "diamond and furs" kind of girl to begin with. But he felt like he owed her this gift. He couldn't marry her yet with Charisse still holding out on their divorce. The least he could do was let her know that if she wasn't his wife she was still the love of his life.

Evan stood up from his desk, walked across the room, and opened his office door.

"I'll be back in a couple of hours, Adrienne," he called to his assistant, who nodded. "If I'm a little late for my three o'clock, let Jim know I'm on my way."

"Yes, Mr. Murdoch."

He then made his way down to his private elevator at the end of the corridor that took him to the lobby twelve stories below. As the elevator's metal doors opened and he was about to step onto the lobby's marble tile, he looked up and felt the blood drain from his head.

"Why, hello, Mr. Murdoch!" Detective Morris drawled with that predatory smile of his.

"H-hello," Evan answered, taken aback.

"Your assistant told me you were busy, so I just decided to grab a quick bite to eat and wait for you down here." He looked around him, gazing at the catwalk overhead. He shoved his hands into the pockets of his baggy slacks. "This is quite a place you got here! All this glass and marble . . . the best that money can buy, huh?"

The elevator dinged and the doors began to close. Evan hopped out before they closed on his shoulders.

"What do you want, Detective?" he asked through gritted teeth, unable to keep his tone polite. He was tired of being harassed by this man. "You called the doctor's office, didn't you? They should've confirmed my and my brother's alibi. We were there the whole time that you said that thing happened to Dante. What else do you need to ask me?"

The detective shook his head. "I'm not here to ask you anything. I wanted to tell you somethin'."

Evan raised his brows. "And that is?"

The detective took a step toward him. His smile widened into a grin. "Dante Turner woke up."

A chill went up Evan's spine.

"He woke up yesterday afternoon. He isn't speaking yet. All the drugs haven't worn off, but the doctors think he'll definitely recover enough to be able to speak. He's *going* to talk again, and when he does, he's going to tell us what happened."

Evan stilled. He could feel his panic rise with each passing second. Dante was awake! Dante was going to talk! He would tell the detective who shot him, and Antonio would be arrested. Paulette's family would be torn apart.

"So, I asked you once," the detective continued, "and now I'm going to ask you again. Is there anything . . . and I mean *anything* you need to tell me about the shooting that happened that night? Is there anything you know that I need to know?"

Evan swallowed loudly. "No, there isn't."

"Are you sure?"

Evan straightened his shoulders and rose to his full height. "Yes, I am sure, Detective."

He watched as Detective Morris nodded, then turned to stare across the lobby at the TV screens that showed commercials from the franchises owned by Murdoch Conglomerated. He grew somber.

"You know, my mama and daddy used to work for you," Detective Morris announced, making Evan confused by the course this conversation was taking.

"Excuse me?"

"My mother and my father used to work at a cookie plant down in Alabama," he explained, turning back to Evan. He spoke louder so he could be heard over the noise from all the Murdoch Conglomerated employees who were walking throughout the atrium, grabbing their afternoon lunches. "I could remember them working there when I was a kid. They would have the smell of cookies on their clothes and in their hair. They would bring home the broken bits for me and my brother to snack on at school. Shit, most of the town worked at that cookie plant or depended on it!" He glanced back at the video screens. "Then, in the early nineties, Murdoch Conglomerated bought the company. Everyone was excited. They thought the plant might expand . . . hire even more people, bring even more money to town. But then you guys shut the whole thing down." He glared at Evan again. "Just turned off the machines, kicked everyone out, and locked the doors one day."

Evan inwardly winced. He didn't know what cookie plant the detective was referring to, but he wasn't surprised to hear that the company had done something like that back then. His father's tactic when he first started to expand Murdoch Conglomerated was to buy out competitors. If he considered them worth incorporating into the business, he'd keep the companies open as subsidiaries, but most he just shut down. Evan wasn't sure if his father had done it sometimes out of spite.

"Mama and Daddy didn't have a job anymore, no pension. Everything in town went to shit," the detective continued. "A lot of people moved to other places if they could, but the ones who stayed had it bad . . . *real* bad. My daddy started drinkin'. He and Mama got divorced." The detective pursed his lips. "I never thought one day I'd get the chance to look in the eyes of the man who did that to my town—to my family."

"I didn't do it, *my father* did. I wasn't the CEO of the company at that time. I was still in junior high, Detective!"

"All the same, you're a lot like your daddy, aren't you, *Mr. Murdoch*?" he snarled with contempt. "Like I said before, any man who gets to where you've gotten in this world can't do it without getting his hands a little dirty, without doing some things that aren't so honest."

Evan blanched. He gazed into the man's cold, gray eyes and realized that the detective wasn't just conducting an investigation into Dante's attempted murder. He hadn't just latched onto Evan because he thought he knew something about the investigation, or because the detective was some racist redneck from the backwoods of Alabama

who was out to put a rich black man in his place.
Evan realized that Detective Morris had an axe to
grind for past wrongs—and he planned on grinding
that axe against Evan's backside.

"Detective, I've told you everything that I know.
Now if you'll excuse me, I have to get to an appointment. And if you continue to ask me questions from
this point on, you're going to have to do it with my
lawyer present. Understood?"

The detective chuckled. "Whatever way you
want it, Mr. Murdoch. Doesn't make a difference
to me."

"Good," Evan said, before walking around the
detective, striding across the lobby while telling
himself that he wasn't running away.

"Damn! Where the hell you been, man?" Terrence called out as Evan opened the glass door
and stepped into the jewelry store. The younger
man pushed himself away from one of the coun-
ters and held up his arms. "I've been waiting for
you for the past twenty minutes!"

"Sorry! Time got away from me."

Terrence nodded before scrutinizing Evan
more closely. "Hey, are you all right? You don't
look so good."

"I'm fine," Evan answered, not wanting to have
to recount his run-in with Detective Morris. He
stared down into the glass case. "So what do we
have? What pieces look the most promising?"

"The hell if I know," Terrence muttered with a
shrug, glancing over his shoulder at a pretty
woman in a tight skirt who was taking jewelry out

of one of the cabinets in the corner and placing several diamond bracelets and necklaces on a velvet-padded cushion. "I asked one of the sales girls to pull a few things. I don't know shit about buying a 'push gift.' I'm nobody's baby daddy—as far as I know. Knock on wood." He rapped his knuckles on the counter. "So I asked her to make some recommendations."

"You've bought jewelry for women before, Terry. This isn't much of a stretch."

"You know damn well it is! When I gave girls gifts, I was basically saying, 'Thanks for the good sex last night. Hope we can do it again sometime.' You're buying a gift saying, 'Thanks for having my baby. I hope you don't hate me after you squeeze something the size of a watermelon out of something the size of a lemon.'" Terrence held up his hands and shifted them back and forth like weighing scales. "One calls for something a lot bigger than the other."

"So you're saying I should have asked someone else to help me do this?"

"I'm saying you should have called Paulette! This is more up her alley, and she's tight with Lee. She knows what she likes."

Evan grimaced and turned his attention back to the glass case. "I couldn't call Paulette for this."

"Why not?"

"It'd just be too . . . too awkward."

"What the hell would be awkward about it? It's just Paulette!"

"Trust me." Evan held up his hand. "It's better if you're here and not her."

Terrence squinted at his brother. "What the

hell is going on with you, Ev? You've been acting real shady lately."

"*Shady?*" Evan's voice went up an octave. He stared at his brother in outrage. "How am I shady?"

"Something's happened . . . something's gone down and you're not telling me what it is."

Evan pursed his lips. He wanted to tell somebody. He wanted to release this lonely burden, but could he do it? *Should* he do it?

"Just *say* it, Ev," Terrence urged. "It can't be that bad! You didn't kill somebody, did you?"

"All right, gentlemen," the pretty blond sales girl said as she walked across the room holding a velvet-lined tray aloft. "I have several beautiful pieces to show you today. I'm sure you'll find something among our selections that will—"

"Would you excuse us?" Evan said, holding up his finger. "We just need a sec."

The young woman lowered the tray. Her smile disappeared. "Of . . . of course," she stuttered.

Evan grabbed his brother by the arm and tugged him toward the shop door. "Let's talk outside," he whispered. When they stepped onto the sidewalk and walked a few feet to a deserted end of the block, he let Terrence go.

"Dammit, *what* is it?" Terrence asked impatiently, eying him again.

Evan sucked in a deep breath and slowly exhaled. He shook his head. *I can't believe I'm doing this,* he thought.

"I didn't . . . I didn't kill anybody," he began tentatively. "But I . . . I know someone who did."

Terrence's brows furrowed. "What?"

Evan closed his eyes. "Antonio . . . He killed someone. He killed Paulette's ex-boyfriend, the guy who was blackmailing her. He basically confessed it to me."

Evan opened his eyes to find his brother staring at him in shock.

"What the . . . what the fuck! Ev, tell me you're joking! Tell me you're lying to me because—"

He shook his head. "I'm not lying, Terry. I wish I was! He told me what he did and how he did it. I looked the guy up online to find a news story about how he died. He was murdered . . . murdered just like Antonio said, but they haven't figured out who killed him. The police are still investigating it. They even questioned Paulette."

"Oh, shit," Terrence whispered, taking a shaky step back, bumping into the adjacent brick wall. "Oh, shit! Oh, Jesus! Did you tell Paulette?"

He shook his head. "No, I . . . I can't. It's not my place."

"*Not your place?*" Terrence shouted. "Not your place? Ev, you have to tell her!"

"I can't, Terry! Not now. Not after what else happened."

"There's *more*?"

Evan nodded. "I kind of . . . I kind of let it slip to Antonio that Dante had tried to blackmail Paulette, too. I told him what Dante had done and within a couple of weeks, Dante was shot."

Terrence cringed. "So you're saying you think Antonio tried to kill him?"

"I don't know! Maybe! The detective said Dante woke up, that he probably saw his shooter, and he could point out who tried to kill him. What if he tells the cops it was Antonio? What if Paulette's husband gets carted off to jail?"

"Ev," Terrence said, staring at him, aghast. "That's not our biggest concern right now!"

"Yes, it is! If he's found guilty of murder, Antonio could get the death penalty, Terry!"

"Look, you're telling me that our sister is living with a man who already killed one dude and might have tried to kill another. *That's* what I'm worried about, Ev! What if he tries to do the same shit to her?"

"He won't hurt her, Terry. He *loves* her!"

"But how do you know he won't kill her?" Terrence shouted. His voice echoed down the street, and Evan furiously motioned for him to keep his voice down. "How do you know that?" he whispered through clenched teeth. "What if he gets pissed off at her one day and decides to come at her with a butcher knife, huh? What if she says the wrong thing and ends up with an electrical cord wrapped around her throat?"

"He won't . . . he won't do that," Evan argued, though his voice lost its forcefulness.

In his heart, he knew he couldn't vouch for anything anymore. He never would have guessed Antonio would kill anyone, but Antonio had done it. Deep down, Evan really didn't know what Antonio was capable of.

"Shit," Terrence muttered again, scrubbing his hand over his face.

"You have to promise me that you won't tell Paulette what I just told you."

"I can't do that, Ev."

"But Terry, if you tell her, she might—"

"I said I can't do that, dammit!" Terrence barked, lowering his hand. "I can't! I'm not promising you anything."

Evan watched as his brother shook his head and muttered to himself. Terrence then abruptly turned.

"Where are you going?" Evan shouted after him. "I thought you were going to help me pick out a gift for Lee!"

"You really expect me to stand around looking at fucking bracelets after you told me that shit? Hell no! I'm out," he said, before waving Evan off.

"Terry! Terry, come on!" Evan called after his brother, then sighed as Terrence continued to stalk toward his Porsche, parked at the other end of the block. "Goddammit," Evan murmured in defeat before walking back into the jewelry store, letting the door swing shut behind him.

Chapter 11
Terrence

Terrence slumped back in the padded booth in the back of the art deco restaurant, his mood as dark as the lighting surrounding him. He sighed before taking a sip of chardonnay from his wineglass and checking the time on his cell phone's screen.

It was fifteen minutes after eight. C. J. was late—again. This time for a dinner date in Adams Morgan. It was the dinner they had postponed at least twice already.

"I should've known this shit would happen," he mumbled as he yanked off his leather jacket and tossed it roughly onto the seat beside him, pushing up the sleeves of his sweater.

He was in no mood to sit around waiting for C. J., not with what he had experienced today. He was still grappling with what Evan had told him, with the weighty secret he now carried. He'd hoped to find some momentary solace from all of it, to get lost in C. J.'s company and the movie they planned to see later that night. But now he was sitting alone with his torturous thoughts and all his worries.

His sister was living with a murderer. Every night she laid her head on her pillow she did it next to the man who had killed her lover. In some way, Terrence could understand Antonio's anger. Finding out that *any* man had blackmailed C. J. into cheating would have enraged Terrence, too, but would he have hunted the man down and killed him in cold blood? And Terrence wasn't as convinced as Evan that Paulette had nothing to fear from Antonio. Was a man like that capable of doing something violent to her if he got incensed again? Terrence couldn't say for sure, and that unnerved him. It made his stomach twist into tight knots. It made him scared for his little sister.

Terrence's phone buzzed. He glanced down at it again to see a text message flash on the screen.

"Running late, baby. Sorry! Stuck in Virginia traffic. I'm on my way," he read.

Terrence grumbled. She was still in Virginia? There was no way she'd make it to the restaurant in the next fifteen minutes—maybe in the next half hour. They probably weren't going to make the movie later, either, and he had even chosen the nauseating chick flick because he had known it was something she'd like.

Terrence reached for the last pumpernickel roll in the bread basket at the center of the table and peered around the restaurant. There was a crowd gathering near the bar on the other side of the room. The stools were full of loud guys and a smattering of giggling women who seemed to be sizing up one another, doing the mating rituals that singles usually did. Meanwhile, the restaurant tables were starting to fill up with other diners, mostly couples laughing and smiling over candlelight. But a few tables—like Terrence's—were occupied by a lone patron.

His eyes settled on a middle-aged woman in a frumpy purple sweater who was leaning over a bowl of turtle soup, staring down at the glowing screen of her e-reader. She dabbed with her linen napkin at some of the soup that dribbled onto her chubby chin. She was too engrossed to look up. More of her soup dribbled onto her sweater, near her oversize bosom. She didn't even bother to wipe that off.

Good God, Terrence thought as he lowered his bread bun from his mouth. *Do I look like her?*

"Can I refill your wine, sir?" a waiter asked as he walked toward the table, gesturing to Terrence's almost empty glass. "You were having the chardonnay, right?"

Terrence shook his head and grabbed his jacket. He eased out of the booth and rose to his feet. "Nah, I'm good," he murmured before stepping away from his table, leaving the waiter to stare at him in bewilderment.

Terrence headed to the bar. He'd be damned if he'd sit around *alone* waiting for C. J., looking like some sad cat lady in a sweater. That wasn't how he rolled!

He walked to the granite bar top, tossed his jacket onto one of the few free stools, and slapped his hand on the edge of the counter, grabbing the spiky-haired bartender's attention. "Double shot of tequila, my man."

The bartender nodded and turned to grab a glass to fill Terrence's order.

"Oh, is that who I think it is?" a familiar voice shouted from behind Terrence, making him turn.

He looked down to find Andre from the gym smiling up at him. Andre was decked out head to toe in a brown leather suit and matching shoes. A maroon silk ascot was at his throat. A mixed beauty with almond-shaped eyes, glowing golden skin, and plump ruby lips who had to be almost a foot taller than he was stood at his side with her arm linked through his.

"Why, it's the epitome of manliness himself," Andre effused, throwing back his head and dropping his hand to his chest in mock awe. "Mr. Terrence Murdoch! Be still my heart, honey!"

Terrence laughed at Andre's theatrics. He was really starting to like this guy.

"What are you doing in town, gorgeous? I rarely run into people from Chesterton around here!" Andre said. "The small-town folks are usually too scared to come to the big city!"

"I was meeting someone for dinner, but"—Terrence paused and shrugged—"they're running late."

"Well, I'm glad I ran into you! I was wondering if you thought about that little offer I made you."

Terrence sighed. "I'm still thinking about it,"

he answered honestly. "It's been a while since I've modeled, Andre. I'm older. I've put on weight since then."

"Oh, hush up, boy! You know you've still got it!" He looked Terrence up and down, letting his appreciative gaze travel over him.

"I've had surgeries."

"Haven't we all?" Andre asked, batting his eyes. "We all need a little touch-up every now and then! I keep my plastic surgeon on speed dial."

"No, I mean *serious* surgery. I'm not the same dude I was ten years ago . . . hell, *six months* ago! I just don't know if I'm up to it again."

"Oh, I know what'll help convince you!" Andre winked as he unwound the woman's arm from his and eased her toward the bar. She'd been silent during their entire conversation, watching them with an amused remoteness. "This lovely goes by the name of Aiko. She's a client of mine, and she can tell you all the wonderful things I do for her and the wonderful money I help her make! Won't you, sweetheart?" he asked, glancing at the beautiful woman beside him.

"Absolutely," she replied in a throaty purr, openly staring at Terrence.

Terrence shook his head and removed his jacket from his stool. He knew where this was going. A situation like this one could land him in a lot of trouble. "Actually, Andre, I was just about to—"

"Now, Terrence, honey, don't be rude!" Andre ordered, slapping his manicured hand on Terrence's broad shoulder. "Offer to buy the young lady a drink and talk for a bit. Is that so hard? Meanwhile, I'll be across the room doing some agent business. Okay?" He then fluttered his fingers and sauntered off, leaving Terrence to gaze awkwardly at the beauty in front of him.

"I'll have a mojito," she said, shrugging out of the denim bolero she was wearing, revealing a studded tank top that dipped so low in the front he could almost see the tops of the dark nipples that were proudly jutting through the cotton fabric of her shirt. She hopped onto the stool next to his, brushing his thigh as she did.

Terrence licked his lips as he gazed at the woman beside him, seeing something a lot more tantalizing than any of the dishes on the restaurant's menu.

Oh, if he wasn't in love with C. J. he would be all over this chick! But he *was* in love with C. J.— very much so. That meant he had to be a good boy. He released a beleaguered breath and leaned toward Aiko so that he could be heard over the bar room clamor.

"Look," he began, clearing his throat. "I'll order you a drink, but I have to tell you, I . . . I have a girlfriend. I'm kind of . . . uh . . . off the market, so to speak."

She cocked an eyebrow. A wry smile crossed her lips. "Oh, really?"

He nodded. "Afraid so."

She leaned toward his ear, filling his nose with her alluring fragrance that was a mix of musk and jasmine. "That's not a problem, because I've got a girlfriend, too," she whispered.

He shifted back and stared at her in amazement. She smirked.

"Well, if that's the case," he said just as the bartender sat his tequila in front of him, "a mojito for the lady!" he called out, making her throw back her head and laugh.

And for two hours, Terrence enjoyed beautiful Aiko's company. They shared crazy modeling stories over several shots of tequila and glasses of mojito, regaling each other with tales about eccentric designers, diva supermodels, and weird photo shoots. Terrence felt like he had a new drinking buddy, but instead of a burly brother with tattoos who liked to talk about sports and cars, it was a gorgeous, five-foot-eleven model who had appeared in a few Revlon ads and had to fly to Tokyo next week for a runway show. In Aiko's company, all thoughts of his earlier conversation with Evan about Antonio and his anger over C. J. going AWOL briefly disappeared.

"Well, damn!" Aiko exclaimed in a low voice as a cute girl with a plump ass in a tight red dress walked by them.

Aiko's arm was thrown around Terrence's shoulders and she leaned against him, all the while letting her lecherous gaze follow the red-dressed, curvy siren's undulating rear end to the other side of the bar.

Terrence chuckled as he threw back his fifth shot. "I know, right?"

"I would *love* to sample a piece of that," she

drawled before flashing her eyes toward his. "Wanna share?"

He furrowed his brows in disbelief, making her suck her teeth.

"I *know* you have a girlfriend and so do I, but"— she leaned toward him—"I won't tell if you won't."

He shifted his elbows off the counter and squinted, wondering if the alcohol was playing tricks with his ears. "Wait . . . I thought you weren't into dudes!"

"I'm not! But I've been known to do a ménage—under the right circumstances."

At those words, his dick perked up a little.

"What do you say?" She wiggled her brows and stuck out her pink tongue, trailing it languidly over her glossy lips. "We can head over there and chat her up? See if she's interested? If she's down, it could be a memorable night."

Terrence sighed. It was tempting, so very tempting. And he was just drunk enough to be willing to do something like that. A year ago, he wouldn't have hesitated, but now . . . but now . . .

"Terry?" he heard C. J. call out to him.

He turned to find his girlfriend glaring up at him with her hands on her jean-clad hips. Her eyes shifted to Aiko, who still had her arm casually draped around his shoulder.

He grinned. "Hey, baby! You finally made it!"

C. J. frowned. He realized he had slurred his greeting. Maybe he was drunker than he thought.

"Terry, I've been calling you and texting you for the past two hours. I've wandered around this restaurant at least four times looking for you! I thought you had left and gone back home!"

"*You called me?*" He reached down and patted his jacket pockets. "Shit, babe, I'm sorry. I think I left my phone at the . . . you know . . . our table. I was so distracted I didn't notice."

"Yeah, I can see that," she murmured, sending a withering glance to Aiko.

He held up his shot glass. "I was having a few drinks here with my girl!" He affectionately slapped Aiko's knee.

"More than a few, Terry," Aiko said with a snort before offering her hand to C. J. for a shake. "It's a pleasure to meet you, lovely," she cooed and then gave C. J. a wink.

"Down, girl!" Terrence hopped off his bar stool. His feet were a little unsteady underneath him. He felt like he was on a gently rocking boat. "This one is already taken—and she ain't into threesomes."

Aiko poked out her bottom lip and pulled her hand back. "Aww, that's a shame!"

"I know, right?" he said with a laugh.

"Let's *go*, Terry!" C. J. said through clenched teeth, making his eyes widen.

"Oh, shit!" He glanced at Aiko, who was snickering. "I think I'm in trouble."

Aiko nodded. "I think you are, too."

He waved at Aiko over his shoulder as he trailed behind C. J., who was already stomping to the restaurant door. "Catch you later, girl!"

"You know my number!" Aiko called back.

* * *

"You know my number?" C. J. repeated while glaring out the windshield and tightening her whiteknuckled grip on the steering wheel. "I cannot believe this shit!"

Terrence slumped down farther in the passenger seat of C. J.'s Honda Civic, adjusting the seatbelt across his chest. He was way too drunk to drive himself home and had no desire to total two Porsches in less than a year, so C. J. was driving him from the restaurant back to his condo. But it didn't seem like it was going to be a tranquil ride. She had been seething quietly for the past twenty minutes, refusing to look at him. He guessed she was tired of staying silent.

"Here I am wandering around that damn restaurant, looking for *your* ass, panicked because I'm so late, and there you are sitting at the bar, getting drunk with some . . . some bitch!" she screeched.

"Whoa!" Terrence said with a laugh. "Calm down, babe!"

He had never seen C. J. this furious. He stared at her and smiled drunkenly. It was actually kind of hot.

"Don't you tell me to calm down, dammit! I can't believe you would do something like—"

"First of all," he began, sitting up in his seat, "*you're* the one who left *my* ass sitting around waiting for you again. This time it was for more than two hours."

"No," she said tightly, "I left you waiting for *forty-five minutes!* I spent the rest of that time staring at dining tables, looking for you, and standing outside calling your cell phone asking where the hell you were! I thought something was wrong, Terry! I wasn't sure if something had happened to you or—"

"Secondly," he continued like he hadn't heard her, "Aiko isn't remotely interested in me! She'd want to fuck you, not me!" He tilted his head thoughtfully. "Okay, *maybe* she'd fuck me if she knew you were involved, but it'd have to be like a . . . I don't know . . . a two-for-one deal."

C. J. paused from glaring at the roadway in front of her to turn and stare at him. "Terry, what the hell are you talking about?"

"And thirdly," he said, reaching out for her. He let his index finger trail languidly over her cheek and then along the neck and collar bone before finally skimming the swell of cleavage he could see under the roadway light. "You're damn sexy when you're mad, baby."

He laughed when she fussily slapped his hand away. She stared out the windshield again.

"Just don't say anything else to me, Terry, okay?" she ordered, gnawing the inside of her cheek. "Don't say one goddamn thing or I'll be tempted to murder you."

At the mention of murder, Terrence fell silent again. His thoughts returned to his sister and Antonio, to his earlier conversation with Evan. He turned to look out the passenger side window, no longer in the mood to talk.

They arrived at his place about twenty minutes later. Terrence had to lean against C. J. as she guided him down the hall to his condo door, bearing his weight and huffing as she did it.

"Where are your keys?" she asked, shifting her purse to her other shoulder and propping him up against the hallway wall.

He shrugged. "Hell if I know!"

He watched as she groused loudly and began to dig into his jeans and leather jacket pockets, shoving her hands into them in search of his house keys.

"Damn, girl!" He chuckled. "Buy me dinner first if you're gonna manhandle me!"

C. J. glowered up at him, not looking remotely amused. "Found them," she muttered after yanking his keys out of his jacket pocket. She turned away from him to unlock his door.

Terrence's gaze lowered to her delectable ass and how plump it looked in her skinny jeans, like a ripe Georgia peach. He wondered what color thong she was wearing tonight. He wondered how long it would be before he could see her in that thong. He reached out and grabbed a handful. Again, she swatted his hand away before shoving open the door.

"Come on," she said, grabbing his arm and yanking him through the doorway. He stumbled slightly on the welcome mat. A minute later, C. J. was dragging him into his bedroom. She reached along the wall and turned on the overhead light, revealing his California king, ebony nightstand, and wardrobe. Terrence tumbled face first onto the bed and rolled onto his back.

"Sit up," she ordered, walking toward him. "I have to take off your clothes."

He lazily shifted upright and gave her a wicked

grin. "Hell, yeah! I was hoping you would. Let's do this," he said as he slid his hands up her outer thighs, but she wrenched his hands away and pulled off his jacket instead.

"Stop it, Terry."

She then reached for his jeans, undid the metal snap, and lowered the zipper. He reached out and tried to do the same to her, making her angrily take a step back from the foot of the bed. "Dammit, I said stop it! We're not having sex tonight! You're sloppy drunk! You are getting in *that* bed and you are going to sleep it off!" She reached for his pants again. "We'll just talk about this in the morning."

This time he shoved her hands away and glared up at her, catching her by surprise. "Don't talk to me like I'm some fuckin' child!"

She stilled.

"Who the hell do you think you are?"

"Your girlfriend, the last time I checked!"

"Well, you better check again! You'd have to be around to be my damn girlfriend, wouldn't you?"

"What does that mean?"

"What the hell do you think it means?"

The anger he had been trying to keep at bay all week, all *month* now came bubbling to the surface. "You're never here! You're too busy playing church girl in North Carolina for your daddy most of the damn time," he sneered. "You don't give a shit about me! Just stop pretending and admit it! So why the fuck are you here, C. J.?" he asked, making her jump back and flinch like he had struck her. "It *has* to be for the sex 'cuz it certainly ain't for anything else!"

"I can't . . . I can't believe you would say that . . . that you would even . . ." She shook her head. "Dammit, I *care* about you! Me being away sometimes doesn't change that! And I thought you cared about me too. Of course, I—"

"No, you don't care about me," he said, feeling the shots of tequila he had imbibed spurring him on with liquid courage. "On the long list of shit that's important to C. J. Aston, it's obvious I rank pretty low."

"But this is only temporary!" she argued, looking hurt. But he wasn't assuaged. He had finally hit a nerve with her after feeling like he hadn't been able to get through to her for weeks. "I told you I was just doing this for my father's campaign, to help him out. It's not gonna last forever!"

"So you say, but how do I know you won't make up another excuse to keep disappearing down there, huh? How do I know you won't just . . . just hook up with somebody else in North Carolina, like your boy Shaun Clancy?"

She dropped her hands to her sides and screwed up her face. "What the hell does Shaun have to do with any of this?"

"I don't know." He narrowed his eyes at her. "You tell me!"

She stared at him, slowly shaking her head again. "I don't know what you're insinuating," she began, "but if it is what I think it is, you're *way* off—and you don't know me half as well as I thought you did."

"Same here, baby." His voice was cool with contempt. He reached down woozily, grabbed her fallen purse from the rug near his bed, and tossed her purse out the bedroom door so that it landed with a thump and a clang on the hallway's Brazilian hardwood floor. "Even more of a reason why you shouldn't be here then, right?"

She followed the path of her purse, then turned around to look at him, staring at him with so much pain in her eyes it almost made him wince. He nearly opened his mouth to take back everything he had just said, but his anger was a lot stronger than his remorse at that moment.

He had turned down an offer for a damn threesome for her! And how many other beautiful women had he rejected and outright ignored because he was in love with C. J.? Hadn't he gone out of his way countless times to show her that he loved her, to show her that she was first in his life? Meanwhile, she couldn't even show up to a damn dinner date on time for him. She had left him sitting alone at that table *again* like some asshole! He wasn't putting up with it anymore.

"Well, fuck you, too, Terry," she spat with tears brimming in her eyes. "Fuck you, too."

He watched as she turned and walked out of the bedroom.

As he listened to her footsteps recede down the hall, he fell back onto his bed and turned onto his stomach. When he heard his front door slam shut, he closed his eyes and fell asleep.

Terrence awoke the next morning on top of his bedsheets with a case of bad dry mouth, a horrendous headache, and the feeling that he had done something really stupid last night. He slowly pushed himself to his elbows and looked down at himself. He was still dressed from the night before. He unsteadily rose to his feet a minute later, only to rush into his bathroom and vomit whatever was left in his stomach into the toilet bowl. When the nausea finally subsided, he downed two Excedrin and stripped off his clothes. He climbed into the shower stall and turned up the water to its highest temperature, letting the scalding hot stream blast his back and shoulders. Terrence emerged from the shower almost an hour later, after the water had gone from hot to tepid. His headache wasn't quite as bad, but he still felt awful, like a wrung-out, dirty washcloth left to dry in the open air.

He stepped onto his bathmat, wrapped a towel around his waist, wiped the fog of condensation from the bathroom mirror, and gazed at his reflection.

"Shit," he whispered before lowering his head into his hands.

He now vividly recalled the stupid thing he had done last night. What he had said to C. J. and how he had kicked her out of his home, tossing her purse into his hall like she was some common hood rat he was trying to get rid of after a one-night stand.

"Shit!" he spat again.

Terrence knew he could be a nasty drunk, but that wasn't the only reason why he had treated C. J. so badly. She'd hurt his feelings, so he'd hurt her in return. Frankly, she'd hurt him quite a few times in the past few weeks, but instead of just saying that he had lashed out at her, which isn't what he had intended to do. That was the major downside about being this deep in love, something he was experiencing for the first time in his life: he felt totally vulnerable, like he was stuck in the nightmare of standing behind the lectern to make a speech and realizing, when he looked down, he was completely naked. He had no real defenses against C. J., against those times she could make him feel insecure, ignored, and outright rejected. So he had acted like a little boy and thrown a temper tantrum. He had done something he now sincerely regretted and, as a result, he may have lost her.

No, he thought, *I didn't lose her. I pushed her away.*

Terrence stalked, barefoot, out of his bathroom and back into his bedroom. He grabbed his cordless off his night table and dialed her cell number, his fingers flying so fast that he wasn't sure if he had called her or accidentally dialed someone else. He listened to it ring over and over again before her voice mail greeting clicked on.

"Hey! This is C. J.! I'm busy right now. Please leave a message after the sound of the beep and I'll get back to you as soon as possible. Thanks!"

"Baby," he said, unable to keep the desperation out of his voice, "I'm so sorry for what I said . . . what I did last night. I didn't mean any of it. I know I fucked up! Please call me back when you get this."

He then hung up.

Terrence dressed, ate breakfast, and waited for his phone to ring, but it didn't. Two hours later, he called her again, only to get her voice message yet again.

"C. J., please call me back!" he said to her voice mail. "I'm sorry, baby! I'll . . . I'll make it up to you, but just . . . just talk to me, okay?"

He then sent her a text with the same message.

But she didn't call or text him back by that evening as he'd hoped. She didn't call him back the next day, either, or the day after that. She never called him back.

Chapter 12

Dante

"Need any help getting in, fella?" the chartered car driver asked, peering at Dante in the reflection of his rearview mirror. He had just pulled up to the curb in front of Dante's building, parking under one of the streetlamps that filled the car compartment with its misty glow. "I know you just left the hospital. If you need help, I can hop out and—"

"Did I say I needed any fucking help?" Dante spat in a hoarse voice before shoving open the sedan's door. He climbed out of the car, dragging behind him a plastic bag filled with the rattling bottles of pills he had to take daily thanks to the bullet that went through his side: antibiotics, an anti-inflammatory, and painkillers. When he stepped onto the sidewalk with his bag in tow and shot to his feet, he immediately winced from the pain.

The doctors had told him he would need some assistance, someone to watch over him and help him with his day-to-day tasks while he recovered. He'd scoffed at their suggestion. Dante Turner had *never* needed anyone in his life to help him, not since he was in diapers. Why the hell should he start now? But he did wonder how he was going to make it up the flight of stairs at the entrance of his condo building with this lingering pain, let alone to and from work every day. He had assured the partners at his law firm that he would return in a matter of weeks. They were expecting him back in the office with a shit-eating grin, ready to deal and get those billable hours. He would have to make it work; he had no other choice. Thank God for the pills! Thank God for the vengeance that spurred him on, that made him refuse to give up until he saw that bitch pay for what she'd done to him.

Dante slammed the car door shut behind him before trudging to the concrete stairs leading to the building's entrance.

He hadn't known she had it in her to do something so low, so down and dirty. He had known Renee—his former partner in crime, lover, and the daughter of the woman he had talked into suing Terrence Murdoch—was angry at him. The last time he had seen her, she had been furious when he told her she was delusional to think he had feelings for her that went beyond the bedroom, that he had just been using her to get to her mother. But she didn't have to shoot him for it. She didn't have to try to kill him!

Thankfully, she hadn't succeeded. Dante wasn't

dead, but he was definitely furious. And he was going to make her pay.

He closed his eyes with relief as he climbed the last stair before shoving the exterior door open. He walked down the short hallway to the elevator and pressed the up button to take him to his floor. The button didn't light up. He pressed it again, jabbing his finger onto the button until his nail bed started to hurt.

"Come on! Come on!" he shouted.

"Oh, the elevator's broken, honey," said a woman wearing dark sunglasses. She was carrying a Yorkshire terrier with a pink bow on its head in her arms as she walked by Dante. "It's been broken all day. They put in a call to have it fixed, but they probably won't get to it until the morning," she explained as she headed for one of the condos down the hall while pulling out a set of keys.

"Shit," Dante muttered before giving one last longing glance at the elevator's metal doors. He then turned and headed to the stairwell to make the long climb up six flights of stairs to his home.

He had already tried to tell the cops that Renee was the one that had shot him—even if they hadn't understood what he was saying.

Soon after Dante had awoken, a detective with a receding hairline and ruddy face had waltzed into his hospital room, looking more eager than a shopper at a Black Friday sale to talk to Dante.

"We want to bring the person who shot you to justice," Detective Morris had said after pulling up a chair close to Dante's hospital bed. "We want to put them behind bars, Mr. Turner, before something happens to you again. But we need your help. Do you remember who shot you?"

Dante had vigorously nodded, or at least he had tried to. The sedatives had been still in his system, making him listless. The breathing tube had been removed, but it had left his throat feeling raw and dry. His voice was little more than a raspy whisper.

"Who was it?" the detective had asked, leaning forward eagerly.

"Re-Renee," Dante had whispered. "Renee . . . Upton."

The detective had squinted his gray eyes at him. "I'm sorry. I'm having a hard time hearing you, Mr. Turner. What did you say?"

"Renee!" Dante had said again. "Renee! *Renee!*"

The detective had shaken his head. "I'm not understanding you."

Dante had watched as the detective reached into his pocket and pulled out a small notepad and ballpoint pen. The detective had flipped the notepad open.

"Can you write it down, maybe?" he had asked, holding out both the pad and pen to Dante.

Dante tried to reach for them, but his hand shook too badly to grab the pen, let alone hold it and write with it. His arm was still too weak. His hand had collapsed back to the bed and he had closed his eyes, overwhelmed.

"It's fine. It's fine!" the detective had said, though he had looked equally disappointed. He had pushed himself up from his chair. "Let me give you some time to get back on your feet, to get yourself together. When you're ready to talk, you can tell me everything," he had said before reaching into his suit jacket again and setting a business card on Dante's hospital tray.

It had been three days since, and Dante still carried the detective's card. He planned to call Detective Morris tomorrow morning, right after he had a good night's sleep in his own bed. Then he would have a long conversation with the detective. If his voice failed him again, he'd resort to damn sign language if he had to! He would do whatever he had to do to make sure Renee suffered.

Dante mounted yet another landing and almost cried in frustration when he saw the number four on the metal door in front of him.

You've gotta be fucking kidding me!

He had two whole floors to climb. He didn't think he could make it.

Dante gripped the metal railing to steady himself, blowing air out of his clenched teeth in sharp bursts. He was clammy with sweat. The pain in his side was horrific. He shoved his free hand into his plastic bag and yanked out a bottle of OxyContin. He popped open the lid and swallowed one of the pills, then another, even though he had already taken one a few hours earlier. He slumped down on the floor next to the door and waited for the painkillers to take effect. After twenty minutes of grimacing and restraining the urge to scream, he finally felt the OxyContin start to kick in. The searing hot pain abated and Dante released a shaky breath. He pushed himself to his feet and slowly started to trudge up the stairs again.

"Just how long are we supposed to wait, god-dammit?" a male voice whispered above Dante as he stepped onto the fifth floor landing.

"It shouldn't be too much longer. She said he was supposed to get out today. She's tight with one of the nurses there," another man replied.

Dante paused at the sound of phantom voices in the stairwell on the floor above him. He peered up to find two men waiting near the sixth floor door. Their shadows fell over him.

"But we can't wait here all damn night," one of the men spat—a big dark-skinned dude with broad shoulders. "I don't care how fuckin' much she payin' or how good that pussy is!"

"Ssssh! Be quiet," the other one said. He was shorter, slighter in build, and had dreadlocks. His back was facing Dante.

"I ain't gotta be quiet! Ain't nobody up here! Nobody's been up here in two damn hours! And I'm not waiting here forever."

"Just give it another hour. We took care of the elevator, didn't we? That nigga lives on the sixth floor. The stairs are the only way he can get up here. He has to come this way. Just chill!"

As Dante listened, he frowned, feeling the hairs on the back of his neck rise.

"We should've did that shit outside like I told you," the bigger one said, crossing his arms over his barrel chest and shaking his head. "We could've just waited for him to walk up to the door and taken care of it then. Now we just standing around here like some—"

"We couldn't do it outside. We'd get caught!

There's too many people around out there! Shit, I almost got caught when I tried to do it at that hospital. I could've gotten arrested. I'm on parole. I'm not doing that shit again!"

Dante blinked. *At the hospital?* He stared up at the men, almost feeling faint.

They're here for me, he finally realized.

"Well, I'm telling you one thing, Renee better hook a nigga up when we finally kill this motherfucka! No more dick teasin'. I want my money and I want that pussy!"

The smaller one sucked his teeth. "You're gonna get it, man. Just be patient! Goddamn! You act like you never had a piece of ass before!"

The bitch is still *trying to kill me,* Dante thought with disbelief. And it looked like Renee wouldn't stop until he was dead. She had actually put a hit out on him. She had guys waiting for him in his own damn building to take him out. But it made sense, he guessed. He knew she was the one who pulled the trigger. Renee knew if he survived the gunshot that he would tell the cops what had happened, so she made it her mission to make sure he didn't survive.

Dante turned and crept back down the stairs, careful not to make too much noise and attract the attention of the two hired thugs on the floor above him.

When he reached the first floor, he raced out the door and down the flight of concrete steps to the sidewalk below, hoping to get as far away from the building as possible. He gave a paranoid glance around his shoulders to make sure he wasn't being followed, that some other thug wasn't lurking in the shadows waiting to shoot him.

He then headed down the block in a direction unknown, officially on the run.

Chapter 13
C. J.

The audience erupted into applause, followed by a few shouts of "Hallelujah!" and "Amen!", shaking C. J. from the listless daze she had been stuck in for the past twenty minutes. She raised her gaze from her lap and clapped along with the crowd, although she had no idea why they were all applauding.

Her father stood at the podium and resumed his speech. She sat in the front row between her mother and brother, pretending to listen. She tried valiantly to concentrate on what her father was saying, but she couldn't. Her thoughts felt weighed down by muck.

C. J. heard her phone buzz, alerting her to a new voice mail. She glanced at the phone screen and saw that it was another message from Terrence. That would make the eleventh message in the past four days and the fourth today—he was getting desperate. She dropped her phone back into her purse, took a deep breath, and tried to focus yet again on what her father was saying, but her efforts faltered when her phone buzzed again five minutes later.

Damn it, Terry! Will you leave me alone?

Her mother frowned under her wide-brimmed, fur-trimmed hat and squinted at her.

"Is that your phone buzzing like a bee?" the older woman whispered.

C. J. frantically dug back into her purse.

"Your father is speaking, Courtney," her mother said, scowling at her. "Would you turn that thing off?"

"I'm *trying* to, Mama," she muttered, before finally retrieving her phone. She tapped a few buttons to place the ringer *and* notifications on mute.

"Well, who's calling you anyway?" her mother asked, leaning over her shoulder and nosily peering down at the phone's glass screen. She wrinkled her button nose. "Who in the world is Terrence?"

"Nobody," C. J. snapped, covering the screen with her hand.

Her mother raised her eyebrows at C. J.'s dismissive tone.

"I mean . . . I mean it's no one that you know," C. J. whispered.

And Terrence wouldn't be someone her mother would get to know, even though C. J. had been prepping for the day when she would eventually introduce him to her family. Thanks to Terrence breaking up with her, it looked like that day would never come.

The older woman looked suspicious, but, thankfully, didn't say anything more. She instead returned her attention to the stage.

Meanwhile, C. J. slowly removed her hand and stared down at Terrence's name, at those eight white letters, and fought the overwhelming urge to excuse herself, disappear into the hallway, and finally call him back. But she couldn't call him back, not after what he had said to her. Instead, she sighed and dropped her phone back into her purse, blinking back the tears that had been hovering close to spilling over all day, maybe *all week*.

What had hurt the most wasn't that he had said the only thing they had now was sex, or that it was obvious she felt nothing for him anymore. It wasn't even his accusation about her hooking up with Shaun Clancy that left her wounded. It was the truth behind his words that she still found it hard to recover from.

Terrence could get downright toxic when he was hurt. She had seen it before; it was his worst trait. But he didn't lie when he got that way. It was like he would take a sip of truth serum and couldn't help blurting out everything he felt, everything he had been secretly thinking all along. And she'd had no idea he felt that way, that he thought those things about her. She'd been so in love with him, so eager to make it work. She had even envisioned marrying him one day! C. J. had thought they had an almost perfect relationship, that he understood her better than anyone else. But what did she know about love, about intimacy? She had only been in one serious relationship prior, and that "romance" had been orchestrated by her own father. She'd had nothing to go by when she hooked up with Terrence, and her inexperience and delusions now left her feeling dumb and utterly humiliated.

I was so stupid!

C. J. sniffed, starting to tear up again. *Dammit,* she thought, frustrated at her own emotions. She'd be damned if she'd cry over him, but it looked like that was exactly what she was doing.

She grabbed her purse to search for a Kleenex, only to come up empty. She sniffed again and wiped at her eyes with her hands, feeling the tears spilling over now. She looked crazy, like a loon, with her smeared mascara and puffy face. Her brother glanced at her in annoyance.

"What are you doing?" he snapped. "Why the hell are you crying?"

She shook her head, then closed her eyes, feeling the tears come down harder. She rose to her feet, making her mother and brother stare up at her in confusion.

"Excuse me," she whispered, rushing down the row and to the exit doors before they had the chance to ask her where she was going. All the while she heard her father's rumbling voice behind her.

Stupid. I was so stupid. So stupid!

The chanting only stopped when she burst through the metal doors and ran smack-dab into Shaun, colliding with his chest and getting a face full of his gray suit jacket.

"Hey now!" he shouted with a laugh. But his laughter tapered off when he saw her face. "Hey, are you okay?"

She quickly nodded and forced a smile. "I'm . . . I'm fine. I just . . . I think I'm catching a cold or maybe a stomach bug. I . . . I should head home."

Instead of letting her go, his hold tightened around her shoulders. "I can drive you if you aren't feeling well."

She stepped out of his embrace and dipped her head. "No. No, that's not necessary, but thank you. Just tell my family I wasn't feeling well and went home if . . . if they ask where I am, okay?"

He nodded as she fled past him to the doors leading out of the auditorium to the parking lot, getting a blast of fall air as she did it.

C. J. sat in her robe and comfortable flannel pajamas, nursing a cup of hot tea and staring at the old movie playing on her living room TV screen. She hadn't left her apartment in two days. She had made up an excuse to her family to explain her absence.

"I have a really bad . . . uh, cold," she'd said on the phone to Victor earlier that week, putting on a fake nasal voice.

"A cold?" he had asked.

"Yeah." She'd paused to bark out a cough. "And it's really bad! I'm taking medicine, but I don't think it's a good idea for me to be around a lot of people right now. I should be good in a few days, though."

"Uh-huh," Victor had muttered.

Thankfully, Victor hadn't asked her any more questions after that, though he had sounded incredulous the whole time.

The truth was she couldn't shake off her heartbreak, even though she knew Terrence had left her with little choice but to walk away. She knew this logically, but that didn't make her ache lessen. It only frustrated her.

C. J. turned away from her television screen when she heard a knock at her apartment door. She lowered her cup of tea to her coffee table, rose to her feet, and tightened her robe belt around her waist. Her brows furrowed as she stared through her peephole. She hadn't been expecting any visitors today. She gaped in surprise when she saw who was standing on the other side of the door.

"Shaun?" she whispered before quickly removing the deadbolt and bottom lock. She swung the door open.

He stood on her welcome mat, holding a large paper cup in one hand and a grocery bag in the other. He wasn't wearing one of his suits today but a wool sweater, jacket, and jeans. When he saw her, his mahogany-hued face brightened.

"Hey!" he said.

"H-hi, Shaun! What . . . what are you doing here?"

"Well, you told me you weren't feeling well and Victor mentioned that you had a bad cold. I knew you were up here in Virginia by yourself, so I brought you some tomato soup and Theraflu. That combo always makes me feel better even when I'm at my worst."

She shook her head in bemusement. "You drove *three hundred miles* to bring me soup and Theraflu?"

"Well . . . yeah."

When she continued to stare at him blankly, his smile fell. His shoulders slumped. "If I'm intruding, I can—"

"No! No, you're not intruding! It just . . . caught me off guard. But this was incredibly sweet of you." She pushed her door farther open. "Please come in."

He nodded and walked into her apartment. She gazed around her, shamefaced that she hadn't tidied up the place. Luckily, nothing embarrassing like an empty takeout container or one of her thongs was sitting around for him to see.

"This is a . . . uh, nice place you have here," he lied, and she choked back a laugh. She knew her apartment was as tiny as a matchbox and decorated just as elaborately, but it was her home.

"Thank you."

"So where should I set this?" he asked, holding up the soup carton and the plastic bag.

"Oh, I can take those!"

"You may wanna be careful with the lid on that, though. I picked it up at the grocery store near here and the only lid I could find was a little bent, so—"

He didn't get to finish. The instant she grabbed the soup carton, the lid popped off, making tomato soup gush over the side, sending a bright red splatter onto his sweater and down the front of his jeans.

"I am so, *so* sorry, Shaun!" she shouted, scrambling to her small eat-in kitchen. She tossed the empty carton in the sink, ran to the paper towel dispenser hanging on the wall, and grabbed several handfuls before running back to him. The soup was now oozing down the front of him and dripping onto her floor.

"It's . . . all right, really," he said as she dabbed at the stain with the paper towels, making a wide circumference around his crotch.

"No, it's not! I made a complete mess of you— and I'm only making it worse."

"It's just soup, C. J. It's no big deal."

She squinted when she realized he was grimacing. "*What?* What's wrong? You look like you're in pain."

"Well, it feels a little hot in some . . . some areas," he said, shifting his stance.

She motioned to his jeans. "Take off your pants."

His eyes widened. "*What?*"

"Take . . . off . . . your . . . pants," she repeated slowly, enunciating each word.

When he continued to look at her uneasily, she rolled her eyes and dropped her hands to her hips. "Look, Pastor Clancy, I'm not trying to seduce you. I'm just not letting you get second-degree burns because you were nice enough to bring me soup that I managed to scald you with. You can take off the jeans in my room, if it makes you feel any better. I'll stay out here. I can wash and dry them for you. Hand them to me through the doorway."

He hesitated before nodding only a few seconds later. She guessed his scalded balls won out.

"Okay," he muttered.

Ten minutes later, she was tossing his jeans

along with liquid detergent into the washer in her kitchen, while he stood alone in her bedroom. She wondered how she had managed to create this mess. C. J. slammed the lid to the washer shut and reached for another wad of towels to clean up the rest of the spilled soup when she heard a knock at her front door again.

"Who the hell is that?" she murmured before striding out of her kitchen.

No one else had made the trek from North Carolina to Virginia to check on her, had they? Once again, she stared through the peephole. This time, her heart dropped. All the blood drained from her head.

"Oh, no! No! No!" she whispered hysterically. "Not today. Not now!"

"C. J.?" Terrence called, knocking again. "Please, baby, open up!"

This was some joke, some weird twist of fate. Why had Terrence chosen today of all days to just show up at her apartment? Of course it had to be the same damn day that Shaun was here with her, not wearing any pants!

"C. J.!" Terrence shouted, pounding his fist on her door again. "C. J., I know you're home. I saw your car parked in your reserved space. Don't make me have to get escorted out of this damn building, because I will stay out here until you answer me, goddammit!"

Despite his threat, she seriously considered ignoring him and hoping he would go away, but part of her longed to talk to Terrence. It was the same part that ached just seeing him on the other side of the door, less than a foot away from her. She was angry at him, but she still missed him. She still loved him.

Because I'm a damn fool, she thought dejectedly.

She took a little solace in the fact that he looked almost as bad as she did. Even in the dim lighting of the apartment hallway, she could see that he needed a shave and there were bags under his eyes like he hadn't slept in a few days.

"Baby, please talk to me! Just *talk* to me! That's all I'm asking!" he yelled, and she felt an imaginary knife twist in her gut.

She closed her eyes and dropped her forehead against the wooden slab.

"Please?" he said in a softer voice.

I'll make it quick, she told herself. She wouldn't invite him in. She wouldn't cave, either, but she would give him a chance to say whatever he had to say, then send him on his way. She was a mature woman. She could handle this.

She unlocked the door before she could change her mind and whipped it open. When she did, he looked at her, stunned, like he hadn't expected her to answer.

"What the hell do you want, Terry?" she asked, crossing her arms over her chest, forcing a hard edge to her voice. "Why are you here?"

He took a tentative step toward her. "I wanted . . . no, I *needed* to talk to you, babe. You haven't returned any of my phone calls or texts. I've been—"

"You tossed my purse out of your bedroom and told me to get out." She inclined her head and raised her eyebrows. "What more is there to say?"

"I didn't mean that. You *know* I didn't mean any of that! I was drunk off my ass!"

"You were drunk—but you know damn well you meant every word you said."

"C. J.," he said, reaching for her, but she stepped away from him, knowing she would probably give in if he touched her. He lowered his hand and shrank back with his head bowed. "Baby, look, I . . . I love you. I love you! You know that! Sometimes I say things when I'm angry that I don't mean. Well, if I *do* mean it, I don't mean it in the way I say it. It's the worst version of what I really feel. But no matter what I said that night, I still lo—"

"Hey, C. J.!" Shaun called out from her bedroom. "Is it okay if I wash my sweater, too?"

Terrence fell silent at the sound of Shaun's voice. He blinked.

"Might as well do both at once, right?" Shaun's muffled voice continued. "C. J., you out there?"

Shit, she thought, raising her hand to her forehead. This is exactly what she had wanted to avoid.

I never should have opened the damn door!

Terrence's jaw tightened. A vein popped up along his brow. "Do you . . . do you have some other . . . other guy in here?"

She quickly shook her head and blew air out of her puffed cheeks.

This is awkward.

"Yes, I do, but—"

Terrence shoved past her, cutting her off and almost making her bump into the adjacent wall. She watched in shock and alarm as he jogged through her living room and down the short hallway that led to her bedroom.

"Terry? Terry, what the hell do you think you're doing?" she shouted after him just as he turned the doorknob and shoved her bedroom door open. "Wait! *Wait!* Don't—"

The words clogged in her throat again at the sight of Shaun standing next to her bed, just in his plaid boxers and knee-high white athletic socks, holding his dirty sweater in his hands. As the door whipped open, he jumped and reached for the peach-colored sheets on her bed, feebly covering his partial nakedness.

For several seconds, the two men stared at each other.

"Who the fuck are you?" Terrence asked him, breaking their silence.

Instead of responding, Shaun continued to gape helplessly.

"Who *the fuck* is this?" Terrence bellowed, turning to her and jabbing his finger into the bedroom. He glared down at her. "What the fuck is this shit, C. J.? I came here to apologize and run in on this?"

C. J. winced, mortified that Shaun was witnessing this and furious at Terrence for making a true ass out of himself. She peered into her bedroom around the door frame. "Shaun, I am so sorry about this! I didn't—"

"*Shaun?*" Terrence yelled with widened eyes. "Shaun . . . as in your *ex-fiancé*, Shaun?" He let out a caustic laugh. "Well, I'll be damned. I guess I was right all along!"

"Stop it, Terry," she said through clenched teeth. "You're acting like an asshole . . . a complete fool! Just stop!"

"*I'm a fool?*" He pointed at his chest. "Oh, I'm a damn fool, all right! I thought I was being paranoid because I was worried you might do some shit like this. Not C. J., not her! But I guess I was right all along, huh?"

"Look, uh . . . Terry, is it?" Shaun said, finally regaining his voice. He tightened her cotton bed-sheet around his waist. "I have no idea what's going on, but I can assure you that C. J. hasn't—"

"Man, shut the fuck up before I shut your ass up!" Terrence ordered, glowering at him.

"Don't talk to him like that!" she screeched, un-able to hold back her own fury, getting sucked in by all of Terrence's rage.

She closed her eyes and took a deep breath, try-ing her best to get herself under control, but it was a challenge. She was fighting the dueling tides of anger and embarrassment, and both left her feeling like the floor was rocking underneath her, like she couldn't get her footing. She couldn't believe Ter-rence was acting like this. Yet again, he was letting the hurricane of his emotions take over and she was left with rain pounding on her head.

"So you're fuckin' him, too, huh? Showing him everything I taught you?" Terrence asked with a menacing gleam to his eyes.

C. J.'s eyes flashed open. She didn't respond to his question, too furious to articulate an answer. Her silence only seemed to embolden him.

"Doing all your new tricks? I bet he—"

"Hey!" Shaun called out, making Terrence whip around again to face him. "Hey, why don't you just back off and leave her alone, all right?"

"What did I say?" Terrence snarled. "What the fuck did I say to you about minding your own goddamn business, huh?"

C. J. watched in horror as Terrence suddenly charged across the bedroom, looking like a jaguar that had locked onto his prey while Shaun was the poor gazelle with no idea he was about to get eaten.

"Terry! Terry!" She frantically reached for his arm, grabbing the fabric of his sweater to hold him back, but he roughly yanked it out of her grip and shrugged her off.

Shaun looked absolutely terrified. He dropped the bedsheet to the floor and clenched his fists like he was prepared to fight, then loosened them after giving it a second thought. He took an unsteady step backward, then another. Terrence gave Shaun a hard shove, sending the other man flying. Shaun landed on his ass near her dresser, his feet becoming entangled in her discarded bedsheets. He held up a hand to shield himself from the impending blows.

"Stop it!" she shouted, running across the bedroom just as Terrence raised his fist. "Stop it, Terry! Don't do this!" She stood between the two men, pressing her palms against Terrence's chest, holding him back with all her might. "Please!"

He looked down at her, and for the first time since he stormed into her apartment, she felt like he really saw her, like he realized exactly what he was doing. He slowly lowered his fist and glowered down at Shaun.

"Fine," he sneered. "You can have her, brotha! Just know that everything she does in *that* bed has my signature written all over it—and I wrote it with my dick!"

"Get out!" she ordered, shoving at his chest

again and pointing to her bedroom door. She was shaking all over, her body flooded with adrenaline. "Just *get out!* Get the fuck out, Terry!" she yelled, shoving at him again. "I can't talk to you when you're like this. I can't stand to look at you when you do this shit. Get out of here!"

She watched as he turned around and walked back toward the bedroom doorway.

"I'd be happy to," he said over his shoulder with finality and ease, like he had already done what he had come here to do. She turned away from him after that.

She knew he had left for sure when he slammed her front door shut behind him, making the entire living room wall shudder.

Chapter 14

Terrence

"Fuck that bitch," Terrence kept muttering to himself as he drove back from C. J.'s apartment, breaking speed limits and barely stopping at red lights. When he arrived back at his condo, full of indignation and fury, he quickly dug out Andre's business card from a pile of discarded receipts and valet tickets on his coffee table. He called Andre and told him that he wanted to try to get back into the modeling game after all.

"Oh, thank you, Jesus!" Andre exclaimed on the other end of the line. "We've *got* to get you to New York right away. I want you to meet the rest of the folks at the agency. I want to get your portfolio *on point*. Watch out, world, Terrence Murdoch is back!"

A few days later, only a couple hours before he was headed to the train station, he called Evan to let him know he'd be back in a few days.

"Why are you going to New York? What's up there?" Evan asked.

"I'm gonna try modeling again. An agency wants me, so I figured I might as well give it a shot."

"*Modeling again?* Wait . . . when did you decide to start modeling again? You never mentioned it before! When did this happen?"

"I don't know. It just seemed like the right time," he said with a shrug, throwing a few more things into an overnight bag. "I'm doing better. My recovery from the accident is done. It seemed like some changes were in order. I'm ready."

"Changes, huh?" Evan fell silent on the other end of the line. "This wouldn't have anything to do with what happened with you and . . . and C. J., would it?"

At the mention of his ex's name, Terrence's jaw tightened. He paused from his packing. "Why the fuck would it have anything to do with her?"

He had already given his brother the gory details of him stumbling upon her and Shaun Clancy in her apartment. He had no desire to relive them.

"Well, it's just . . . you never mentioned modeling again before and . . . and then you guys break up and you're off to New York to start a new career! I thought she . . . well, she might have something to do with this."

"Well, she doesn't," Terrence answered succinctly before closing the zipper on his bag. "Fuck that bitch!"

Terrence repeated the phrase again as he boarded the Acela Express train from Virginia to New York City. While he reclined in his leather chair, he tried to block out visions of what C. J. was doing while in bed with Shaun Clancy. As the train sailed through D.C. to Baltimore and then Newark, he was plagued with visions of what Clancy might be doing to *her* on her peach-colored bedsheets, which probably still smelled of Terrence's aftershave.

He bet C. J. had had a good laugh at his expense, carrying on an affair right under his nose. He wondered how many times she had claimed to be held up by some last-minute meet-and-greet for her father or church event when she really was getting freaky with Clancy somewhere, doing things she wouldn't even do with Terrence.

Fuck that bitch, he thought again as he fought the urge to punch his fist through the Acela's double-paned glass window. Instead, he turned up the volume of the angry hip-hop tune playing through his headphones. He turned it up so high that his eardrums almost burned.

When he arrived at Penn Station, his muscles were rigid and the tension in his neck was almost painful. He was breathing like he had just run a marathon. He climbed up the stairs and onto the sidewalk and glanced at the exterior of Madison Square Garden just as he heard a horn blare and pounding dance music. He turned and saw Andre in a blue Audi illegally parked along the curb. The tiny man lowered the tinted window and frantically waved at him.

"Come on, before the cops get on my ass!" Andre called.

Terrence jogged a few feet, threw open the door, and hopped inside. The car pulled off the curb seconds later with a squeal of tires just as one of New York's finest started to walk toward its bumper.

"How are you doing, gorgeous?" Andre asked with a smile, expertly handling midday New York traffic with awe-inspiring ease.

"I'm good," Terrence answered, slumping back into the plush leather seat, gazing at the Manhattan scenery outside his window. He hadn't been to New York in a while. The city usually gave him a rush, an endorphin high the minute he set foot in Manhattan or the other boroughs, but he wasn't feeling it today.

"*Good?* Just good? Why aren't you excited?" Andre raised his gold-tinted sunglasses from his face to perch them on his shiny bald head. He looked Terrence up and down. "Are you okay?"

Terrence nodded and turned back to face him. "Yeah, I'm fine. Why?"

Andre squinted, scrutinizing him even more closely. "Well, frankly, you're looking a little worn, my dear . . . more worn than high heels from Payless after a hard night of partying! Seriously, you could carry luggage in those bags under your eyes! What've you been doing to yourself, sweetheart?"

Terrence shrugged listlessly, making Andre shake his head.

"I'm gonna have to make you an appointment *today* with my aesthetician on the Upper West Side. There is no time to waste!"

Andre grabbed his cell phone from the dash-board.

"Siri, give me Stephan!" he yelled, calling up the miracle worker's phone number.

"Calling Stephan," the phone answered back.

As Andre talked on the phone about microder-mabrasion, vitamin C masks, and oxygen blasts, Terrence glared at the pedestrians outside his win-dow. Again, his thoughts floated back to C. J.

He wondered how long it had taken her to restart things with Clancy. Had it only started re-cently, or had it been soon after she started going back to North Carolina? Had it been when Ter-rence started to sense that something had changed between them, or was it as far back as when he was still in the glow of their new relationship, when he still thought they were blissfully happy? Those questions haunted him, and he suspected he'd never get any answers.

"*Five o'clock?* Oh, thank you, Stephan! You're a life saver, honey!" Andre cried. "Yes, we'll be there. Don't worry . . . All right. See you then." Andre blew a kiss into the phone and hung up. He pursed his lips and shook his head in exaspera-tion, returning his attention to the busy street in front of him.

"Thank goodness he could do it! It wasn't easy. Stephan's a hot commodity in these parts, honey, but he was willing to cut me a favor."

Terrence didn't comment.

"Look, Terrence, I'll help you out this time, but you know better than anybody that you can't come up here looking a mess! You have to bring your A-game. You may have been the belle of the ball in

Chesterton, but remember there are plenty of pretty faces here on Fashion Avenue! If you want to go far, you have to take care of yourself . . . *your looks,* more importantly."

"I know," he said, adjusting his seat belt. "I've just had a . . . a hard couple of days, that's all. I've had a hard time sleeping."

And eating, he wanted to add but didn't.

Since his fight with C. J., he hadn't had much of an appetite. Since catching her with Clancy later, his appetite had all but disappeared. At this rate, getting back to his old modeling weight wouldn't be much of a challenge.

"Well, we can't have that," Andre said with another slow shake of his head. "You're no spring chicken anymore! No hard partying, no drugs, keep the drinking to a minimum, and eight hours of sleep a night! All right?"

Terrence nodded, though he knew tonight would likely be another sleepless night for him.

Less than a half hour later, Andre was dragging Terrence around the agency, introducing him to the other agents, showing him the wall of postcards displaying the models the agency represented. It was all a blur of bright lights and fake people. Terrence realized as he shook hand after hand, as he stripped down to his boxer briefs and some assistant took his measurements, as one person after another stared at him and examined him like he was a lab specimen, that despite what he had told Evan this morning, his heart wasn't in this. Yet his heart *had* to be in it if he really was going to do this. He had to get himself under con-

trol and in the right frame of mind, or coming to
New York would be a complete waste of his and
Andre's time.

"Okay, let's get a few Polaroids of you, shall
we?" a waifish blonde with a pixie haircut said as
she held up a camera.

Terrence allowed her to drag him toward an adjacent wall and position him like a cut-out paper
doll.

"All right, lovely! Give us a few poses," one of
the fellow agents said. Andre had told Terrence
her name, but he had forgotten it already.

Terrence looked at the three pairs of eyes staring up at him. He shifted and made a half-hearted
attempt at a few poses that drew frowns and furrowed eyebrows.

"That's the best you can give us, darling?" an
agent with a British accent called out, puckering
her lips and glaring at him over the top of her
glasses. "How Andre described you, I was expecting the second coming of Tyson Beckford . . . and
frankly, I'm not seeing it."

"He's just warming up. Hush up, girl! Give him
a chance," Andre said, waving her off. "Come on,
Terrence, show us what you got, honey!"

Terrence tiredly closed his eyes, took a deep
breath, and opened them.

"All right, let's try this again," the assistant said,
gazing through her viewfinder, taking more pictures.

But Terrence couldn't focus. His mind kept
drifting. He thought about C. J., about Clancy,
about C. J. *with* Clancy. He thought about how he'd

been shocked to discover he could finally fall in love with someone, only to have that love come back to bite him in the ass!

He did a few more poses for them, but it wasn't much better than what he had done before. He could tell from the look on Andre's face that he was disappointed.

"Well, let's try your walk," Andre said. "Maybe you're just a little rusty in front of the camera."

"Are you sure he can walk, darling?" the British agent asked. A condescending sneer was now on her thin lips.

Terrence wasn't surprised that she had posed the question to Andre and not him. He was just an object now. He had ceased to exist as a person.

"He's done Paris and Milan," Andre snapped. "I think he can do our showroom! Watch a runway god at work!"

She snorted in response. "If you say so, darling."

A minute later, Terrence stood at the end of the long hallway, feeling exhausted and ridiculous. But he pushed back his shoulders and told himself to do this, to just get *through* this! Besides, if he was going to start modeling again, he would have to do this all the time.

He started to walk down the hallway, fairly confident that he had his pace and his posture on lock. But he saw from the looks on their faces that something was wrong. They stared at him as if he had stumbled and fallen face first on the carpeted floor.

"*What* was that?" the British agent shouted.

Andre narrowed his eyes. "Something's off, honey. Walk up and walk down again."

Terrence grimaced and did as Andre said, walking up and then down the hallway a second time, feeling the burn of the halogen lights overhead bearing down on him along with Andre and the British woman's intense stares. The uneasy looks on their faces remained.

"Are you . . . are you limping?" the British woman asked, then nodded in response to her own question. "He's limping! Good Lord, Andre! Your client has a limp!"

Shit, Terrence thought, realizing that his secret was out.

"He . . . he just hurt himself at the gym or something!" Andre insisted with a wave of his hand, looking flustered and trying his best to hide it. "That's all it is! He'll be fine in a week. No problem."

Terrence felt sweat trickle down his back. He lowered his head, unable to meet their eyes anymore. He nervously licked his lips. "No, it's . . . uh, it's not from the gym," he confessed. "It's from the car accident I had in February. I damaged my leg. I've had the limp ever since."

Andre's mouth fell open. The British woman's eyebrows raised by about an inch.

"It's not a *bad* limp," he quickly added. "Most people don't . . . don't notice . . . at first."

"Well, we noticed!" The British woman snorted again. "There goes your runway god, Andre . . . and more than half your potential bookings."

She then turned and walked away, laughing to herself.

* * *

"Why didn't you tell me you were in an accident?" Andre barked at him as they drove to his facial appointment.

"I *tried* to tell you, but you kept blowing me off. I told you I'd been through some stuff, that I had some surgeries," Terrence argued. "*You* told me it didn't matter!"

"I thought you meant nose contouring . . . maybe liposuction! I didn't know you meant *rebuilding bones*!" Andre exclaimed. "What the hell am I supposed to do with you now? Who the hell wants a model who can't walk? And you can barely pose!" He sucked his teeth. "Might as well put you in Sears and JCPenney's ads."

Terrence eyed Andre, feeling his fury rise, but he didn't say anything in response to Andre's putdown. Shame overrode his anger. He had worried that if he tried to model again, his accident would come back to haunt him . . . that some glaring imperfection would come to the forefront and everyone would know for sure that he wasn't the model he once had been. Now Andre knew the truth and had reacted accordingly.

When they arrived at the salon, Andre parked his Audi, threw open the driver's side door, and walked toward the glass doors, all the while talking on his phone and barking something to Terrence over his shoulder. Instead of following him, Terrence walked right past him.

Andre blinked in astonishment as he watched Terrence stride down the sidewalk.

"Terrence!" Andre called after him. "Terrence, where do you think you're going?"

Terrence didn't respond. He just kept walking, tugging up the collar of his jacket, feeling the cold blast of wind from the Hudson River snake its way between alleyways and skyscrapers before sweeping around his hunched shoulders.

"Well, you can forget about me representing you!" Andre yelled. "And I'm taking your facial!"

Terrence didn't know where he was headed, he just needed to get away from here. His overnight bag was still at the agency, but he didn't care, he wasn't going back. He kept walking from block to block to block, following the length of Broadway until he reached Times Square, oblivious to the blazing signs advertising Bubba Gump Shrimp Co. and Madame Tussaud's. His cell phone rang and he ignored it. A few people tried to hand him flyers and tickets as he walked by, and he ignored them, too. He just wanted to get away, to forget what had happened today, about what had happened that week. He wanted to disappear.

Finally, long after it had gotten dark and the bright lights of Manhattan had eclipsed whatever lights were in the sky, Terrence got tired of walking. He spotted an entrance to a hotel in Midtown and pushed through the revolving doors.

"Welcome to the Horchow Hotel," the front desk attendant said eagerly with a grin. "How can I help you?"

Terrence ignored him and went straight to the bar several feet away. He walked down a short flight of stairs and saw that it was already filled with patrons. He peeled off his wool jacket and walked up to the bar.

"Patrón," he muttered in a barely audible voice, too weary to speak louder.

The bartender nodded and turned away, wiping a set of shot glasses with a hand towel. "Right away," he said.

Terrence looked to his right to find a woman two stools away staring openly at him. She was petite with a heart-shaped, pretty face and long red hair done in a single braid that hung over her shoulder. She was wearing a short dress with spaghetti straps despite the cold temperature outside. The dress revealed her freckled shoulders.

"Hey," she piped with a ready smile.

"Hey," he answered tiredly just as the bartender handed him his shot.

"Visiting New York?"

He nodded.

"Me too! I'm supposed to be meeting a friend here for a drink, but . . . it looks like she stood me up. Some friend, huh?" she said with a self-deprecating laugh.

He didn't respond.

She twirled her straw in her glass, making the ice cubes clink. "Are you drinking alone, too?"

He nodded again before taking a sip.

"Mind if we . . . uh, drink together? I just hate drinking alone!"

It was on the tip of his tongue to tell her no. But the truth was he didn't want to drink alone, either, with only his thoughts, doubts, and regrets to keep him company. He could use a little distraction, if only briefly.

"No, I don't mind," he said, rising from his

stool and taking the one directly beside her. "I'll keep you company."

He learned that her name was Daphne McHale and she was from Utah. She was visiting New York for the first time to attend a teachers' conference. They talked about all things inconsequential, trading jokes and flirting harmlessly. One hour faded into the next. The bar room filled with more people, and Terrence glanced down at his wristwatch and realized that it was past midnight.

"Hell, it's getting late. I should probably book a room," he said with a chuckle.

She lowered her straw from her mouth. "You don't *need* to book a room, Terrence."

"I do if I don't want to have to sleep in this damn lobby!" he exclaimed, pointing to one of the nearby banquettes. He then slapped a few twenties on the marble bar top to cover his tab.

"I *mean*," she said with a smirk, easing toward him, fingering the V-neck of his sweater, "you can stay with me . . . in my room, if you'd like."

He eyed her. "Are you asking me what I think you're asking?"

She laughed and gazed into his eyes. "Without saying it outright . . . yes. But if there's any confusion about what I'm asking, I can just say it. Will you come to my room and spend the night with me?"

He hesitated only briefly before he nodded. "Sure."

A few minutes later, they walked to the elevators. When they stepped inside the compartment and the doors closed, Daphne pounced on him like a ravenous dog that had just spotted a mutton chop. She wrapped her arms around his neck and plastered him with kisses as they ascended to the twenty-second floor, where she was staying.

"I'm going to show you the time of your life tonight, big boy," she said as she rubbed his dick through his jeans. She lifted his sweater, raked her fingernails over his bare stomach, then kissed him again.

He told himself not to think. He told himself, most of all, not to think about C. J. But he hadn't kissed a woman besides C. J. in about six months, hadn't sucked on another woman's tongue or felt another woman's breast in the palm of his hand. Instead of basking in the newness of Daphne's body against his, he was bothered by how unfamiliar it felt. Daphne was shorter than C. J. and slim rather than curvy. Her breasts were perky but smaller. Her ass was firm, but not as round. She even tasted different. Every time he touched Daphne, he was reminded of another body he was no longer touching, and it infuriated him. He couldn't even fuck another woman without being reminded of his ex! But he would be damned if the memory of C. J. held him back from this. He was going to get laid tonight, even if it killed him.

Finally, the doors to the elevator opened. They tumbled out, and Daphne grabbed his hand and led him down a couple of hallways, giggling drunkenly, before they finally reached her door. She put her room key card into the lock, twisted the door handle, and shoved the door open.

"Let's have some fun," she whispered, beckoning him with her finger.

Terrence trailed in after her, letting the door slam shut behind them.

Two hours later, Terrence stepped off the hotel elevator on the eighteenth floor with his newly procured room key in hand. He had a pounding headache. His eyes felt like they were filled with sand. He sluggishly did the walk of shame to his hotel room after the brazen revenge fuck he hadn't enjoyed half as much as Daphne had advertised.

He had left Daphne slumbering alone and naked in her bed, deciding not to wake her to say good-bye. Instead, he dressed as best he could in the dark and walked out of her hotel room, quietly shutting the door behind him. Now, Terrence staggered into his own hotel room with a burning sensation in his chest that had nothing to do with the four shots of tequila he had downed at the hotel bar. He strolled across the carpet, tugging his sweater over his head as he did it. He stood in the center of the room, bare-chested, glaring out the floor-to-ceiling windows at the view of Midtown Manhattan and the New York City skyline that twinkled and glowed with an optimism that seemed to mock him.

Today had been an absolute disaster—just as he had feared it would be. He had been a fool to think he could rewind the clock, that he could go back to being the self-assured man he had once been. And with just the silence of the hotel room surrounding him, the voices of doubt that he had refused to listen to all day, that had emerged soon after the car accident, were screaming loud and clear right now.

You're never going to go back to the way things were! You thought you were hot shit but you're not!

Why don't you just take your sorry ass back to Chesterton and live off your trust fund, pretty boy? That's all you're good for!

He gritted his teeth and closed his eyes, feeling himself sinking under some unseen current. He needed to talk to someone. He had to get someone to talk him down off this imaginary emotional ledge or he would send the chair at his hotel desk careening through the floor-to-ceiling windows.

Terrence reached for the hotel phone on the desk to call his brother. He glanced at the clock on the nearby night table. It was almost three o'clock in the morning. Evan would probably think something was wrong if he called him this late, but he *had* to talk to him. He had to get these voices to shut up.

Terrence began to punch numbers into the dial pad. It wasn't until he dialed the last number that he realized who he had been really calling in his hour of need—and it wasn't Evan.

Hang up, he told himself as he listened to the phone ring on the other end. *Hang up before she picks up—or that motherfucka Clancy picks up.*

But he didn't. He listened to the phone ring over and over again. He listened until she picked up on the fourth ring.

"Hello," C. J. answered groggily.

At the sound of her voice, something inside Terrence broke. He sat down on the edge of the bed when he felt his knees buckle underneath him.

Damn, he missed her!

"Hello?" she said again, clearing her throat.

He closed his eyes and bowed his head, imagining her on the other end of the line. Before he woke her up, she would've been sleeping on the left side of the bed. That was the side she usually slept on when he stayed over or when she came to his place. Her face and eyelids would be a bit puffy. She'd be wearing an oversize white T-shirt and nothing underneath.

Terrence wanted to tell her everything that had happened today and how it had shaken him. He wanted her to reassure him and tell him it was a minor setback. So what if he couldn't model again?

"Come on, honey! It's not like you really wanted to be a model again anyway," she would say with a smile. "It's no big deal."

He wanted to yell at her and bitch her out for betraying him, for hooking up with that pussy Shaun Clancy—for breaking his heart. He wanted to hear her explain herself and cry and beg him for forgiveness.

He wanted to tell her that he was pissed at her and furious, but despite what she had done, he still loved her. He wanted her back. He wanted them to get back together.

But he couldn't. All the words piled up in his throat like cars stuck in a traffic jam at the Lincoln Tunnel. Instead, he continued to listen to her breathe, to the sound of the phone rubbing against her pillow and cheek. He felt like a fool all over again.

"Hello?" she repeated, now sounding irritated. "Is anybody there?" She grumbled, then released a loud breath. She mumbled something he couldn't decipher, then she hung up.

Terrence kept the receiver to his ear until the line began to bleat, until he had no choice but to hang up.

Chapter 15

Leila

Leila held her breath and clenched her hands in her lap as she watched the woman sitting in front of her slowly open the cardboard box, then remove the tissue paper packaging.

"Oh, Leila," Audrey said, picking up one of the pink, metallic envelopes, "these are just . . . just gorgeous!"

Leila exhaled, breathing a sigh of relief. *"Really?* You really like them?"

"I don't like them. I *love* them!" Audrey exclaimed, pulling more of her custom-made invitations out of the box and grinning. Her green eyes brightened as she ran her hand over the parchment, lighting up her plump, pale face. "I figured they'd turn out nice, but never thought they'd be *this* nice! Can I . . . Can I open the ribbon on this one? I don't want to mess it up."

Leila laughed. "You can do whatever you like, Audrey. They're your invitations!"

Thank goodness Audrey Wilcox liked the final product. The invitations to her daughter's thirteenth birthday party were one of the few design projects that Leila had done that month. Her new company had looked well on its way to being in the black only a few months ago, and now it was firmly in the red. She was still hemorrhaging clients, which confused her. She had thought Chesterton would be a prime place to open a graphic arts and stationery business since the town and its surrounding county was filled with start-up businesses and upper-middle-class people who loved to host parties and had plenty of money to spend. But she seemed to have been sorely mistaken. She hadn't secured any new clients in almost a month and was now trying to think of different ways to give a lifeline to her failing business.

"I would ask, though," Leila ventured as Audrey continued to smile at the birthday invitations, "to please spread the word that you really liked what I did for you. If you refer a new client to Leila Designs, I could give you a discount on any future design work."

"Oh, no problem, Leila! I'd be happy to!" The middle-aged woman slowly shook her head in awe at the invitation she held, sending her page cut flying around her face. She fingered the black-and-silver, polka-dot ribbon. "My daughter, Zoe, is going to love these! I'm so glad I didn't listen to my friend Maggie and have someone else make the invitations. That was the best decision I ever made!"

"I'm . . . I'm sorry . . . *what?* You said your friend told you to get the invitations made somewhere else?"

Audrey paused. Her grin faltered. "Huh?"

"You said your friend Maggie told you to get your invitations elsewhere. Did she suggest another designer in town?"

Leila had wondered if maybe that was the culprit behind her business problems. Maybe there was another, larger design firm offering bargain-basement prices for similar work.

"Oh, dear," Audrey whispered. Her pale face grew considerably paler, draining of all color. "Did I . . . did I really say that out loud? I am *so* sorry, Leila!"

"Sorry about what?"

"Well," Audrey began, shifting uncomfortably in one of Leila's leather office chairs, "Maggie Sutter is a . . . a friend of mine."

Maggie Sutter . . . Maggie Sutter . . .

Leila struggled to remember where she had heard that name before.

Now I remember, she thought.

Maggie Sutter was the woman who had canceled a consultation a few months ago where they were supposed to discuss invitations, save-the-dates, and menus for Maggie's winter bash. She had been very abrupt when she did it, giving no real reason why she had canceled.

"She told me that I would be better off giving my money to another designer," Audrey continued, "someone more . . . more acceptable."

Leila squinted. "I'm sorry, but . . . I don't think I'm following you. Acceptable in what way?"

Audrey hesitated again.

"Please tell me," Leila said. "If there's bad buzz about my business going around, I'd really like to know."

Audrey released a loud breath. "Look, Leila." She caught Leila by surprise by reaching out to gently pat her hand. "I don't care what you do in your private life. Like I told Maggie . . . it's none of my business! But ever since Maggie's sister's husband left her for that two-bit slut waitress at Hooters, she's been hell-bent on taking a stand against people having affairs."

Leila's breath caught in her throat. Her eyes nearly bulged out of her head.

"And it doesn't help much that Maggie's a friend of a friend of Charisse Murdoch. I swear those women can act like a little gang sometimes! She said Charisse said we all have to stick together . . . all us *wives*, I mean. But I don't cotton to that type of thinking!" Audrey rushed on, when she saw the furious expression on Leila's face. "If a man doesn't want to be with his wife anymore, you can't force him to be, can you?" She waved her hand dismissively. "And that whole bit about you being a former prostitute and a coke addict, I didn't believe it for one second! That was just too over the top! I *knew* those were rumors Charisse had to have cooked up. Evan Murdoch wouldn't get engaged to a prostitute!" she said with a shrill laugh.

Leila took a trembling breath. She was clenching her hands in her lap so tightly now that she swore the fingernails were digging into the flesh.

Her palms might start to bleed. She had secretly suspected all along that Charisse was behind this. After all, Charisse had made it her mission to make Leila's life miserable. But Leila had no idea that psycho would follow through with it—or that she would take it this far!

She told everyone I was a hooker and a cokehead, Leila thought. *No wonder they don't want to do business with me!*

"You're absolutely right," Leila said, forcing her voice to stay even. "Well, I'm glad you like the invitations, Audrey. Now if you'll excuse me, I have another client coming in the next few minutes," she lied.

"Oh!" Audrey said, nodding. "No . . . no problem. I should be going anyway."

An hour later, Leila was sitting behind her office desk, rubbing her pregnant belly and still fuming, when her cell phone rang. She glanced at the screen and frowned when she saw it was Isabel's school.

Her daughter had started the new private grade school only a month ago. It was Evan and Leila's alma mater. Leila never would have been able to afford the tuition on her own—not without the help of a big scholarship like the one she had received when she had attended almost twenty years ago—but now that she had Evan's financial help, she could send Isabel to Queen Anne Academy without financial aid. She appreciated Evan's generosity, but had been hesitant to accept it.

"She's a bright girl, Lee. If Izzy gets a good education there, what difference does it make who pays?" he had asked with a laugh.

It makes a difference to me, she had thought while watching him write the tuition check. It was yet another thing that emphasized the imbalance in their relationship. It was yet another thing that Evan could control.

"Hello?" Leila now answered, picking up after the second ring.

"Hello, is this Ms. Hawkins?" a gravelly voice replied.

"Yes, this is she."

"This is Eleanor Fairchild, the principal at Queen Anne Academy. I'm calling in regard to your daughter, Isabel."

"Yes? Is everything okay?" Leila adjusted in her chair, feeling a hint of alarm. "Is she all right?"

Leila got a flashback to the last time she had received a call from school about Isabel. It had been to tell her that they couldn't find her, that she had run away.

"Isabel is fine, Ms. Hawkins . . . in a manner of speaking."

"I'm sorry? *In a manner of speaking?* What . . . what does that mean?"

"It means we've had a little incident here with Isabel and one of our other students. They were fighting on the playground and had to be pulled apart by two of the teachers on recess duty at the time."

Leila's mouth fell open. "Izzy *was fighting?* Are you sure?"

Her daughter never fought! At least, she hadn't in the past.

"I am sure, Ms. Hawkins. Both girls suffered a few cuts and bruises, but they're all right—for the most part. Both are now sitting in my office. They have been suspended for the day and maybe for the rest of the week, pending review of the incident. I haven't decided yet."

Leila dropped her head into her hand and sighed. "I'm on my way to get her," she said. "I'll be there in less than thirty minutes."

Leila swung open one of the heavy oak doors and walked down the short corridor leading to the academy's front office. As she walked under the series of stone archways and past portraits showing the founders of the private school, she felt a little queasy, much like how she felt the first day she had set foot on the school grounds when she was nine years old. She'd been a nervous little girl back then, gangly and carrying a backpack that almost outweighed her. She'd been wearing a uniform that didn't quite fit because her mother couldn't afford anything better. She had almost gnawed her lip raw that day, not knowing what to expect as she slowly walked to her homeroom. She felt the same way today, unsure of what exactly to expect when she walked into the principal's office.

She rounded the corner and found a young woman with dark hair parted severely down the middle, sitting at a desk while classical music played on an iPod dock perched on a file cabinet nearby. A view of the school's basketball and tennis courts was visible from the office window. Leila knocked on the door frame to get the young woman's attention.

"Yes?" the young woman asked, turning away

from her laptop screen and peering up at Leila expectantly.

"My name is Leila Hawkins. I'm . . . I'm here to pick up my daughter, Isabel Hawkins."

The young woman nodded curtly. "Yes, I'll let Ms. Fairchild know that you're here." She then rose from her desk and walked the short distance to a closed door with a gold plaque.

"Eleanor Fairchild, Principal" was displayed on the plaque in large black letters.

The young woman knocked.

"Come in," a scratchy voice answered. The young woman leaned her head inside and whispered something Leila couldn't hear. A few seconds later, the door opened wider and Leila saw Ms. Fairchild standing in the doorway. She was tall and thin, with knobby shoulders that showed prominently through her navy blue sweater. Her gray hair was cut short so that it looked like a wisp of feathers around her narrow head.

"Ah, Ms. Hawkins!" Ms. Fairchild said, holding out her hand to her. "Thank you for coming!"

The young woman stepped aside and Leila stepped forward to shake Ms. Fairchild's hand. The old woman's grip was light. Her hand was cold, bony, and limp.

"Please come inside."

Leila stepped into the expansive office and instantly spotted her daughter. When she did, she cringed.

Isabel's plaid jumper was ripped on one side. The two pigtails that Leila had neatly combed, brushed, and greased into place that morning were now in complete disarray. Isabel also had a scratch on her left cheek near her eye.

"Izzy? *Baby?* What in the world . . ." she breathed, rushing toward her daughter's side. She grabbed Isabel's chin and stared at her cheek.

Isabel lowered her eyes

"The other student looks just as bad as your daughter, if it's any consolation," Ms. Fairchild said, linking her hands in front of her.

Leila side-eyed the older woman. "Not really," she muttered before slowly kneeling down on the Afghan rug beside Isabel's chair, grunting as she did it. "Baby, *why* were you fighting? What happened?"

Isabel didn't answer her, but kept her eyes downcast.

"May I speak with you privately, Ms. Hawkins?" Ms. Fairchild asked.

"S-sure." She turned back to Isabel. "Wait outside for me. Okay?"

Isabel nodded.

A few minutes later, Leila was sitting in one of the armchairs facing Ms. Fairchild's large mahogany desk. The older woman closed her door and strolled across her office, pausing to pull a dead leaf from a bouquet of tea roses that sat on a nearby table.

"I wanted you to know that I have decided to suspend Isabel for the week. It may seem like a harsh penalty, but in light of her short time here at Queen Anne, I want her to understand that we do not accept that kind of behavior at this institution," Ms. Fairchild said, taking a seat behind her desk.

Leila nodded. "Yes, I understand. Izzy won't do this again. I'll make sure it!"

Just as soon as I find out why she was fighting in the first place, Leila thought.

She still didn't understand it. Her daughter was usually so soft-spoken and gentle. She wasn't a fighter. But she had been behaving differently lately.

Ms. Fairchild pursed her wrinkled lips and leaned forward in her chair. "I don't know if you've had time to peruse our school handbook, but Queen Anne actually has a zero-tolerance policy toward fighting, Ms. Hawkins. We want to condition our young men and women to exhibit exemplary behavior, to be upstanding citizens in this world. Fighting does not fall in that category."

"Yes," Leila repeated tightly, "I understand. As I said, it won't happen again."

"But," Ms. Fairchild continued with a sigh, like she hadn't heard Leila, "I am willing to bend that policy for Isabel for a number of reasons. One being that she seems to be a young lady with much potential based on her test scores and the initial feedback from her teachers. I think she could do quite well here at Queen Anne."

"I think so, too," Leila said softly, rubbing her belly in slow strokes.

"Also, I kept in mind her connection to the academy," Ms. Fairchild continued. Her wan face broke into a skeletal smile. "One of her teachers made me aware that she was a legacy student—of one of the more *esteemed* legacies at our institution. I was surprised you didn't include that information in her application!"

Leila stopped rubbing her belly. She shrugged. "I didn't think it mattered that I had attended Queen Anne. I wasn't sure it would help her admission."

Ms. Fairchild inclined her head. "You also attended our school?"

"Uh . . . yeah! Yeah, I was a student here back in the nineties."

Ms. Fairchild still looked confused.

"Isn't . . . isn't that what you were referring to when you said Izzy was a legacy student . . . because I went here?"

"Why no! But I'm pleasantly surprised to discover Isabel has *two* legacy connections! I was referring to Isabel's stepfather, Mr. Evan Murdoch! You see, the Murdochs have a long history here at Queen Anne and we are *very* appreciative of what they've done for our school. Offering a scholarship fund for underprivileged students, providing money for auditorium renovations. Why, just last year Mr. Murdoch donated *fifty thousand dollars* to build our new music wing! It will be finished in the spring. When it's done, please tell him that we'd love to give him a tour—if he has time available, of course."

Leila was now at a loss for words. She opened her mouth and closed it. She opened it again. "So you're . . . you're allowing Izzy to stay at Queen Anne because . . . because you think she's a Murdoch?"

Ms. Fairchild blinked. Her smile disappeared. "Well, I wouldn't . . . I wouldn't put it quite *that* way, Ms. Hawkins."

Really? Because that's exactly *how I would put it,* Leila thought angrily, but didn't say it aloud.

She threw her purse strap over her shoulder and pushed herself to her feet. "Thank you for everything, Ms. Fairchild. I'm taking Izzy home now. We'll see you in a week."

Fifteen minutes later, Leila was driving off the Queen Anne Academy grounds back to the Murdoch Mansion. She glanced at her daughter, who sat slumped in the passenger seat beside her. "What were you thinking? Why in the world were you fighting, Izzy?"

Isabel didn't respond, but instead continued to glare out the windshield.

"Answer me!" Leila yelled, making the little girl jump in her seat.

"I don't . . . I don't know," Isabel finally mumbled, lowering her eyes.

"You don't know? *You don't know?*"

Leila furiously shook her head, trying her best to rein in her temper but not succeeding. She pulled onto the road leading to the Murdoch Mansion.

"Izzy, I don't know what has gotten into you lately. First, Evan catches you stealing my jewelry, and now I get a call from your new school saying that you were fighting some other girl on the playground. And now you're suspended! This behavior is unacceptable, young lady!"

Isabel's bottom lip began to quiver. Her eyes started to water.

"Are you acting out because of the baby? Are you trying to get attention? Is that it? Or . . . or is it your dad? Did he put you up to this, too?"

Isabel shook her head.

"Then what is it?" Leila drew to a stop in the driveway and turned to face her daughter. "Why are you acting out like this?"

Isabel closed her eyes as tears spilled onto her cheeks. "Stacey . . . Stacey said you were a ho," she whispered.

"What?"

"She said you were a ho!" Isabel screamed, opening her eyes and glaring up at her mother. Her words came out between sobs and hiccups. "Stacey said that her mom said that you were a ho! And Stacey was telling everybody on the playground that they . . . that they shouldn't play with me because . . . because I'd grow up to be a ho just like . . . just like *you!*"

Leila stared at Isabel in shock.

"Oh, honey," Leila whispered, reaching for her daughter, wanting to break into tears herself. She wrapped an arm around her. "Oh, baby, I . . . I didn't know. I'm so—"

Isabel shoved Leila away. She unbuckled her seat belt and flung open the passenger-side door. Leila watched helplessly as her daughter rushed up the stone steps to the mansion and pounded her small fists on the French doors until the housekeeper opened them. She rushed past the older woman, who looked at her aghast.

Almost two hours later, Evan strolled into their bedroom, only to find Leila pacing in front of their bed muttering to herself. She had just left Isabel's bedroom twenty minutes ago, finally getting the little girl to calm down, only to get herself stirred back up again.

Evan furrowed his brows when he saw her. "What's wrong?"

"I'm gonna kill her," Leila mumbled, curling her hands into claws. "I am going to fucking *kill her*!"

He shrugged out of his suit jacket and tossed it onto the bed. "Kill who?"

"Your goddamn wife!" she shouted, making him jump. She dropped her hand to her lower back and continued to waddle back and forth on the plush carpet. "That bitch has it coming to her! I don't care if you fuck with me, Evan, but you don't fuck with my child . . . my Izzy! I've had enough of this shit from her! If I wasn't seven months pregnant, I'd march straight to her house, yank her through the door, and kick her ass!"

"What are you talking about? Why do you want to kick Charisse's ass?"

Leila stopped pacing long enough to glower at him. "She's going around town telling everyone that I'm a whore! She said I used to be a hooker and cokehead! She told them that they shouldn't do business with me. That's why my clients are leaving in droves! Now she's even got the kids at Queen Anne saying that they shouldn't play with Izzy because she's going to grow up to be a ho just like her mama!"

"Jesus," he exhaled. "Are you sure Charisse really did all that?"

"Of course, I'm sure! You think I would just pull this shit out of thin air? Someone told me she's doing it!"

"Okay," he said, holding up his hands. "Okay, just . . . just calm down, baby."

"Don't tell me to calm down!" she shouted, feeling the cords stand up along her neck. "Don't you dare tell me to calm down, goddammit!"

"Look, I just don't want this shit with Charisse to send you into early labor, okay? It's not worth it! Take a deep breath."

She closed her eyes and did as he suggested. She breathed in and out and rubbed her stomach, feeling their baby girl shift.

"I'll talk to Charisse," he said. "I'll take care of this."

"No," she said firmly, opening her eyes and shaking her head.

"Lee, come on! If I talk to her and tell her to back off, she'll—"

"I said no, Evan!" she shouted, now beyond frustrated. "Don't talk to her about this. I don't need you to be our go-between! Don't *wave* your magic Murdoch wand!" she said, illustrating her words by waving her hand in the air. "Dammit, just stay out of it! *You* back off!"

He flinched, looking hurt.

Leila hadn't meant to yell at him, but frankly, she was getting tired of this—of *all of this*! She couldn't go anywhere without being reminded of Evan or his money or his powerful family. She wasn't seen as Leila Hawkins anymore. Who cared that she had grown up in Chesterton, had once held down multiple jobs to pay the rent, and had been the head of her own household only months ago? All they cared about was that she was Evan Murdoch's pregnant mistress, his live-in whore! Even Isabel's life seemed to be inextricably linked with the Murdochs, her name now tied with theirs— whether she liked it or not.

This isn't what I signed up for, Leila thought, shaking her head ruefully. She'd had no idea when she and Evan started on this path that her life would turn into this . . . that she would feel like a woman who had lost her identity and all sense of control.

She took another shaky breath. "I'm sorry," she whispered. "I'm sorry, Ev. I didn't mean to lash out at you like that, but I'm just . . . just tired. I'm tired of all this bullshit!"

She left it at that, not wanting to say any more, worried at how she might hurt him more than she already had if she told him the full truth.

"I know," he said, wrapping his arms around her. She dropped her head to his shoulder and he rubbed her back. "I know. I hate seeing you upset like this. Really, I can talk to her and—"

"No, Ev," she said, raising her head to gaze at him again. "I mean it! She's trying to get a reaction out of me and definitely trying to get a response from you. I refuse to give in to her!"

She knew responding to Charisse's baiting was a no-win game. Even if Leila was justified in wanting to exact revenge for everything Charisse had done to her—the sabotage and rumors—no one else in Chesterton would see it that way. To them, Leila was still Evan's mistress, trying to take Charisse's rightful place in the Murdoch household. It would only make things worse for her and Isabel.

"Promise me that you'll stay out of this, Ev."

He pursed his lips.

"I know you want to help and I . . . I appreciate it, but I don't want you to get involved. Promise me that you won't."

"Fine," he grumbled.

"No, not 'fine.' 'I promise.' I know how you are. I want to hear you say it!"

The bedroom fell silent as she waited for his response, wondering if he would really agree to her request. She watched as Ev took another deep breath and nodded.

"I promise," he finally said.

Chapter 16

C. J.

C. J. squinted into the bright lights from the film crews gathered three feet below her—all clustered around the small raised stage on the Aston Ministries grounds. Despite her unease, she forced herself to keep her smile firmly in place.

Her father had wanted to hold the press conference at the courthouse soon after the paternity results were read aloud in court by the presiding judge. The results showed Reverend Pete Aston wasn't the father of Rochelle Martin's baby. Even Martin's lawyer had held a press conference at the courthouse, announcing that she would be forced to drop her lawsuit, explaining that she wasn't a villain but a greatly misunderstood young woman. But Reverend Aston's new PR Svengali, whom he had hired for his congressional campaign, believed in giving a show. She had suggested that he hold his press conference at the church instead.

"It gives it more authority and presence," she had said, her blue eyes alight with inspiration. "And having that big glass church in the background will look absolutely *amazing* on camera!"

So this is why C. J. was chattering her teeth in high winds and forty-degree weather, waiting for her father to step up to the podium and begin to speak among the clicking of camera shutters and those few reporters near the stage. She pursed her lips as she raised the collar of her wool coat to block the wind, all the while trying to smooth her wayward locks with her hands.

"I want to thank my lovely wife, Sarah, for standing by me and believing from the very beginning that I was a man of my word and a man of God," Reverend Aston finally began. "I want to thank my son, Victor, and my daughter, Courtney, for all their love and support. I would also like to thank all the parishioners and those voters out there who believed me from the very beginning."

C. J. watched out of the corner of her eye as Victor stood on the opposite side of her father while the older man gave his speech. Victor donned a full-on plastic smile for the occasion. He was hand-in-hand with his wife, Bethany, who gazed up at him adoringly—the poor, deluded woman. Bethany even leaned her head against Victor's shoulder. They looked like the perfect couple.

If only everyone knew the truth, C. J. thought.

She then glanced at Shaun, who stood directly next to her, who was smiling politely at the cameras as her father continued to speak.

Though I guess I'm not much better.

Standing at her side, Shaun seemed very much like her boyfriend or even her husband. Her father's "people" had put him on the podium next to her specifically for that reason, although they had pretended it had been for something else.

"Symmetry," the young PR flack had explained with his bleached-white grin. "It just looks more balanced with him standing next to you."

Uh-huh, I bet, C. J. had thought sarcastically.

She knew that was a crock of shit! They wanted everyone watching the press conference to think that C. J. was with Pastor Clancy, that he was her boyfriend. They wanted everyone to believe that Reverend Aston not only had the perfect son and daughter, but also children with perfect significant others. C. J. couldn't work up the energy anymore to rebel against these lies. She was too exhausted to care. She hadn't had a decent night's sleep in almost a week, not since Terrence had stormed out of her apartment.

That next morning, after she had apologized to Clancy a million times and cried her eyes out, she had resolved that she would erase all memories of Terrence Murdoch. She finally was ready to move on and let him go—or so she'd thought. It was more than a week later and she still hadn't managed to do that.

C. J. now grimaced as the wind picked up ferocity, making her hair whip around her shoulders again. She crossed her arms over her chest as her father started to accept questions from the reporters who were all shouting simultaneously.

"Are you planning to file a defamation suit

against Miss Martin now that the truth has come to light, Reverend?" one reporter asked.

"I wouldn't be much of a Christian if I blindly sought revenge," her father replied.

"Praise the Lord!" C. J.'s mother exclaimed while wrapping an arm around her husband.

"So the answer is no," he continued. "I don't plan to file any more lawsuits. I plan to stay as far away from court as possible. I will simply pray for Miss Martin, focus on spreading the good word, and concentrate on my campaign."

The questions continued like this for the next fifteen minutes; all the while C. J. struggled to pay attention, to keep her grin in place.

At least Terrence had stopped calling her. He had gone from calling her constantly to not calling or texting her at all. And she had no interest in reaching out to him, either.

What she had seen that day in her apartment was not the man she had fallen in love with. It was not the man who had wooed her with moonlit picnics in Macon Park and conversations that could go on for hours without awkward pauses. Back then, Terrence had been sweet and tender, open and loving. He wasn't the callous asshole who had charged into her apartment, acting like some chest-thumping, raging gorilla.

Where was the Terrence she had known and loved?

Gone, she realized reluctantly. *He doesn't exist anymore.*

And because that version of him no longer existed, their breakup was for the best and probably inevitable. They weren't compatible anymore, like two disparate jigsaw pieces that no longer fit together. Terrence would go back to his playboy ways and fly off to Europe or the Caribbean with some beautiful video vixen on his arm.

And I'll come back here, she resolved as she gazed up at the towering glass edifice of Aston Ministries headquarters. *The video vixens can have him!*

So why was she still so unsettled? Why did her thoughts keep drifting back to him?

"C. J.," Shaun said, gently touching her shoulder.

She turned to him, startled from her heavy thoughts. "Huh?"

"The press conference is over," he said, gesturing to the front lawn, where the reporters were starting to disperse. "I wasn't sure if you noticed. You seemed like you were out of it."

"I guess I drifted off for a bit." She glanced around herself again. "I hope no one else noticed."

"I wouldn't worry. I don't think they did."

She continued to smile blankly, barely listening to him. He frowned.

"Are you okay?" he asked.

"Yeah, I'm . . . I'm fine. I'm just a little . . . uh . . . cold. That's all." She shoved her hands into her coat pockets.

"That wasn't what I meant."

Her smile teetered as he took a step closer to her.

"I haven't spoken to you since last week," he whispered. "I wondered if you were . . . well, I wondered how you were doing after what . . . what happened. I wanted to call you to see if you were all right, but I figured you needed some time to your-self."

C. J. gazed up at him as if seeing him for the first time. How was it possible that Shaun seemed to understand her better than her own man had?

"I did need some time alone. Thank you, Shaun. Thank you for sensing that. Thank you for . . . for everything."

"It's not a problem," he said with a shrug. "I—"

"No, I mean it." She reached out and grabbed his hand. He glanced down at it, at their inter-twined fingers, and for a few seconds she consid-ered letting his hand go, but she didn't. She held on tight. "You've been incredibly sweet and kind and patient with me . . . probably more than I de-serve. You're a good man, Shaun."

He chuckled. "So you keep telling me."

"No, you are. You're a *good* man."

And you were probably the right man for me all along, she thought.

She stood on the balls of her feet, leaned for-ward, and lightly kissed his cheek, making his eyes widen, catching him by surprise. There was no pas-sion or love behind the kiss, certainly not the love that she suspected he felt for her. C. J. admired Shaun, but she still didn't love him. But the kiss was the only real thanks she could offer him, besides her words. At least, it was all she could offer him for now.

I could learn to love him if I tried harder, though, she told herself, ignoring the fact that she had told herself this same lie six years ago. *I probably won't love him like I loved Terry, but I could learn to feel some-thing close to it.*

She squeezed Shaun's hand again, then let it go.

"I need to head back to my office. I've got a few phone calls to make," she said. "Wanna meet up for lunch later, maybe?"

"Sure! How about one o'clock?"

"One o'clock it is." C. J. then gave a genuine smile, the first she had all day. She headed to the stage stairs. C. J. began to walk back toward Aston Ministries, feeling a little lighter in her step, but she was halted by the sound of her brother's booming voice.

"C. J.!" he called out to her. "C. J., wait up!"

She contemplated pretending she hadn't heard him, but she slowly turned around instead. She found her brother striding toward her, still smiling, which immediately made her suspicious. She glared back at him.

"If looks could kill," he muttered, laughing at her facial expression.

"What do you want, Victor?" she snapped.

"Oh, nothing! I just wanted to tell you that you did a good job at the press conference."

She eyed him, now even more suspicious. "A *good job?*"

He nodded. "Don't look so shocked, Court! I can give out compliments every once in a while. It's good to see you finally falling into line. I'd doubted you'd ever be able to do it, but I have to say"—he paused to look her up and down—"I'm pleasantly surprised."

"What are you talking about?"

"I mean that little show you put on up there . . . holding Shaun's hand and giving him that little kiss on the cheek." He gave her a slow clap. "It was so adorable, a perfect touch! Next time, though, do it at the end of the press conference, not after the whole thing is over. We'd like to get a moment like that on camera."

"I wasn't doing it for the damn cameras, Victor! I wasn't putting on a performance."

"Of course you weren't . . . and I adore my wife, too," he said sarcastically before glancing over his shoulder at Bethany, who stood more than twenty feet away with their mother and father. Bethany turned to him and blew him a kiss. Victor pretended to catch the kiss and winked at her. He then turned back around to face C. J. "We all have stories we like to tell. We just have to make them believable."

"I don't know how many times I have to tell you this, but I'm not like you."

He chuckled again and patted her on the shoulder. "Of course you aren't! Not yet, anyway."

At his words, her blood ran cold.

"But with time . . . you might be. You just might be, Courtney," he said before heading back across the field toward his wife.

Chapter 17

Evan

"Would you like me to wait for you here, Mr. Murdoch, or should I just come back and get you later?"

Evan leaned his head back against the leather cushion and sighed as his driver, Bill, pulled into one of the condominium's many parking spaces. "You can come back. I'll call you when I'm ready. I have no idea how long this will take."

Evan watched as Bill nodded in the front seat. "No problem, sir." Bill then unlocked the door and pushed it open, about to head to the back to open Evan's car door.

"Oh, and Bill?" Evan said, making his driver pause.

"Yes, sir?"

Evan pursed his lips as he stared outside his

tinted window. "Our visit here today is just between you and me, okay?"

Bill turned completely around to face Evan. He paused and squinted his dark eyes, perplexed. "I'm sorry, sir?"

"We stopped on the way home to grab dinner somewhere . . . a bite to eat. If anyone asks, that's what you should say," he ordered, although the truth was that Evan didn't know who would be asking Bill such a question; he just wanted to make sure that Bill had an answer ready. Evan didn't want this visit to get out to anyone, especially to Leila. He didn't know what might happen if it did.

Bill gradually nodded. "Of . . . of course, sir."

A couple of minutes later, Evan was walking down one of the condominium's many corridors, grimacing as he did it. He made furtive, guilty glances over his shoulder before finally stopping in front of one of the doors and ringing the doorbell. He heard the bell chime on the other side. He nervously swallowed the lump that had formed in his throat. A few seconds later, the door opened.

"Ev!" Charisse exclaimed.

She stood in the doorway wearing an oversize pink wool sweater that revealed one of her creamy, bare shoulders. Her blond hair was pulled into a loose ponytail atop her head. A few tendrils fell around her face, softening her look. She smiled warmly.

"You came!" she gushed.

"I said I would," he answered flatly in return.

She pushed the door open wider. "Come in."

He followed her command.

He knew Leila had told him not to get involved

in her dispute with Charisse, to let her handle it, but that just wasn't in his nature. He could see how it was affecting Leila and, by extension, affecting their relationship and him. How could he *not* get involved? It was his job to take care of her now, of his family. He *had* to do this! So he had called Charisse out of the blue earlier that week to let her have it.

"You need to stop this shit!" he had said to Charisse over the phone. "You're not only fucking with her, but you're messing with her daughter now. She wants to kick your ass!"

Charisse had chuckled in reply. "Well, she knows where to find me."

"I'm not kidding! She's really pissed off and, frankly, you're pissing me off, too. I've tried to show you some patience considering . . . well, considering . . . uh, everything," he had said, not wanting to bring up her sexual abuse at her father's hands. "But I can't do it anymore. This shit has got to stop, Charisse! You need to let this go. You need to let *me* go!"

She had fallen quiet on the other end of the line. "I don't know if I can do that, Ev."

"You're going to have to. I don't love you anymore. Do you hear me? I don't want you anymore! I don't want to hurt you, but it's the truth."

"Prove it," she had said.

"*Prove it?* What the hell does that mean?"

"If you're so sure you don't love me and don't want me, then you won't mind us talking over dinner. You won't mind me making my case to you alone, with no interruptions from anyone—

including that mistress of yours. And then after I say what I have to say, if you still want us to go our separate ways, I'll grant you your divorce."

"Charisse, are you serious?"

"I'm very serious! If it's over like you say it is, then this shouldn't be a problem for you, should it?"

"Yeah, right. You've done this before. You said we were going to talk things over and then when the time came, you refused to go forward with anything!"

"Well, not this time. *This* time . . . I mean it."

He had sucked his teeth. "This is stupid, Charisse . . . a total waste of fucking time! It would be much easier if you would just—"

"Humor me, Ev," she'd said with laughter in her voice. "Have dinner with me."

He had hesitated. "So you promise that if I do this, you'll grant me a divorce? This shit will be over?"

"I give my solemn promise."

He had groused with defeat. "Fine. When should I come over?"

"Would you like something to drink?" Charisse now asked as she guided him through her living room into the small dining room adjacent to her eat-in kitchen.

"No," he said, shrugging out of his wool coat and tossing it onto the back of her love seat. "And you shouldn't be having anything to drink, either."

He watched as she rolled her baby blues and opened one of the doors of her stainless steel refrigerator. She rummaged inside, moving things around on the shelves. She then withdrew a small dish filled with butter before slamming the door shut. "I was just offering you water or sparkling cider, Mr. Buzzkill. Nothing alcoholic. Don't get your panties in a twist."

"Water is fine," he mumbled, looking around him. She quickly filled a glass and handed it to him.

Soft jazz music played on her stereo in the living room, a fire burned in her enclosed glass fireplace, and he could see a copper pot of tomato sauce bubbling on one of the burners. She was actually cooking! Charisse hadn't cooked anything for him in years, not since the early days when they had started dating.

She's going all out for this one, he thought with raised brows. But it was a waste of time and effort. He was just doing what he had to do for her to move on and sign their divorce papers. Though Leila probably wouldn't appreciate his methods, she would certainly be happy with the outcome when he told her they could finally get married.

"So how are things at the office?" Charisse asked, grabbing a loaf of French bread and a knife from the counter. She placed it on a wooden cutting board and began to slice off a few pieces. "Still conquering the world one food franchise at a time?"

"We're getting by," he muttered, removing his suit jacket and tugging at the knot in his silk tie. If he had to be here, he might as well get comfortable. He walked toward the granite kitchen counter where Charisse now stood. He leaned an elbow against it, watching her work.

He had to admit that she was an alluring woman when she wanted to be. Seeing her in leggings, sweater, and bare feet, he remembered what he had seen in her all those years ago, what had attracted him to her in the first place. This version of Charisse had been absent for quite a while, hidden behind martinis and bitchiness.

Evan had one vivid memory of her standing in her kitchen of her old apartment, laughing through her tears at something funny he had said while she chopped red onions for the dish she was making him. She had laughed and cried so hard that she had nicked the tip of her finger with the knife and had had to get a Band-Aid.

"Kiss it and make it better," she had said with an exaggerated pout.

He had kissed the tip of her finger and then leaned forward to give her a sultry kiss that landed them both in the bedroom only minutes later.

He now watched as Charisse added butter to one of the bread slices she had just finished slicing, then held it out to him. He took it and chewed.

"Homemade garlic herb butter. One of your faves," she said with a wink. "See, I still remember some things."

Too bad you only started to remember now—when it's too late, he thought, but he didn't say it aloud. He wondered if Charisse had been the woman now standing in front of him throughout their marriage, whether it would have still fallen apart. Would he and Leila even be together now?

It makes no difference either way. It's probably all an act anyway.

"So how are things at home?" Charisse asked with mock innocence, inclining her head. He reached for another bread slice and popped it into his mouth. "Tranquil, I hope."

"No thanks to you," he said between chews, making her chuckle.

"Oh, come on, Ev! If you two were really meant to be, what I said or did shouldn't make much of a difference, should it? Because you guys are *so in love*," she said in an exaggerated breathy whisper, placing a hand to her heart and fluttering her lashes. "Admit it! You thought the grass would be greener on the other side, but it didn't turn out that way, did it?"

Evan lowered his eyes to the kitchen countertop, turning away from the truth in her words.

She was right. He *had* thought that his life would be much better with Leila versus Charisse—free of rancor and drama. He'd thought it would be damn near perfect! He had loved Leila and wanted her for almost forever, and now he finally had her. This should be their happy ending, but it hadn't turned out that way. And the issues they faced weren't just due to Charisse. When he got Leila, he also got her jealous and vindictive ex-husband, rebellious daughter, and meddling mother who *always* expressed her opinion on their relationship. And now they were having a baby, but instead of drawing closer to him, Leila seemed to be pushing him farther away. This isn't how he had planned it. This isn't what he had envisioned or hoped for.

Charisse sniffed the air. "Is that a whiff of regret I smell?" She laughed again, making him glare at her.

"Can't help but stir up shit, can you?"

"I'm not stirring up shit! I'm just pointing out the obvious."

"No, what you've been doing to Lee over the past few months is stirring up shit."

She made a *tsk-tsk* sound. "That's simply fighting for what's mine, Ev!"

"I'm *not* yours . . . not anymore."

She leaned toward him so that they were almost nose to nose. "You say that . . . but I'm not so sure," she whispered, gazing into his eyes.

Charisse eased toward him by another inch, and his eyes drifted to her glossy lips. Her lips were only a sliver away from touching his when he remembered who this woman really was. She had slept with his brother Dante. She was systematically intimidating and harassing his fiancée and refusing to grant him a divorce. He also remembered what he was here for, to sever ties with his wife once and for all because he was in love with Leila. Evan quickly took a step back.

"What are we eating?" he asked, turning away from her and heading to the dining room table. He pulled out a chair and sat down. "It smells good, whatever it is."

Out of the corner of his eye, he saw Charisse shake her head in exasperation before turning to the oven. "Spinach-feta shells with minted tomato sauce," she said. "Another one of your faves."

For the rest of the evening, Evan was diligent about keeping his distance from Charisse so nothing like what had happened in the kitchen could happen again. He expected her to use the meal as a chance to "state her case," to make arguments for why he should be with her and not Leila, but she didn't. She kept the conversation innocuous, even polite, not mentioning any of the past acrimony between them—the lying, the bitterness, and the affairs—or how she felt about him asking for a divorce.

By the time they finished their meal, he had a full belly and was even somewhat happy. He had done what she had asked and now, if Charisse stuck to their agreement, they could finally go their separate ways.

He wiped his mouth with his dinner napkin, pushed his chair back, and rose from the table. "Well, thank you for the meal. I should be heading home, though." He glanced at his watch, then looked across the table at Charisse. He put his suit jacket back on. "I guess I'll be receiving the signed divorce papers from you sometime this week."

"Sure," she said, pausing to take a sip from her water glass, "after I do one last thing."

"What's that?" Evan frowned as he watched Charisse rise from the table and walk toward him.

"This," she said just before linking her arms around his neck, catching him by surprise. She then stood on the balls of her feet and raised her lips to his.

Evan started to pull back, to shove her away and unwind her arms from around his neck, but she held tighter onto him, pressing her lips more firmly against his.

"Don't fight it, Ev," she whispered hotly against his lips.

Despite his wife's urging, he could have . . . *should* have fought it. He should have tried harder to remove himself from her embrace, but he didn't. He didn't know if it was the nostalgia of the moment—making him remember how beautiful and sexy she had once been. Or maybe it was the distance and tension he had been feeling for months with Leila. Or maybe it was because he knew this was Charisse's last stand and she would not give up until he gave in, but he surrendered to the moment. He relaxed and let Charisse kiss him.

He let her dart her tongue inside his mouth, and God help him, he met her tongue with his own. Her hold around his neck tightened as she leaned back her head and their kiss deepened. She pressed her breasts against his chest. He wrapped his arms around her back, drawing her closer.

"See, Ev. I knew you still loved me!"

At her words, he recoiled as if he had been bitten by a poisonous snake. He withdrew his arms from around her waist and took an unsteady step back. He stared down at his wife, who was grinning up at him triumphantly.

"We shouldn't have done that," he said with a gasping breath, shaking his head. "I . . . I didn't want to do that."

"Yes, you did! You wanted it and so did I. Admit it, Ev!"

"You didn't bring me here just to talk!" He

wiped his lips on the back of his shirtsleeve, wanting to get the taste of her out of his mouth. "I was so fucking stupid! You'd planned this all along, didn't you? You brought me here to play these . . . these fucking mind games! You thought you could seduce me into coming back?"

"No, you idiot! I brought you here to find out the truth . . . to see for myself what you refuse to admit to me and to yourself—that you still want me, Ev. And now I know for sure that you do."

He clenched his jaw. "One kiss doesn't prove that."

She laughed. "So you claim."

"Look, I came here and ate dinner with you. I held up my end of this stupid bargain. Sign the fucking divorce papers, Charisse. *End* this!"

"Oh, don't worry. I'll keep my word. Besides, I know now that even if I don't have your ring on my finger anymore, I still have a hold on you, Evan Murdoch. And that's all I needed to know." She smirked. "I wonder if Leila would be interested in knowing it, too."

"Don't you dare mention any of this shit to Lee!"

She laughed again.

"I mean it, Charisse!"

"Like I really want to fucking talk to her!" she huffed as she crossed her arms over her chest. "Believe me. I would be perfectly happy to never see or speak to that bitch again."

He took another shaky breath and turned to head to Charisse's front door.

"Thank you, Evan!" she called to him. "I feel so

much better about all this. You've taken a load off my shoulders."

He cringed.

Charisse may have had a load removed, but with that kiss, he felt like he had just dragged a new load onto his back.

Chapter 18

Dante

Dante opened the car door and glanced cagily around him before stepping onto the broken concrete sidewalk. Nothing looked out of sorts. It was the same old drab D.C. neighborhood of his childhood. The same small two-story houses were in various states of disrepair, from crumbling brick to torn panels of siding to broken windows with black trash bags taped over the missing windowpanes. The lawns were more dirt and rubble than grass. At the end of the block was the same streetlamp with its innards exposed, showing a tangled mass of disgorged wires resembling multicolored intestines. A pair of wilted Converse sneakers dangled from one of the phone wires overhead and the same four dudes leaned against the buckling wire fence as they played a game of craps on the sidewalk, blocking the path of all those who walked by. Well, Dante could reluctantly admit that they probably weren't the *same* dudes from his childhood, but they might as well have been.

"Same broke mofos," Dante mumbled derisively. "Same piss-poor houses."

Though prosperity had come to other parts of D.C. with gentrification by young hipsters who had moved into the city in the past decade, that prosperity had not arrived here. Nothing had changed in this neighborhood—in this far from glamorous enclave in Ward 8.

He shut the car door behind him and raised his hoodie to cover his head as he made his way to the house nestled near the end of the block.

He had moved into his mother's old home a little more than a month ago after kicking out the renters and bouncing from hotel to hotel for a few weeks before that. He hadn't returned to his condo. He was too scared to do it, unsure whether he would find another group of thugs waiting around to put a bullet in his head. He hadn't returned to the law firm, either, making vague excuses about his recovery and needing more surgeries.

"We're deeply sorry for what's happened to you, Dante, but . . . you've been away for two months," one of the partners had explained. "We're going to need some medical records to explain your absence . . . for legal purposes, of course."

"Like a doctor's note?" Dante had snapped. "I was shot, Edgar! I didn't get the flu. Hell, it was on the local evening news. I could send you a goddamn TV clip!"

"Please don't be flippant," the old man had grumbled. "We believe that you were shot! Dear God, who would lie about something like that? But we need insurance document copies . . . X-rays . . . something to explain why you've been gone for so long . . . why you're *still* gone! You understand, don't you?"

Dante had seethed silently on the other end of the phone line, wanting to unleash a curse-filled tirade against his boss. He wanted to tell Edgar that his hair plugs looked ridiculous and that he hated his puffy, marshmallow-like face. He wanted to tell Edgar that Edgar's young trophy wife had confessed the same when she had sneaked off with Dante to give him head in one of the filing closets during the law firm's Christmas party last year. But he didn't tell Edgar any of this. Instead, he had counted to ten and said, "Sure, I'll get something to you in a few days."

"Wonderful!" Edgar had exclaimed.

But Dante hadn't sent him the documents. In fact, he hadn't spoken to anyone at his law offices—or anyone at all—in quite a while.

The last phone call he had made was to Detective Morris about the investigation.

"She's still after me," Dante had explained to the detective.

"*She?* She *who*, Mr. Turner?"

"The woman who tried to have me murdered! She had some guys waiting for me at my place! I need a police guard, someone to watch me twenty-four-seven to make sure it doesn't happen again."

"I'm . . . I'm sorry, but I'm not following you, Mr. Turner. What woman?"

"I told you . . . the bitch who's trying to kill me! Her name is Renee Upton and she's pissed off that I dumped her and wouldn't take her to Barbados or some shit, so now she wants to take me out permanently. She tried it in the parking garage in July and it didn't work. She won't give up until I'm dead."

"Because you wouldn't take her to Barbados?" the detective had drawled.

"*And* because I dumped her!" Dante had explained, annoyed to have to keep repeating himself. The phone line had gone silent on the other end, and Dante had wondered if the detective was still there. "Hello? *Did you hear me?* I said she tried to kill me!"

"Yeah, I heard you, Mr. Turner," the detective had said with a loud sigh. "Look, are you sure it was this woman who shot you in the parking garage and not some . . . someone else? Maybe someone else might be involved."

"Detective, I *saw* her. She shot me. She ran. I'd swear on it!"

When his pronouncement was met by more silence, he had grumbled impatiently. "If you need her address, I can give it to you. I want her arrested and I want protection until she's taken care of . . . until she's behind bars."

"All right," the detective answered grudgingly. "I'll follow up and get back to you."

"*Get back to me?* But what about the police protection?" Dante had shouted into the phone. "I need someone to watch my back!"

"I can't promise you that, but I can tell you that

I'm taking this allegation very seriously. I'll follow up on it. You just sit tight."

But the police still hadn't made an arrest, which left Dante dumbfounded and filled with impotent rage. He had given them her address. He had practically pointed a neon arrow in Renee's direction, but nothing had happened. The detective had called him last week to tell him they couldn't find her.

"She wasn't at her home and her mother said she hasn't seen her in days."

"And you just took Mavis's word on that? That old bitch is lying! She knows where she is!"

"But we can't prove that, Mr. Turner."

"So you're telling me Renee's just going to get away with this? She tried to kill me *twice* and she's free to walk the streets?"

"No, I'm telling you that we'll keep pursuing her until we find her or . . . until we get a better lead," the detective had said.

"What better lead?"

"I mean you stay in touch just in case you remember anything else that may help us in the investigation."

"*What else?* I told you everything I know!"

"Well, maybe when you think about it some more, when you think more carefully, you might remember that night a little differently," the detective had said cryptically. "Other people had a reason to hurt you, Mr. Turner. Someone else might be involved in this."

"Who the hell else would be involved?"

"I don't know . . . business associates. Maybe

even one of your brothers. Evan Murdoch seemed like a promising lead."

Dante had squinted. *"Evan?"*

Evan had threatened him, but he didn't believe for a second that his pussy brother was actually capable of murder.

"Look, I'm just speculating, but, again, you get back to me if you remember things differently."

As Dante now strode on the cracked cement outside the home of his childhood, he shoved his hand into one of the pockets of his hoodie. He squeezed the paper bag filled with pill bottles that rattled rhythmically with each step he took and he almost exhaled with relief.

Dante's world had been turned completely upside down. He could no longer go to his condo. He could no longer go back to work. He couldn't comfortably show his face in public for fear of being spotted by someone who meant him harm, but at least he had his Oxy—his painkillers. The pain had subsided a while ago, but his need to feel the numbing sensation that came each time he swallowed those pills still hadn't gone away. It made him forget his unspent fury and sense of helplessness at his situation. He would gulp down two or three or four at a time with a glass of O.J., fall back into one of his mother's old, musky recliners, stare at the television, and let the world float away. He'd finally drift off to sleep with visions of carnage and revenge dancing in his head.

I'm coming for you, Renee, he would think with a

satisfied smile as he nodded off, *you heartless bitch! And you're next on my list, Evan. You thought you could take my rightful place as head of the family and cast me out? You've got another thing coming, motherfucka! And don't think I forgot you either, Leila, or you, Paulette. You bitches will get your justice due one day, too!*

In his dreams, he would dole out punishments to all of them like they were Halloween treats, dropping off one poison candied apple after another. He would pay them back for how they had wronged him and make them suffer worse than he had. But those fantasies faded as soon as he was awake. In the real world, Dante was absolutely powerless. He was a pill-popping addict cowering in his mother's run-down home. And he had no idea how he could bridge the gap between his revenge fantasies and reality.

He reached up and threw open his mother's wrought-iron gate, wincing at the loud squeak it made. He bounded up the concrete steps, then looked up and paused.

A young woman of eighteen or so stood on his front porch, leaning against one of the wooden posts, wearing a tight leather jacket and equally tight jeans. She didn't scramble off the porch when she saw him. She looked like she had been waiting for him this whole time.

He had seen this young woman before, lounging near his car, walking past the house. It was hard to miss her with her bright purple braids streaming down her back. He had worried that she had been following him, but he had pushed those worries aside as paranoia.

She's not following you but just happens to live in the neighborhood, he had told himself.

She was curious as to who had moved into Mary Turner's old place. Besides, Renee didn't know he had lived in this neighborhood more than a decade ago. There was no way she could have tracked him down here.

But now, staring at the girl in front of him, he wondered if he had been wrong.

"You Dante?" the girl called out, tossing her long braids over her shoulder, pushing herself away from the porch post. She walked toward the wooden stairs and stood in front of him, blocking his path.

He shoved his hand into the hoodie's other pocket where a Glock 19 Gen 3 sat with a full magazine. He had bought it soon after he figured out Renee had put a hit out on him. It was small enough to carry without detection, but big enough to pack a punch, according to the gun dealer who had recommended it to him. He carried it with him at all times now.

"Who wants to know?" he called back to her, wrapping his hand around the grip and putting his finger on the trigger, ready to pull out the gun at a moment's notice.

"Kiana Lacey," she said, strolling down the steps toward him, bouncing on the treads of her scuffed tennis shoes. "But everybody around here calls me Kiki."

She gave a charming smile that made her face go from unassuming to pretty—but Dante wasn't fooled. He didn't know who this girl was and he didn't trust her. And unless she could give him a good reason for why she was standing in front of him, keeping him from getting to his front door, he might put a bullet in her.

She stopped a foot away from him. "You never heard of me?"

"No," he answered succinctly.

The girl's smile fell. "Daaaaaamn!" she exhaled, then sucked her teeth. "I thought Grandma told you about me. She said she did!"

Dante slowly shook his head in bemusement. "What the fuck are you talking about? I don't know your grandmother, kid."

"Oh, yes, you do!"

"Look, I can assure you that I don't, *Kiki*," he snarled with a curl in his lip. "So if you could get the hell off my property, I would appreciate it."

"I ain't goin' nowhere!" He watched as she defiantly crossed her arms over her chest. "My grandmother's name was Mary Turner and you knew her. She *lived* here!"

Dante paused. "Did you . . . did you say Mary Turner?"

"Yep, she was my grandma!"

He shook his head again. "That's impossible! Mary Turner didn't have any grandchildren. She was my mother and she only had one kid—*me*! And I don't have any goddamn kids!"

She sucked her teeth again. "Yeah, well, I wouldn't be too sure about that."

His hand loosened on the gun's grip. *"What?"*

She took another step toward him. The smile was back. She stared up at him unflinchingly with caramel-colored eyes. "Wassup, Daddy?"

* * *

Dante watched as Kiana or Kiki walked casually around his kitchen, opening cabinets and slamming them shut, like she had done it dozens of times before. She then bent down and threw open the door to his refrigerator, shoved around a jar of mayonnaise and a jar of pickles on one of the metal shelves, and sighed dejectedly.

"Shit," she muttered under her breath before giving him a withering glance over her shoulder, "ain't you got any food in here?"

He didn't respond but instead raised his beer bottle to his lips and took a long drink.

She pulled out the jar of mayo and a plastic bag filled with a few slices of American cheese and slammed them both on the counter.

Dante remembered it all now. His mother *had* told him that he had fathered a child a long time ago, but he hadn't believed her.

"Michelle Lacey came 'round here with a little baby, Dante," his mother had told him over the phone during his first semester at Rutgers University when he was eighteen years old. "She says it's yours."

But Dante had dismissed Michelle's claims. She had dated quite a few guys that winter, when they had hooked up. She even had a reputation on their block for being ready and willing for whatever guy showed her the barest amount of interest. Dante wasn't surprised that she claimed the baby was his, considering he was the only dude in their neighborhood who was going to college—on a full scholarship, no less. Of course,

Michelle would want to latch onto the *one* guy with some potential, who seemed like he was going somewhere! But Dante wasn't having it.

"It's not mine! She's full of it," he had told his mother, shouting over the music his roommate had been playing in their dorm room.

"But it *is* yours, honey," his mother had insisted. "It gotta be!"

"Why? Just because she told you it was? Come on, Ma! Don't be gullible."

"No, it's just . . . I can see it . . . in the . . . in the eyes. I think she's yours."

He hadn't known what she had meant at the time: *"I can see it in the eyes."* But he knew now what his mother had meant. Kiki had the same eyes as his father, George Murdoch. Terrence was the only other person who had inherited that trait from their father. Now it looked like there was another.

"Why are you staring?" Kiki asked as she pulled out a loaf of bread and began to make a sandwich.

"No reason," Dante said, adjusting in his chair at the kitchen table and leaning back. "You just look like someone I know."

"My mom used to say I looked a lot like you." Kiki slathered one of the bread slices with mayo. "Grandma said it, too." She paused to gaze at him. "I can't see it, though."

"How is your mother?" Dante asked politely, drinking more beer.

"Dead," Kiki blurted out, slapping her cheese onto her sandwich. "One of her hustler boyfriends killed her. He got high one day and stabbed her. Did it about a year ago. I never liked that motherfucka. Told her he was a piece of shit, but she didn't listen," she sneered, throwing the two bread slices together and cutting them in half with a butter knife.

Dante winced. "I'm sorry to hear that."

He watched as she shrugged and bit into her sandwich. "It's okay. She wasn't much of a mother anyway. By the end, she was a junkie, too—and I fuckin' hate junkies."

Dante reached for his pill bottle in his hoodie pocket and lowered his eyes.

"So you still working as a lawyer?" Kiki asked between munches.

"No, I'm on a . . . uh, break for now."

"Is that why you moved back here? Grandma told me before she died that you lived in some nice place out in Virginia. I was surprised to see you up in here."

Dante raised an eyebrow. "My mother told you a lot about me, didn't she?"

But she didn't tell me anything about you, Dante thought.

His mother had carried on a relationship with this young girl seemingly for years and had never mentioned it to him. Then again, she hadn't told him who his real father was until the week before she died. His mother was accustomed to keeping secrets.

Kiki nodded at his question and took another bite. "Yeah, she told me that you were divorced . . . that you didn't have any other kids . . . that you didn't want me," she said, glaring at him again.

He pursed his lips. For the first time in his life, Dante felt an inkling of guilt. He could remember how much it had hurt to be rejected by his father. It pained him to now realize that he had done the same to his own daughter.

"Look, uh . . . Kiki," he began feebly, "when your mother got pregnant—"

"I hate it when people say 'she *got* pregnant'! Like she *got* a cold. What the fuck is that about?"

"I . . . well, I . . . I was a teenager when it . . . uh, happened," he continued, ignoring her sarcasm. "I was very young."

"Like every other dude around here ain't a daddy by nineteen," Kiki said dryly between chews.

"But your mother and I weren't that serious. I wouldn't even call us boyfriend and girlfriend. We were just—"

"Save it." Kiki held up her hand, stopping him. "Just save it. I don't wanna hear it." She finished the last of her sandwich and wiped the crumbs off her palms. "I didn't come here for some story or excuses. I came here to ask if I could stay with you."

Dante's mouth fell open. "You want to live here with . . . with *me*?"

She nodded. "I was staying with my girl at her place a few blocks from here, but she got two kids. Her baby screams all day and all night and her man is messed up! He keeps trying to push up on me. He told me I couldn't keep living there for free. He said either I had to pay rent or fuck him. And I don't have no money, so . . ." She raised her empty hands.

When Dante continued to stare at her blankly, she pushed herself away from the counter and sucked her teeth.

"Look, I wouldn't be here long, just until I got myself situated. I know Grandma has that other room. I could stay there. You wouldn't even know I was here."

Kiki *really* wanted to live with him. Even though he felt guilt for deserting her, he didn't feel enough to want to share his mother's home with her. She may have been his daughter, but no one else knew that. How would it look to let some teenage girl move in with him? And what if she stumbled upon the secret stash of prescription pills he kept locked away in the bathroom cabinets and found out about his addiction? What if Renee discovered that he was living here? Would it put Kiki at risk?

"You . . . you barely know me, Kiki. I barely know you."

"So you're saying I can't live here?"

"What I'm saying is—"

"Dammit, I knew you were gonna say no! You never helped me out before, why the hell should you start now, right?" She then turned on her heel and strode toward the kitchen entrance. Dante watched helplessly as she stormed down the hall toward his front door.

He grimaced. "Kiki! Kiki, wait!"

"Fuck you!" she barked before swinging the front door open and slamming it shut behind her.

Chapter 19

Terrence

"So where are all the drinks?" Terrence gazed at the buffet table in front of him, grabbed one of the bright pink petit fours from a ceramic platter, popped it into his mouth and chewed. "Is that all you got . . . lemonade and iced tea? Is the lemonade at least spiked?"

His little sister, Paulette, sighed loudly as she shifted one of the tiered sterling silver trays on the table that featured mini cupcakes decorated with pearls and little plastic rattles. "It's a baby shower, Terry! Why the hell would the lemonade be spiked?"

"But you invited dudes to this thing," he grumbled, reaching for one of the mini cupcakes, only to have Paulette slap his hand away. "We're all

adults! You're telling me a man can't get a goddamn Corona?"

"Yes!" she said before rearranging an assort-
ment of folded linen napkins that one of Evan's
maids had set on the table. "That's *exactly* what I'm
telling you!"

He closed his eyes and sighed. "Then why the
fuck am I here?"

"You're here," she said while turning to face
him, "to celebrate our brother and Lee having a
baby together . . . his *first* baby, mind you. So please,
Terry"—he watched as Paulette reached up, adjusted the collar of his shirt, and pursed her lips—
"*please* try to act like you're in a good mood."

Terrence frowned. His brow clouded over.
"What do you mean 'try to act like you're in a
good mood'? Who said I wasn't?"

"She means don't sulk around like you have
been for the past month or so," Evan called out as
he strolled into the room, carrying a large box
with a silver bow on top. He set it on the table with
a pile of several other gifts. "This day is for Lee,
me, and the baby. Don't bring down the room."

Terrence's eyes widened comically. "Well, excuse the hell out of me! I didn't know my mere
presence brought the room down. I just can take
my gift and get the hell up out of here, you know!"

Paulette closed her eyes and shook her head,
sending her curls flying around her shoulders.
"I'm not doing this. I am *not* doing this! Not
today!" She sighed and threw up her hands. "I'm
supposed to be hosting this thing. I have to check
on Lee and see if the rest of the party guests need

anything. You guys can take care of this yourselves."

"Take care of *what*?" Terrence asked as he
watched his sister's receding back. She sauntered
out of the salon in a huff, in a cloud of emerald
green silk. She didn't answer him. He turned back
to his brother. "Take care of what? What the hell is
she talking about?"

"Look," Evan began, placing a conciliatory hand
on Terrence's shoulder, "we all know you're still
torn up about your breakup with C. J."

At the mention of C. J.'s name, Terrence's pulse
quickened. It had been eighteen days, fourteen
hours, and twenty-two minutes, and his mind still
leapt back to the moment he pushed open her bedroom door and found Shaun Clancy standing in
his boxers next to her bed. He still remembered
the heartache and sense of betrayal that had overwhelmed him that day, the rage that left him with
an almost irresistible desire to beat Clancy senseless. And he would have beaten Clancy senseless—
if C. J. hadn't stopped him.

"We know how much you miss her," Evan continued.

Terrence shoved Evan's hand off his shoulder.
"I don't fucking miss her! Why the hell would I
miss her? Fuck that bitch!"

"Terry," Evan said, taking a deep breath and
looking very tired, "*please* stop saying that! You
know you don't mean it."

"Yes, I do mean it! She cheated on me. I don't
give a shit about her!"

"You *do* give a shit about her. You love her.
That's why you're still so pissed."

Even though he knew his brother was right, Terrence opened his mouth to deny it, but Evan waved his hand dismissively.

"And from what you told me, you kicked her out of your apartment, and *then* she hooked up with that other guy a few days later. I don't know if I would necessarily call that cheating."

Terrence sucked his teeth. "Man, I don't need you to replay what I—"

Evan held up his hands again. "I'm just saying that I get how you feel. I understand! I've been there. Believe me! But you can't let it take over like this, Terry. She's obviously moved on, right? You've got to move on, too."

"Like you're one to give love advice! You're still married to one chick while you're living with another," Terrence snapped, then immediately regretted the words after they flew out of his mouth.

"Actually, Charisse mailed the signed divorce papers back last week," Evan answered proudly. "Once a judge signs off on them, we're officially divorced. I'll only have one woman in my life from now on."

Terrence narrowed his eyes at his older brother. "And how the hell did you manage to pull that off?"

Evan shrugged. "I just talked to her."

"*Talked to her?* Riiiiiight." Terrence gave a mirthless laugh. He knew his brother well. Evan was lying through his teeth. "Some shit went down. Probably some shit I don't wanna know about."

"I don't know what you mean," Evan replied, his voice going robotic again like it always did when he lied.

Terrence shook his head in exasperation. "Of course you don't! You never do, do you, Ev?" He then shoved past his brother and walked back into the great room with the rest of the baby shower guests.

Two hours later, Terrence was slumped in a wingback chair in a corner of the great room while Leila and Evan sat in front of the limestone fireplace, opening baby shower gifts and pretending to be delighted by some ugly onesie and matching yellow blanket that would probably be tossed in the trash as soon as all the guests left. Several people sat on the chairs and on the sofa throughout the room, gushing over every item that Leila held aloft.

Everyone seemed so happy, so content. It was downright sickening!

"*Evan's right,*" a voice in his head said as he gulped from his third glass of lemonade, which was spiked with vodka thanks to Terrence secretly raiding Evan's liquor stash. "*You are stuck in a bad mood.*"

I'm not in a bad mood, Terrence argued as Leila opened yet another package and held up yet another onesie that made everyone in the room "ooh" and "aww."

I'm just realistic.

He didn't care that Charisse had signed the divorce papers and that Evan and Leila could finally get married. He knew their relationship was doomed to failure, just like Terrence and C. J.'s relationship, and like Paulette and Antonio's. The Marvelous

Murdochs, or M&Ms, had some genetic disease that made them incapable of maintaining relationships for the long haul. Evan and Paulette could live in la-la land and not acknowledge that truth, but Terrence refused to drink the Kool-Aid and do the same. He'd rather drink the lemonade instead, which is what he did, finishing what was left in his glass.

But part of him, the part that was more self-aware, told him that all of this was a lie. His breakup with C. J. had left him teetering on the brink of a bad mood that threatened to go full dark. He was on the cusp of real depression again, the same depression that had swept over him soon after his car accident. He could see the signs that his former therapist had told him to keep an eye out for: the irritability, the social anxiety, the drinking, the self-loathing, and the desire to just sit in a room alone all day with the only light coming from the television screen. He did that for hours at a time nowadays. Yesterday, he'd barely made it out of bed.

I should just leave, he thought, gazing down into his empty glass, feeling equally empty. *I'm not doing anybody any good staying here. I should just take my ass back home.*

"Hey, Terry, what's up? What are you doing hiding over here?" someone asked, making Terrence look up.

He found Antonio smiling down at him, holding a plate covered with crustless sandwiches.

"I'm not hiding," Terrence lied, staring at Antonio cagily, feeling the vodka kicking in. "I'm just chillin'."

Antonio's smile disappeared. He squinted. "Are you okay, man?"

"I'm fine! Are *you* okay?"

"Sure, why wouldn't I be?" Antonio asked, now frowning.

On the other side of the room, Leila continued to open presents, but Evan was no longer paying attention to the floral box she was currently unwrapping. His gaze was drawn to the other side of the room where Terrence sat and Antonio stood.

"I don't know!" Terrence exclaimed with an exaggerated shrug and a drunken snicker. "Who knows what could set off a dude like you! Just let me know ahead of time, though, just in case I need to break out a bulletproof vest."

Antonio's frown deepened. He set down the plate he was holding on a nearby end table and took a step toward Terrence. "What the hell are you talking about?"

"Nothing," Evan said, speaking for his brother, suddenly striding toward them and making several of the party guests look up at him in surprise. "He didn't mean anything by it, Tony. He's obviously drunk. Don't listen to him."

Terrence laughed. "Oh, I meant every damn word! I meant don't put me in a body bag just because you—"

He was stopped mid-sentence by Evan, who grabbed him by the upper arm and yanked him up from the chair. "Shut . . . your . . . mouth," Evan ordered with a firm iciness into Terrence's ear as he dragged him from the room.

"Get your goddamn hands off me!" Terrence

yelled, trying to yank his arm out of Evan's grasp, but his brother's grip only tightened.

Now the entire room of thirty or so people was watching them, including Leila and Paulette, who had been reading aloud the card that had been attached to the gift Leila had been opening.

Evan tugged Terrence into the corridor and then into one of the empty sitting rooms before finally releasing him with a shove.

"Are you out of your goddamn mind?" Evan asked his brother, shutting the door behind him, looking like he was struggling not to yell or punch him in the face. "Why the fuck would you bring that shit up with Antonio? Why would you do it here, Terry—of all places? Why would you do it with *his wife* standing on the other side of the room, with two dozen people hanging around?"

"Sorry if I thought our sister's welfare was more important than your fucking baby shower, Ev!" Terrence slurred, holding out his arms. "My bad!"

"This has nothing to do with Paulette, and you know it! This has nothing to do with her welfare. This is all about your girlfriend and your breakup and you feeling sorry for yourself! You're acting like a little boy left to play alone in the sandbox!"

"Fuck you! I don't have to listen to this shit!"

"You're ruining my day and Leila's day with your bullshit, Terry," Evan continued, undaunted, "and you're coming dangerously close to ruining Paulette's marriage!"

"Like I have to try to ruin her marriage! Their marriage has been fucked up for a while now. That doesn't have shit to do with me!"

"No, it's not fucked up. Unlike you, they're acting like adults . . . *grownups,* and they're making it work! They're trying to piece their lives back together. They're happy, Terry! Paulette doesn't need you to—"

"They're happy?" Terrence barked out a laugh. "Well, good for them! And all it took was for Antonio to kill her ex-boyfriend and get away with murder! We should all be so—"

"What?" Paulette asked.

The two men whipped around and found their little sister standing in the now open doorway. The pink card with the teddy bear on front of it that she had been holding fell from her hand to the floor. Her mouth hung open. She was blinking furiously like she couldn't quite see what was in front of her.

Watching his sister there and witnessing the look of shock on her face, Terrence immediately sobered. His stomach plummeted.

"Wh-what did you just say?" Paulette repeated, taking a hesitant step into the room. "Did you say Antonio killed someone? That he . . . he . . ." Her words drifted off. She looked utterly devastated.

"Sweet Pea," Evan whispered, walking toward her.

She furiously shook her head and raised her trembling hand to her mouth. "He said . . . he said he didn't do it! Tony said that he didn't . . ." Her eyes flooded with tears. She turned away from her brothers and rushed from the room.

"Paulette!" Evan shouted as he ran toward the doorway. "Paulette, wait!"

He paused as he stood in the threshold and turned his ominous stare to Terrence. "Are you happy now? I hope you're proud of yourself!" he spat before rushing down the hall after their sister.

Terrence sighed and lowered his head. "Shit," he muttered.

Chapter 20

Leila

Leila looked around the clubhouse banquet room, pausing at the entrance. Several of the committee members were standing around the long wooden table in the center of the room, talking in small groups and sampling fruit, croissants, and tea from the complimentary banquet set up in the corner. Leila watched as Lauren Gibbons-Weaver turned, spotted Leila lingering in the doorway, and waved. Leila waved back, then anxiously glanced down at her phone screen, seeing if there was a text message or voice mail waiting for her from Paulette.

"Girl, where are you?" she muttered, then looked over her shoulder to see if she saw Paulette racing down the corridor.

Paulette was late to the country club fund-raising committee meeting, but she hadn't called to tell Leila she would be late.

Paulette had assured Leila that she would be attending today's meeting, especially since the fiasco that had happened with Charisse a few months ago. Charisse seemed to stay at a distance when Leila and Paulette were together, as if she had no desire to battle both women at the same time. But now it looked like Leila would have to go in there alone, and a confrontation with Charisse was inevitable, especially now that Charisse had, by some small miracle, finally signed the divorce papers. That woman would be bitterer than a dish of mustard greens doused in vinegar.

Leila had promised herself that she wouldn't be goaded by Evan's soon-to-be ex-wife. She told herself not to let that woman "drag her down into the gutter," as her mother, Diane, would say. But she had often fantasized about grabbing a fistful of Charisse's blond hair, punching her in the face, and slamming her head onto the ground over and over again. Leila didn't know if she could keep that promise to maintain the moral high ground and keep her hands to herself if Paulette wasn't there as reinforcement.

"All right, ladies," Tilda called out, and the voices in the room died down to a murmur. "Let's call today's meeting to order, shall we?"

Leila puffed air through her cheeks, turned from the doorway, and darted into the hall. Her thumb flew across the screen as she dialed Paulette's cell number. She frowned as she listened to the phone ring on the other end.

"Paulette, hey, it's Lee," she said, keeping her voice down to a whisper so as not to disturb the committee meeting that was already in progress. "I was just calling to see if you're on your way or if you're still coming to the meeting today. I hope . . ." She sighed. "I hope everything is okay. Even if you aren't coming, let me know you're okay. All right? Bye."

Leila hung up and lowered the phone to her side. She hoped Paulette wasn't avoiding calling her back because of what had happened at the baby shower that weekend. She had asked Evan why Paulette and Antonio had abruptly left the event, even though Paulette was supposed to be hosting.

"Something came up with Nate," he had explained while giving one of those painted-on smiles that always made her wary, that always made her suspect he was lying to her. "Nothing big! They just needed to head home early."

But that wouldn't explain why Paulette still hadn't called Leila back in days. It didn't explain why, when Leila had caught a glimpse of Paulette as she left the party, the younger woman had looked almost in tears.

Leila dropped her phone into her crocodile handbag. She was about to turn to head back to the banquet room when she saw Charisse striding down the corridor, heading straight toward her. Leila fought the urge to roll her eyes.

"Hello, Leila!" Charisse called out, whipping off her sunglasses. "How are you today?"

Leila didn't answer her but instead continued to glare at her openly.

Charisse laughed. "Well, well! I see *someone* skipped her etiquette classes." Charisse's fake smile stayed firmly in place. "A word of advice: If you're really planning to be the wife of a man of Evan's stature, you're going to have to learn these things. When someone says hello to you, you're supposed to greet them back."

"Don't start with me, bitch," Leila said through clenched teeth. "You're lucky I don't slap you across the face for the shit you've done these past few months. Scaring off my clients . . . spreading rumors about me at my daughter's school . . . Who the fuck do you think you are?"

"I'm Charisse *Murdoch*, at least for the time being." Charisse took a step toward her. "And *you're* lucky I don't slap you across the face for stealing my husband."

"I didn't *steal* him! By the time I showed up, you two were barely a couple—a fact you keep ignoring. You cheated on him. You dogged him out repeatedly, and he got tired of it. Now you're getting a divorce. Move on!"

Charisse shrugged and pursed her lips, seeming unmoved by Leila's words. "I guess I'll have to, since Evan seems to be in complete denial of his feelings. But I know the truth, even if he won't acknowledge it. The passion that we once had is still there. We could make it work, but I can't force him."

Leila sucked her teeth and dropped her hand to her hip. "What the hell are you talking about? He doesn't feel anything for you, you psycho!"

"Oh, yes, he does! I felt it when he kissed me."

Leila's heart stuttered at those words, lurching

to a stop and then picking back up again milliseconds later.

"Ev tried to hide it, of course," Charisse continued, glancing down at her manicured nails. "He's so emotionally repressed that he'd practically need a cattle prod to feel *anything!* But that kiss got to him. I saw it and I felt it, too. He can say whatever the hell he wants, but he's not over me—just like I'm not over him."

"He . . . He . . . Evan *kissed* you?" Leila asked breathlessly, trying to comprehend everything that she was hearing, but she couldn't. She felt hot all over. Sweat sprouted on her brow and upper lip. The pantyhose she was wearing felt too tight. She felt the urgent need to sit down.

Evan kissed Charisse, she thought, allowing it to settle in. *Evan kissed Charisse. Evan* kissed *her.*

Charisse raised her brows. "He didn't tell you? Oh, who am I kidding!" She waved her hand and chuckled. "Of course he didn't! He didn't tell me what he was doing with you, either. Evan likes to keep those secrets, doesn't he?"

"You're . . . you're lying," Leila said, vehemently shaking her head in denial, almost gulping for air. The room felt like it was spinning around her. "You tell nothing but lies! You've been doing it for months! Ev wouldn't . . . he wouldn't have—"

"You know I'm not lying, Leila. I'm telling you the truth and nothing but the truth. He kissed me after we had dinner together over candlelight. I made pasta shells and freshly made herbal garlic butter for him just last week—just like old times. It's one of his favorite recipes. I could give it to you if you'd like."

Leila blinked. *Garlic* . . . She could remember Evan coming home with the smell of it all over him last Wednesday. She had even made a joke about it.

"Whoa, trying to ward off vampires!" she had said, leaning toward him and wrinkling her nose.

"Huh?" he had asked.

"You reek of garlic, baby! Did you swallow a whole clove?"

"No," he had said with a chuckle. "I guess the restaurant where I went at lunch put too much in the pasta. I won't eat that dish again."

He lied, she now realized, utterly devastated. Evan had *lied* to her!

Leila watched as Charisse smirked. "So how does it feel to be the last to know this time around?"

Leila couldn't respond. She was too shocked to be angry, at least at that moment. Lucky for Charisse, it gave her plenty of time to walk around Leila and head to the banquet room.

"Tell Ev I said hi!" she called over her shoulder before sauntering into the room, leaving Leila standing dumbfounded in the hallway.

By the time Evan walked into their bedroom several hours later, Leila had already cleared out her walk-in closet. Her clothes, hangers, and shoes were piled in a four-foot-tall heap on their bed. Some of it had tumbled from the bed to the carpeted floor, making a tangled mass of shirts, sweaters, leggings, and shorts that resembled a cloth octopus. Suitcases sat open on the footstool at the end of the bed, already filled to the brim with more clothes. She had run out of suitcases to use, so now she was shoving her things into black garbage bags. One leaned against her closet door.

Evan paused from removing his necktie as he stared at the room and all its chaos. His brows knitted together. "What are you doing?"

"I'm moving out," she muttered with heavy breaths as she dragged the now filled trash bag across the room and sat it beside her suitcases.

"Moving out? Moving out *where?*"

"I don't know where. Maybe to one of the guest rooms or guesthouse. Maybe to a fucking hotel. I don't care! I just . . . I just need to get out of here," she said, waddling back into her closet, feeling pain radiate across her groin. But she ignored the pain and started to clear out yet another shelf. She rubbed her stomach, calming her baby girl, who was shifting anxiously. Leila stared at the five shelves still filled with clothes and glanced at the piles and bags of clothes several feet away.

Since moving in with Evan she had accumulated so many things.

So much crap, she thought with disgust. But she would get rid of all the baggage she had taken on since they got together. *I'm done with this shit!*

"What do you mean you don't know, Lee?" He charged toward her closet and braced his arms against the door frame, blocking her path. "What the hell is happening?"

"Get out of my way," she said tightly, turning toward him.

"Not until you tell me what the fuck is going on! Why are you moving out?"

She gripped the wooden shelves and closed her eyes. "Did you really kiss her? Did you kiss Charisse?"

She opened her eyes in time to see his face fall.

"She told you?" He sighed and shook his head. "She didn't waste any time, did she?"

So it was true! At the realization, her stomach turned.

"I should have known she'd tell you," he continued, muttering to himself, "even when I asked her not to. Of course she would! She wouldn't miss the opportunity to gloat about something like that."

"You asked her not to tell me?" Leila's voice choked and came out in a strangled whisper. Tears pooled in her eyes. "You kissed her and tried to hide it?"

"I didn't kiss her," he said impatiently. "She kissed *me*! Well, I guess . . . I guess you could say we kissed each other. It was the only thing that was standing in between her sticking to her guns or granting me a divorce, so I just—"

"You kissed her, Evan!" she screeched. "Stop acting like it was nothing! Like it wasn't important! You kissed *your wife* when you told me that you didn't want anything to—"

"But it *was* nothing, Lee! It didn't mean anything!"

"It means something to me!" She pointed at her chest. "It means something to me, goddammit!"

"But it shouldn't," he snapped, glowering at her. "Look, Lee, I know this is upsetting. I know how it seems at face value, but stop seeing it that way! We want to be together, right?" he began in a measured voice, infuriating her even more. "We want to get married. In order to do that, I have to be divorced. This was the minor obstacle to that. Don't get distracted by this one thing, Lee! Don't you see that Charisse is just trying to manipulate you again? Don't get muddled in the petty details that don't—"

He didn't get to finish. The jaw-rattling slap across his face stopped him cold, catching them both by surprise. He raised his hand to the spot on his cheek where she had hit him. She dropped her hand to her side and started trembling as tears flooded onto her cheeks and down her chin.

"My feelings and my hurt and *your betrayal* aren't 'petty details,' Evan," she said, pointing at her chest again. "You *hurt* me and I'm not . . . I am *not* giving you the chance to do it again! I'm not going to be married to or live with yet another man I can't trust . . . who doesn't respect *me*!"

He lowered his hand from his face. His jaw tightened. Instead of looking contrite, he looked furious. "So you're going to leave?" he asked in an eerily calm voice. His gaze darkened. "I did this . . . I did *all of this* to make you happy, to be with you. And now you're just going to walk out on me . . . on us?"

That was his response to her admission of heartbreak and devastation?

Leila shook her head and shoved past him, no longer concerned with packing her things. She just needed to get out of that closet, that room. She had to get away from Evan or she would start screaming. She would start pelting him with punches, and she wouldn't be able to stop.

"But you were never invested in us, were you, Lee? What I did was never good enough!" he shouted after her. "You always had one foot out the door, ready to leave whenever I wasn't perfect! Whenever I pissed you off! You were just waiting for an excuse to walk away," he said, stopping her in her tracks, making her angrily turn to face him. He charged toward her across the bedroom. "If it wasn't your past shit with Brad, it was your current shit with Isabel! If it wasn't Isabel, it was some drama with Charisse! You were always, *always* looking for a fucking excuse to end it." He laughed coldly. "You were *never* invested in this! Just admit it."

She shook her head, feeling all her fury drain from her as she gazed at the man she once loved, whom she *still* loved, but could no longer trust. "You know that's not true."

"And now you think you can just . . . just walk away, walk out on me *yet again*? Is that what you planned to do? But this time you wanna do it with *our* baby, right?"

They were only inches apart. He towered over her. Evan's face contorted with so much rage she barely recognized him.

"But let me tell you something, Lee. I'm not just rolling over and accepting it this time. You are *not* walking out and taking my kid away from me. It's not gonna happen! You have no idea what you're up against. You don't want to tango with me, baby! I will come after you with everything I've got," he said with a flat iciness. "You fucking hear me? I will get the best goddamn lawyers in town to—"

"To what, Ev? Sue me? Have my baby taken away? *Have me thrown in jail*?" She stared up at him. "Is that what you'd really do to me?"

His hard visage softened. He took an unsteady step back. It was as if he realized exactly what he was saying and whom he was talking to. He lowered his head.

"You can bully me and threaten me all you want, but I can't stay here." She turned and reached for the door handle. "I'm moving to one of the guest rooms. I'll let you know what I decide to do after that when I figure it out."

"Lee," he began, squeezing his eyes so tightly shut that it looked painful. "Lee, *please* don't do this."

But she didn't know what else to do.

"I have to, Ev. I have no other choice," she said as she opened the door, stepped into the hall, and shut the door behind her.

Chapter 21

C. J.

C. J. felt lower than the gum wrapper now beneath her heel as she stepped out of her car and walked across the lot toward the doors of Aston Ministries, but she told herself to take a deep breath, push back her shoulders, and paste on a smile.

"What's that saying?" she mumbled to herself as her high heels clicked along the asphalt. "Fake it until you make it?"

She would have to do that today.

It had been more than a month since she and Terrence had broken up, but the pain was still raw, like an open wound that still had yet to heal over. She didn't know why her healing was dragging on for so long, why she didn't feel incrementally better with each passing day. She had tried to focus on other things, supporting her father's congressional run, getting involved in her church again, and going out to dinner at least twice a week with Shaun. His presence was comforting, but with every joke he told she thought of a dirtier, funnier joke that Terrence had once told her. Every time that Shaun held her hand, she thought of a caress that Terrence had given that had made her shiver all over. It was worse at night when she was alone. She would replay all their moments together, all the things she and Terrence had told each other. She remembered the future she had envisioned with Terrence at her side.

She just couldn't let him go.

When they had first started dating, she had joked that she could never be away from Terrence for too long. "I have to get my Terry fix," she had said with a laugh. Now she knew it wasn't a joke; she felt like a junkie going through withdrawal.

But I have to move on, C. J. told herself. *I have to accept that this is the life I was meant to lead; the life I was meant to have.*

She gazed up at the church's glass exterior.

This was the church that her father had built, where she had received her first baptism, and where she had attended Sunday school as a child. This was the place where Shaun served as assistant pastor, and Shaun still professed to love her.

"I can see us together, C. J.," he had told her just last night as they sat at the restaurant table, gazing at each other over candlelight. "God showed it to me. I've seen it! That's why I never lost hope that you and I would get back together. You don't believe me?"

She had shrugged in response, not knowing what to believe.

"In my vision you were my wife and we had two kids, and a dog . . . a little schnauzer."

"I'm not really a dog person," she had confessed with a shake of the head.

"Okay, maybe the vision was a little off. Maybe God meant for us to have a cat instead," he had said, making her laugh.

So, even after everything she had put him through, Shaun still wanted to make her his wife and the mother of his future children. Shaun and Aston Ministries not only held her past, but they could very well hold her future—if she'd let them.

She paused as she neared the doors, tightening her belt around her waist. So why did it still not feel like she was at home here? Why was she still hesitant to plant roots again? Was it because of Victor and his warning that she would one day become like him? Or was it something else, something more?

"Don't you dare push me!" a woman screeched as one of the doors swung open. C. J. jumped back to keep from getting hit by the door. She watched as a brawny security guard gripped the yelling woman around the forearm.

The woman looked disheveled. Her hair was in a loose ponytail at the nape of her neck and she wore a red velveteen tracksuit that was shiny at the elbows and frayed at the hem. She balled her hands into fists and pounded into the security guard's shoulder. "I'm holding a baby! You could've hurt my damn child!"

C. J. squinted and looked more closely at the

woman. She realized that there was a baby—a squirming infant—in the pink cotton sling across the woman's chest. C. J. could see the tufts of the baby's black curly hair at the top of the bundle.

But the guard didn't look fazed by the baby or the young woman's warning. Instead he continued looking down at her. His broad shoulders blocked her path and kept her from re-entering the doors as she tried. She darted around him, going to his left and his right, but each time he held out an arm.

"Ma'am, I think you better get out of here or we're going to have to call the cops!"

"To hell with you!" she declared with tears in her eyes, finally giving up. Now the infant began to wail. "To hell with *all* of you! You call that a church? You call yourselves Christians? If you were, you wouldn't treat me this way! You wouldn't do this!"

The guard let out a gust of air through his flared nostrils and turned back toward the glass doors. "I said get out of here. That's your last warning," he muttered before stepping through the doors and shutting them firmly behind him.

The woman turned, mumbling to herself. She cradled the baby's head and bottom through the sling, rocking it softly to calm its wails. "It's okay, honey. It's all right," she cooed, before wiping away a lone tear from her cheek.

That's when C. J. realized who she was. She was Rochelle, the woman who said C. J.'s father was the father of her baby. But the paternity tests had proven that she had lied. So why was she here?

The woman looked up and realized C. J. was

standing only a few feet in front of her. She glared back.

"What are you looking at?" she snapped, still gently bouncing the baby.

"N-nothing," C. J. stuttered, embarrassed to have been caught staring.

The woman sucked her teeth and strode toward C. J. As she passed, C. J. watched something tumble from the baby's sling to the parking lot asphalt. She realized it was a pink pacifier.

"Hey!" she called out, bending down and grabbing the pacifier. The woman stopped in her tracks. "Hey! You dropped this!"

The woman paused midstride and turned back to C. J., who held the pacifier out to her. C. J. watched as her glare disappeared, like a mask of defensiveness had been ripped off of her face. Her stony features softened, and C. J. got a glimpse of the beautiful woman she must have been a year ago, back when she was still working at Aston Ministries. She could see why it was plausible to many that this woman could have had an affair with her father.

"Thanks," she said, taking the pacifier out of C. J.'s hand.

"Excuse me," C. J. began hesitantly, "but are you . . . are you Rochelle Martin?"

The woman eyed her again. "Yeah?" she shouted over the crying baby. "Who's asking?"

"Um, my name is . . . uh, C. J. . . . I-I mean Courtney Aston. I'm . . . I'm Reverend Pete Aston's daughter."

Rochelle's eyebrows shot up in surprise. "Oh,

yeah?" She looked C. J. up and down. "I can kinda see the resemblance. Your daddy told me about you, you know?"

C. J. took another step toward her. "He *did*?"

Rochelle nodded. "He said I reminded him a lot of you."

C. J. gazed at her, taken aback.

"He said we were both strong-willed," Rochelle elaborated, twisting her mouth into a wry smile. "I guess that's why things didn't work out too well for me and your daddy. I wasn't good at following orders."

C. J. frowned. "So you're still sticking to the story that you and my father had an affair?"

"It's not a story! I didn't make it up! It *did* happen. Just because he's not the baby daddy doesn't mean nothing ever happened between me and him."

C. J.'s stomach muscles tightened. Her father had sworn to her that nothing had gone on between him and Rochelle. Had he lied to her yet again?

"But you don't believe me," Rochelle continued with a sad shake of the head. "That's okay. No one else in that damn church did, either, even though *everybody* knows the real truth about your father. I wasn't the first woman he had on the side and probably won't be the last. I know that now. In fact, the only person who seemed like he would even believe me was Shaun." She lowered her eyes and gazed at her infant. The baby's wails had died down to a few soft whimpers and hiccups. "But now even *he* won't even talk to me. He let them kick me out!"

"Shaun?" C. J. squinted. "You don't . . . you don't mean Pastor Shaun Clancy, do you?"

Rochelle nodded. C. J. was once again caught by surprise. Shaun had known about her father's affair with his young parishioner?

Why hadn't he said anything to me?

"He told me he would have my back! He promised it to me, but I should have known he was full of shit just like the rest of them."

I'll have your back . . . It was the same promise, the very words he had said to C. J. in the beginning.

"I'll always have your back, even if it means standing up to Victor," he had told her.

"I just wanted him to see the baby," Rochelle insisted, cradling the baby's head again. "I wasn't going to do anything. I just wanted him to see her, because if Reverend Aston isn't her daddy, then he *has* to be! It can't be anybody else!"

"Who . . . who is 'he'?" C. J. asked, now even more confused. "Who are you talking about?"

Rochelle paused and gazed at her as if that was the most ludicrous question in the world. "I'm talking about Shaun! Shaun's her daddy!"

Ten minutes later, C. J. walked down the hall of Aston Ministries, still feeling shell-shocked, like she had just stumbled away from a car wreck and barely survived. She had talked to Rochelle a bit longer, learning more details about what had happened with the young woman and Reverend Aston, about what *later* happened between her and Shaun. Now C. J. wished she could wash her brain of all she knew. She wished she could bleach it clean, but she couldn't. She approached one of the doors in the corridor and hesitated only briefly before knocking on it.

"Come in," Shaun called out.

She slowly pushed his door open, revealing the austere-looking office of a seemingly simple man she had once respected, one she had been trying to convince herself she could someday grow to love. She watched as he looked up from a note he was scribbling on the yellow steno pad as he flipped to a page in the Bible. It was probably notes for the opening reading he would give that Sunday.

When he saw C. J., his face brightened.

"Hey!" He rose from his desk and lowered a ribbon to bookmark the section in the Bible that he was reading before closing its pages. He walked toward her. "What have you been up to?"

He stepped forward and kissed her cheek. She recoiled, making his dark face crease into a concerned frown. "What's wrong?"

"You knew," she blurted out, unable to hold in the secret long enough to step through the doorway. She shoved past him and into his office. She then turned to glare at him. "You knew this *whole* time and you didn't say anything?"

"What are you talking about?"

"I'm talking about Rochelle! Rochelle Martin! *Remember her?* You knew she was cheating with my dad. She came to you and confessed everything! She turned to you when she could turn to no one else."

He continued to stare at her. Shaun made no denials, and she knew that any hopes she'd had that Rochelle had been lying about everything had been dashed.

"You were supposed to counsel her, Shaun—not screw her! How . . . how could you?"

He lowered his eyes. Shame marred his face.

"Answer me!"

She watched as he reached for the door handle and closed his office door.

"Have a seat," he said, walking toward his desk and gesturing to the chair facing it.

"I'd rather not." She crossed her arms obstinately over her chest. "Whatever you have to say to me can be said just as easily while I'm standing."

"Fine," he muttered. "Have it your way." He sighed and gripped the back of his leather swivel chair. "Look, C. J., I'm not . . . I'm not asking you to agree with what I did, but—"

"You're damn right I don't agree with what you did! I thought you were better than this!" she yelled, jabbing her finger at him. "I thought you were better than *them*! But you're just like Victor! You're just like my dad!"

"No, I'm not!" he boomed, then took another deep breath, bringing himself back under control. "I can acknowledge when I make a mistake, C. J. Because that's what it was: a mistake. That . . . that *thing* that happened with Rochelle and me happened during a period of spiritual weakness." He cleared his throat. "At the time, Monica and I were fighting. We were arguing all the time about what she wanted out of our relationship . . . how she wanted to get married. Rochelle was someone who I confided in, and she confided in me about . . .

about your father. We sought . . . we sought solace in each other, and it led to something more. But it was brief. It only lasted for a week or two. I realized it was wrong and I ended it. I'd push it out of my memory if I could!"

"But you *can't* push it out of your memory, because now she has a baby—*your* baby."

"A baby that she swore was your father's only weeks ago! That baby could be anybody's," he spat, making C. J. cringe.

Seeing her reaction, he lowered his eyes again, looking embarrassed.

"I just . . . I just mean that she's slept with lots of people, lots of different men. She told me that she slept around a lot before she was saved, and I suspect she was still doing it after." He gazed at C. J. again. "C. J., please don't let this come between us. I told you, I made a mistake. And we all make mistakes, right? Did you ever consider that maybe I was so patient and forgiving of *your* sins because I wasn't perfect, either? Remember when I told you that I never expected you to be Snow White and I didn't need you to be? Remember when I told you I *still* loved you despite everything you told me you've done . . . despite you walking out on me? I still want to put a ring on your finger someday—if you'll have me."

She slowly shook her head. "But what about Rochelle, Shaun? What about her daughter?"

"What about them?" he asked impatiently, curling his lip in disgust.

C. J. fell silent. Once again, she was struck speechless.

He took another step toward her and placed a hand on her shoulder. "Look," he said, dropping his voice to a soothing tone, "I'm ashamed of what I did, but nothing between us has to change. My feelings for you are still the same, as well as my intentions toward you." He inclined his head. "I still want to make you my wife. God's ordained you for me, C. J.! One day I will have my own church and you will be my first lady. I made a mistake and I admitted it. But don't let that taint your opinion of me. We're moving *forward*. Don't let this hold us back. Please?"

Her shoulders and her heart sank. It would be so easy to agree to what Shaun was asking, to forget everything she knew and to pretend, like him, that Rochelle and her baby didn't exist. They could do it. Even if Rochelle went public with her claims, no one would believe her. They would just think she was lying again. But C. J. knew if she did what Shaun was asking, she'd be proving her brother right. She would be a liar and pretender just like him.

I don't want to live my life that way, she thought, knowing what she had to do.

"I'm sorry, Shaun, but I . . . I can't." She took a step away from him, removing his hand from her shoulder.

"C. J.," he called after her as she turned and walked out of his office and down the corridor.

"C. J.!" he called again as she walked past the receptionist desk where her brother stood.

"Hey, Court, I'm glad I ran into you. I need you to stop by my office later to discuss that breakfast you're attending next week," he said, but she didn't respond.

Instead she walked out the glass doors and to the parking lot. She pulled out her car keys and raised the remote to unlock the car door, prepared to make the long trek back to Virginia, knowing that she would probably never set foot here again.

Chapter 22

Dante

"*Mr. Turner?*" Lindsey, the receptionist at the front desk squeaked as Dante shoved open the glass door of Nutter, McElroy & Ailey law offices. She squinted at him behind her lenses as he strode past her. "Mr. Turner, is . . . is that *you?*"

He didn't answer her but instead continued undeterred to his destination, feeling fury propel him through the front lobby and down the hallway.

Dante knew he didn't resemble the debonair lawyer Lindsey or any of the other law firm associates was used to seeing. He wasn't wearing one of his expensive suits and had skipped getting one of his one-hundred-dollar haircuts. He instead looked like a vagrant who had just wandered into the law offices off the street to come beg for change.

Dante wore his signature hoodie, which smelled of beer and an acrid musk thanks to the many days he had skipped washing it. His full beard and hair were scraggly and knotted. Dark circles were under his eyes from his lack of a good night's sleep in months. But he didn't care. The moment he had read the email from the firm's partners notifying him that he was "no longer a member of the law firm due to his unexplained and extended absence," he ran from his mother's house and leapt into his car. He would have come there in his socks and his boxers if he had to, even though he knew he was probably risking his life by showing up here.

Dante now reached the end of the hall and pushed the door open, catching Edgar McElroy and Steven Nutter by surprise. Steven hopped off the edge of Edgar's desk. Edgar dropped the coffee cup he had been holding, splashing himself with scalding hot French roast, making him shout out in pain.

"Dante? What . . . what are you doing here?" Steven stuttered, staring at the younger man in amazement.

"You fucking fired me!" Dante exploded. "After all that I've done for this firm? After all the billable hours I've given you? After busting my ass for . . . for almost *eight goddamn years,* you fucking fired me?"

Steven raised his hands. "Now, Dante, please calm down. You—"

"No, I'm not going to fucking calm down! I got shot! I almost died and you fired me! Who the hell does that?"

"You were absent for more than three months!"

Edgar said, finally rising to his feet. He reached for the box of Kleenex on his desk and wiped feebly at the brown spot now marring his shirt. "We asked you to provide proof of your . . . your disability and you refused to do so." He loudly cleared his throat and walked from behind his desk. "We—"

"You want proof?" Dante said, raising the bottom of his hoodie, revealing his bare stomach where the scarring from his bullet wound still looked red and raw. "Here's your fucking proof! Would you like to see the bullet, too?"

"For God's sake, Dante! Put your shirt down," Steven said with a grimace as he turned away, covering his eyes. "There's no need for that!"

"We are sorry for what happened to you," Edgar continued. "But we have several associates at this firm who have experienced their own mishaps and—"

"Mishap?" Dante bellowed. "Did you really just call me getting shot a fucking mishap?"

"—and losses," Edgar continued, undeterred. "But they all checked in. They didn't go missing in action. They let us know what was going on and returned to work in a timely fashion." He pursed his wrinkled lips. "You know how competitive our field is, Dante. We need all of our associates at the top of their game." He sighed. "I'm sorry, but . . . we had no other choice. We had to let you go."

"B-but we're providing you with a nice severance package," Steven piped, "in light of your . . . your eight years of working with us."

Dante clenched his fists at his sides, feeling as if he might explode into a million pieces. He wanted to march across the room, grab Edgar's stapler, and beat him and Steven to death with it. He wanted to shove both men through the office window and watch as their bodies sailed thirteen floors to the concrete walkway below. Instead, he forced himself to take a long, slow breath. He forced himself to smile.

"Sure, I . . . I understand," he said before walking across the room to Steven. He held out his hand for a shake. "I appreciate everything that you've done for me, and I'm . . . I'm sorry you had to fire me, but I get that you had no choice."

Steven gazed at Dante's hand cagily, like it might zap him with a charge if he touched it. Finally, he shook it. "Yes, we're . . . we're very sorry, too."

Dante then turned to Edgar with his hand also extended for a shake. "It was a pleasure working with you, Edgar."

Edgar didn't hesitate. He raised his fat chin and shook Dante's hand, giving it two firm pumps. "I'm sorry we had to let you go, too, son. But you know how it is. Lesson learned. I just hope there are no hard feelings."

Dante shook his head. "Of course not." He walked back toward the office door, but paused in the doorway. "Oh, before I leave, there's something I wanted to tell you, Edgar."

Edgar raised his brows. "What's that?"

"I fucked your wife—on *several* occasions . . . particularly that time that you were at that law conference in San Diego. We did it eight times that weekend."

Dante watched as Edgar's face drained of all color. Steven's mouth fell open in shock.

"One night, she took a hit of ecstasy and got really into it. She sucked my dick until her jaw was sore, then told me to fuck her up the ass on the baby grand in your living room. She said it was the best sex she's had in quite a while. Well, at least since your prostate surgery. She said you've had a hard time getting it up since then." His smile broadened. "I just wanted you to know that. You guys have a good day now."

He then turned and strode into the hallway, leaving both men speechless.

Dante climbed into his Jaguar, slammed his door shut, and shoved his hand into his pocket to retrieve his painkillers, seeking the chemical solace that they offered. He shook three into his palm and then tossed them into his mouth like Tic Tacs. He gulped them down without water, feeling them lodge in his throat as he swallowed. He then gazed into the bottle and saw that there were only a half dozen left. He would have to buy more. His doctor had already cut him off, rightly suspecting that he had developed an addiction to OxyContin. He had already moved on to another doctor, who had cut him off, too. Now he was going to one who was willing to write him a fake prescription, but at a steep price. Now that Dante was officially unemployed, he didn't know how long he would be able to keep paying for his drug habit, to keep paying for a condo that he was still too scared to go home to.

He put his key into the ignition, turned on the engine, and pulled off with the screeching of tires.

Dante realized belatedly that he probably shouldn't have told Edgar about the affair he had been having with the older man's wife, especially not in such graphic detail. Talk about burning bridges! But he had been furious at how smug Edgar had been, how he had placed all the blame on Dante for what had happened. It wasn't his fault that he had been shot. It wasn't his fault that Renee was still trying to kill him and the police *still* hadn't arrested her. He didn't care that he had burned any metaphorical bridges. He was mad enough to set the whole damn village on fire!

Dante's hands tightened around the steering wheel as he drove. He fought to get his rage under control so that he didn't start randomly rear-ending the cars in front of him. He drew to a stop at the stoplight and told himself to count to ten yet again. He then glanced out his side window. When he saw who was parked along the curb a few feet away, he blinked.

Dante watched as his brother Evan strode along the sidewalk toward his Lincoln Town Car, looking every bit like the refined millionaire that he was.

"What the hell is he doing here?" Dante wondered aloud. And then he realized that he wasn't too far from Chesterton—only a few miles away, in fact. It wasn't too shocking to see Evan there, but still . . . Dante's mouth still hung open limply.

The driver held the rear door open for Evan and smiled. Evan muttered something to him before climbing inside the car, and the driver nodded. Dante watched as the driver slammed the door shut, then strode to the front of the vehicle.

Watching his brother, Dante was flooded with fury all over again. Here he was at his lowest point and Evan was going about his business like nothing had changed in his life. And nothing probably had changed for Evan. He was still CEO of Murdoch Conglomerated. He was still living with and fucking Leila Hawkins on the regular—the same woman who had outright rejected Dante. Evan was still worth millions of dollars. His life was perfect while Dante's life was the complete opposite—a steaming pile of dog shit!

"Son of a bitch," Dante spat under his breath, feeling like he could rip the wheel from the steering column. If it was the last thing he did, he would make sure that Evan suffered, that he felt just as low as Dante felt right now.

Someone behind him blared a car horn, snapping Dante out of his daze, startling him. He turned to glance over his shoulder at the driver behind him—some elderly man wearing a baseball cap and bifocal lenses—pointing up.

"Just telling you the light's green!" the old man shouted with a wave and a smile.

Instead of pressing on the accelerator, Dante gave the old man the finger. He finally pulled off at top speed through the intersection.

Dante arrived back at his mother's house, still furious at the world, but too tired to do anything about it. He wanted nothing more than to go inside, collapse into his recliner, take another Oxy, close his eyes, and go to sleep.

He slammed his car door shut and turned to the walkway leading to his home, but paused mid-stride when he saw a familiar face peeking at him from around one of the porch's wooden posts. His shoulders sank.

"Wassup, Daddy!" Kiki called out to him as he slowly walked up the porch steps.

She had traded her leather jacket for a hoodie much like his own. Her braids were pulled back from her face today. He hadn't seen her since the last time she had come to the house and made her dramatic announcement that he was her father.

"What the hell are you doing here, Kiki?"

"Well, damn!" she exclaimed with a mischievous smile. "Hi to you, too!"

She stood back to let him unlock the front door. He shoved it open and Kiki trailed in behind him, as if he had invited her inside. He was too tired to point out that he hadn't.

"I repeat . . . why are you here?" he asked.

"I still need a place to crash, and I was hoping that maybe you changed your mind." She flopped back onto his couch and crossed her legs before dropping her feet on the coffee table.

He slammed the front door shut, then collapsed into the recliner facing her.

"No, I have not changed my mind."

"Come on, Daddy! You can't help me out just a little?" she cried, dropping her feet to the shag rug.

"No, I cannot."

"Shit! It ain't like you did anything for me for the past eighteen years! The least you could do is—"

"Look, stop it with the fucking guilt trips!" he exploded, leaning forward in his chair, making her fall silent. "Stop trying to make me feel bad for being a shitty father! I *know* I was shitty, but I had a shitty father, too, goddammit! He didn't do me any favors, either! I had to bust my ass for everything that I got, Kiki, for everything that I am! And even then nothing was promised to me. It all fell apart! It was taken away from me!" He paused and glared at the room around him. "That's why I'm back in this fucking shithole, hiding like a rat in a sewer."

Kiki shifted on the sofa and squinted her caramel eyes at him. "What do you mean? Who are you hiding from?"

He sighed and shook his head, wishing she would just leave so he could take his damn pill. "Nothing," he mumbled.

She eyed him silently for a long time. "So that's why you moved back to Grandma's? Cuz you're hiding out? What happened?"

He lowered the release on the recliner and leaned back with his feet up, closing his eyes and resting his head back against the suede padded cushion.

"Come on, Daddy! Tell me what happened. I promise I won't tell nobody!"

Might as well tell her the truth, he thought. What did he have to lose that he hadn't lost already?

"I pissed off some crazy bitch who wants to kill me. She shot me once," he said pointing to his torso, "and she sent some thugs to my place to finish the job."

Kiki's eyes widened. *"You for real?* She really shot you?"

"Does it look like I'm joking?" he asked dryly.

Kiki started to laugh and clap her hands. "Damn! My daddy's more of an O. G. than I thought. So what you do to her? You shoot her, too?"

"I don't even know where the hell she is," he replied with his eyes still closed. "The police can't find her, either. They haven't arrested her."

"And they ain't going to! Besides, you don't get the police to handle some shit like this. You keep that shit *in house.* You take care of it yourself!"

Dante opened his eyes and stared at his daughter. "What am I supposed to do? Hunt her down like some assassin? Shoot her with poison darts?"

"No, you pay dudes to do it for you! *Duh!*" Kiki shrugged. "I know a couple of them in the neighborhood that would do it for less than a grand. All they need is a name, address, and where she likes to hang out. They could take care of it for you."

Dante cocked an eyebrow. Was Kiki serious?

"You *really* know a couple of guys who could kill her for me?"

She nodded again. "Just tell me when you want it done and how much you're willing to pay."

"And you're willing to just help me out like that?"

She chuckled. "Well, yeah, if you . . . you know . . . let me move in with you and . . ." Her words drifted off as she gazed down at her nails.

"And what?"

"Let me drive your Jag . . . *just a little?*" she asked, giving him another grin.

He didn't believe for one second that Kiki had a pipeline to a group of guys who could take out Renee, but he would pretend to oblige her. Maybe if he did, she would finally leave him the hell alone.

"Okay, fine. Get them to kill her for me and you can live with me and drive my car."

"Really?"

He nodded.

"Thank you, Daddy!" She hopped off the couch and skipped across the room. She wrapped her arms around his neck and kissed his scruffy cheek before he had a chance to shove her away.

"Trust me," she said. "I'll take care of it for you. That bitch won't know what hit her!"

Chapter 23

Terrence

"So how long do we have to stay here, anyway?" Terrence's date asked within seconds of them setting foot on the ballroom's tiled floor.

He paused to cock an eyebrow at her. "We just got here and you're already asking when we're going to leave?"

His date shrugged and tossed her long, dark, curly tresses over her shoulder while wrinkling her nose. "You told me we were going out dancing tonight. I thought you meant to a club downtown. I had no idea it would be in a place like this!" She curled her glossy pink upper lip into a sneer like she was gazing at a vista of the city dump instead of couples sitting at the banquet tables and dancing on the parquet dance floor. "*This* is completely wasted," she said, gesturing to herself, making Terrence glance down at the dress she was wearing.

Though most of the women in the room wore stylish cocktail dresses and evening gowns, Terrence's date, Amaya, had chosen to wear a short, skin-tight shimmering snakeskin dress with panels cut out of the back and side and black stilettos that made it look like she was walking around on stilts.

Though the drop-dead gorgeous beauty's attire drew several appreciative stares from the men around the room, and even Terrence reluctantly had to admit she looked damn good in that dress, it was obvious what she wore was not appropriate for the occasion. She seemed better fit for twirling around a stripper pole than taking a few spins on the dance floor with him at tonight's fund-raiser.

"I'm here to represent my family," Terrence whispered to Amaya as he held her elbow and guided her across the crowded room to their reserved table. "I told my brother I'd make an appearance."

Evan had originally planned to attend the event himself with Leila, but he'd had to back out at the last minute.

"You're offering me free tickets?" Terrence had asked. "I'm surprised you're even talking to me after that thing that happened at the baby shower a couple of weeks ago. I thought you were still pissed at me."

"I was . . . but then I realized you aren't the only one who's been acting like an asshole lately," Evan had said with a resigned sigh. "I figured I should show some compassion, and Lee and I won't be able to make the event anyway."

"Why? What happened?"

"Just . . . stuff. We're going through something right now."

"Uh-oh." Terrence had furrowed his brows. "*Something*? What does that mean?"

"Like I said before, you aren't the only one who's been an asshole. I fucked up. Lee and I are in a bad place, and it's my fault. I don't know if we'll make it through," Evan had whispered on the phone, his voice heavy with emotion. "Going to a banquet is the least of my concerns. So you go and enjoy yourself. At least *one* of us should."

So in addition to Terrence breaking up with C. J., now Evan and Leila were going through "something," and Paulette and Antonio's marriage was so screwed up it wasn't even worth talking about. Terrence was sure of it now: His family was cursed romantically.

"Look, we at least have to stay for an hour or two," Terrence now explained to his date. "It's not that big of a deal, is it?"

In response, Amaya grumbled, "Fine. Whatever!" He held out a Chiavari chair for her. She plopped onto the satin cushion. "I guess I'll just have to be *bored*, then."

He watched as she pulled her phone out of her satin clutch and started to scroll her acrylic, bejeweled nail across the screen.

Probably checking how many people liked her latest photo on Instagram, Terrence thought dryly.

"I need a drink," he said. "Do you want anything?"

"Cosmo," she mumbled, not looking up from her phone screen. "Wait, make it an apple martini."

He nodded and walked across the ballroom to the throng already gathered around the bar. He stepped up to the counter a few minutes later when a spot came open and gave the bartender their orders. As he waited, he hummed and drummed his fingers on the granite countertop to the beat of the music the band was playing. He became lost in thought.

Had dating always been hard? He had been out of the game for less than a year, but he didn't remember it being this trying or painful. His first date with C. J. hadn't been this bad, had it? Their conversation had flowed easily. He could remember laughing with her the whole time and telling her stories about . . .

Forget C. J., dammit, he ordered himself. *Remember . . . that's over and done with!*

C. J. wasn't thinking about him while she was gallivanting around Raleigh with her ex, was she? So why the hell should he waste his time and thoughts on her? Besides, he was here tonight with Amaya in an attempt to finally move on, to take his therapist's advice and try his best not to keep obsessing about his and C. J.'s breakup, endlessly replaying what she had done and what he had done wrong.

"You know that obsessing leads to nowhere, Terrence," his therapist had said at their session last week.

He was seeing his therapist again, something he had been reluctant to do. But after what had happened at Evan and Leila's baby shower, he realized the situation was getting out of hand. He couldn't take care of this on his own. His therapist was even suggesting that they might consider meds for his depression to help in the long term.

"One in ten people take antidepressants," she had explained to him in that calming voice of hers during their last session. "There's no shame in it. Whatever it takes to help you live a healthy life, right?"

He had nodded grudgingly in agreement. "Whatever it takes."

So here he was attempting to live a "healthy life," trying diligently to put the past aside and enjoy his new date. Unfortunately, Amaya's stank attitude wasn't making it easy.

"Thanks," Terrence said, grabbing the glasses that the bartender finally handed to him. He turned to head back to his table with the hope that a little alcohol might improve her mood. As he did, he unwittingly bumped into someone's shoulder, spilling the other party's drink onto the tiled floor.

"Shit! I'm sorry," he said, jumping back.

"Oh, that's okay," the woman replied with her back to him, leaning down to dab with a cocktail napkin at a spot of white wine now on her gown.

When Terrence heard the familiar voice, his stomach dropped.

It seemed to happen almost in slow motion. He watched as C. J. looked up from her drink now puddled at her feet and turned to face him. "It's my fault," she continued distractedly. "I should have looked where I was . . ."

When their eyes met, her words drifted off.

"What . . . what are you . . ." He shook his head, fighting to get the words out. "What are you doing here?"

"I'm covering the event for the paper." She held up the notepad and pen in her other hand and gestured toward it with her empty wineglass. "I'm working for the *Chesterton Times* again."

Seeing her standing there, Terrence felt waves of emotions: shock, elation, longing, and then finally, anger.

What the hell is she doing back in Chesterton?

He had shaved, dressed, and finally dragged himself out of the house to go on a date. He was trying to move on and forget about her, and she had the nerve to show up on his turf, tonight of all nights?

"Why are you working with the *Times* again? I thought you were helping your father with his campaign."

She pursed her lips and lowered her head. "I think I've given all that I could give to Dad. I had to walk away from that . . . that situation. I couldn't do it anymore."

"*Oh, really?* And ol' Pastor Clancy is okay with you being up here?" Terrence asked, his voice dripping with sarcasm. "Considering the last time you got away from him, I'd think he'd want to keep a closer eye on you this time around."

She raised her eyes and glared at him. "Stop it, Terry."

"Stop what?"

"You know damn well there was nothing going on between me and Shaun Clancy!"

"No, I don't know. I know what I saw when I—"

"You were seeing things that weren't there, because it's what you *wanted* to see," she argued. "You had changed. You were a different guy and didn't want to be in a relationship anymore! Just admit it, Terry! You exceeded that month-long shelf life that you *always* have with women—"

"*A shelf life?*" he repeated with disbelief. "Are you fucking kidding me?"

"—and you wanted to end it between us, but instead of just . . . just coming out and saying it, you—"

"You really think that's what I wanted?" he choked, staring at her in disbelief. He took a step toward her so that they were only inches apart. "You really fucking think I wanted to go through that—through *this?* You think I enjoy feeling this way, like my . . . my goddamn chest has been cut open and my damn heart's been ripped out? You think I want this shit?"

She fell silent. He saw the same pain and confusion reflected in her eyes that he now felt. "I didn't know what you wanted anymore, Terry," she whispered.

"There you are!" Amaya called out as she walked toward him. "I was wondering where the hell you'd disappeared to. I've been sitting at that table for almost forever, Terry!" She took the martini glass out of his hand and took a sip. She then gazed down at C. J.

"Hey," she said, giving a half-hearted wave.

"H-Hello," C. J. answered softly, looking a little wounded at seeing him here with another woman.

He felt wounded, too—almost broken.

Terrence yearned to put down his shot glass and pull C. J. close, to drag her across the ballroom so that they could finish talking, so that he could hold her and kiss her, tell her that it was obvious this was all a big misunderstanding and that he had been too pigheaded and stupid to tell her that he missed her so much it hurt. He wanted to tell her that they should start again. But he didn't. It all felt too raw. And with Amaya standing next to him and the band playing on stage and the people laughing and shouting around them, the moment felt . . . wrong.

"I'm Amaya!" He watched dumbly as his date introduced herself to C. J., as she tossed her long hair over her shoulder and took another sip from her glass. "Are you a friend of Terrence?"

"You could . . . could say that, I guess," C. J. answered unsteadily.

"Oh, really?" Amaya looked between the two of them. "How do you know each other?"

"We . . ." he began, then couldn't find the words.

"It's complicated," C. J. said. She then glanced down at her notepad. "It was nice meeting you, Amaya, but I really should get going. I'm covering the event, and I have a few people I need to talk to. You guys have a . . . a good night." She then walked around the puddle of white wine and fled, leaving Terrence feeling numb.

"Complicated, huh?" Amaya narrowed her eyes at him over the lip of her glass. "What's so complicated about it? Did you guys hook up or something?"

He didn't answer her. Instead, he silently headed back to their table, not looking behind him to see if Amaya followed.

"What *is* this?" Amaya asked, prodding her dessert with her fork. She wrinkled her nose. "Is it like a Jell-O?"

Terry didn't answer her, instead he sipped from his champagne glass and kept his gaze focused on a spot on the other side of the room, the spot where C. J. now stood, talking to a couple as she scribbled on her notepad.

He should have left more than an hour ago, but instead he had lingered at the banquet table, not eating the dinner that cost almost two hundred dollars a plate, ignoring everyone around him—including Amaya.

He kept replaying what C. J. had said. *"I didn't know what you wanted anymore, Terry."*

But was it really a question? Did she even have to ask? It was so obvious what he had wanted. That had never changed from the moment he'd met her!

"*Hello!* Are you even listening?" Amaya said, waving her hand in front of his face.

"Huh?" he said vaguely, lowering his glass from his mouth.

"God, were you paying attention?" she cried, making him shake his head.

"No, what did you say?"

"I asked what the hell am I eating." She grabbed

the leather-encased menu that sat in the center of the table listing the entrees for that night. "I tried to figure it out, but this shit is in French. I don't speak French."

"No clue," he murmured, setting his glass back on the table, still gazing across the room.

Amaya loudly groused and slumped back into her chair. "Are you going to stare at her the whole damn night?"

"Stare at who?"

"At that woman! The one at the bar we spoke to earlier. You've been staring at her the whole time, Terry!" She poked out her lower lip in a pout. "You're making me feel like you don't even wanna be here with me."

Probably because I don't, he thought.

Amaya crossed her arms under her double-D breasts and stuck out her chest. "I mean . . . if you're going to act like this the entire night, I can just leave. You can go over there and talk to her!" She leaned toward his ear. "But be careful. Don't mess up and miss a good opportunity, Terry," she whispered saucily. "You might regret it later."

He pursed his lips and slowly nodded. "You're absolutely right, Amaya. My apologies."

She smiled just as he pushed back his chair and rose to his feet, catching her by surprise.

"I'm sorry for wasting your time, but I've gotta do this. I'll hook you up with an Uber driver later to make sure you get home safely, okay?"

She let out a mousy squeak of outrage as she watched Terrence turn away from their table and walk across the room. He headed straight to C. J., who was now talking to another man.

"No, really! I'm not that much of a dancer, but thanks for asking," she said shyly.

"Oh, come on, girl! Just one dance?" the man asked, smiling and moving his shoulders to the rhythm of the music. He held out his hand to her. "I bet we could—"

"Sorry, brotha, but I believe I've reserved a dance with the lady for this song," Terrence interrupted.

The other man's eager smile faded. C. J. turned to stare up at Terrence, stunned.

"*Terry?* I . . . w-what are . . ."

He grabbed her hand and dragged her toward the dance floor, not giving her a chance to finish.

When they reached the other slow-dancing couples, he pulled her against him. She still looked bewildered. Her delicate brows furrowed as she frowned.

"We're going to have to take this slow," he said, wrapping his arms around her waist. "My leg still isn't what it used to be. You won't catch me doing the merengue anytime soon." He chuckled to himself as he gently rubbed her back.

Feeling her softness and warmth against his fingertips gave him a dull ache. He longed to do a lot more than just hold her close, but he stoically fought that urge.

"Terry, what are we doing? Why'd you ask me to dance?"

"Because I'm trying to finally talk to you—not fight with you—and this seemed to be as good a time to do it as any."

She hesitantly placed a hand on his broad

shoulder and fell in step with the music. "What did you want to talk about?"

He cleared his throat. *Where to begin?* There was a long list of questions he had, doubts, and frustrations, but it was probably best to cut straight to the point.

"So nothing was really going on between you and Shaun?"

She rolled her eyes and loudly exhaled. It sounded more like a groan. She dropped her hand from his shoulder and let it hang limply to her side. "Is that why you came over there and dragged me out here? To ask me that damn question again?" She tried to shove back from him, but he held firmly onto her.

"Please, just answer it. I need to know!"

"For the last time . . . *no!* No! Jesus, Terry, he was just there because he was bringing me soup and cold medicine. I accidentally spilled soup all over him and he was cleaning himself up while I washed his clothes. That's it!" She paused. "Then you walked in and . . . well . . . lost your shit. Nothing happened! I wasn't interested in Shaun. I'm especially not interested in him now!"

"What does that mean?"

"Nothing," she said tiredly.

"No, tell me. We're talking now; we're not arguing. Talk to me."

She sighed. "Look, it's a long story, but the gist of it is that Shaun's not . . . he's not the guy I thought he was. I used to think he was the odd man out at Aston Ministries, but he's more like Dad and Victor than I realized. I guess I'm the only odd man out over there."

"So where does that leave you?"

"Ostracized." She laughed sadly. She tried to put up a mask of apathy, but Terrence knew how losing her family again had to hurt. "I accept it, though. I can't be what they want me to be so I'm back to being alone."

"You're not alone, C. J. As long as I'm around, you're not."

"But how long will you be around? The way you've been acting lately doesn't—"

"You told me that you didn't know what I wanted anymore, but what I wanted was you, C. J. I *still* want you. I *still* love you! None of that's changed!" he shouted over the rising sound of trumpets and saxophones on stage.

"You say that now, Terry, but how do I know you're telling the truth? You told me that all we had was sex. That's it," she said, glaring up at him. "You said—"

"I said a long list of stupid, immature shit because I was angry, depressed, and feeling rejected."

Her glare disappeared. Her face softened.

"I miss you, baby. I'm tired of being apart. I hate it. I fuckin' hate it! I barely eat! I can't sleep. I'm annoying the shit out of everybody around me! I'm back in therapy because it got so bad. I want to be *done* with this."

She stared at him mutely.

"Do you want to be done with this, too? Do you still love me like I love you?"

He felt sick to his stomach as he waited in anticipation of her answer. Gradually, she nodded. "Of course I do. I've always loved you, Terry."

The heavy blanket of gloom that had been

thrown over him for almost two months was yanked
off. He grinned. "Well, okay." He pulled her even
closer to him so that they were pressed torso to
torso. "Then let's do this."

She squinted. "Let's do wha—"

She was cut short when he abruptly lowered
his mouth to hers. With that, with the exception
of C. J., the entire ballroom and all the people
within it seemed to disappear.

Their kiss was just like Terrence remembered
from the countless other kisses they had shared—
with a little added spice that came from his pent-
up longing for her. When their tongues met, she
let out a soft moan and linked her arms around his
neck, inadvertently dropping her notepad and
pen to the parquet floor. She tilted back her head
and the kiss deepened even further. She nipped
his bottom lip and licked the inside of his mouth.
Terrence clasped the back of her neck, then let his
other hand slide from the small of her back to her
bottom, grabbing a handful, feeling her rub against
his groin in a slow, sensual rhythm that had nothing to do with the music.

Their ardor drew several inquisitive stares and
raised eyebrows from the couples around them. A
few began to whisper and chuckle among themselves.

"Damn, get a room, you two!" one drunken
man playfully shouted before being swatted on the
shoulder by his wife.

Terrence drew on what little willpower he had
left and tugged his mouth away from C. J. She
stared up at him dully with heavy-lidded eyes.

"Come on," he rasped.

"Huh?" She licked her kiss-chapped lips just as he tugged her yet again, this time off the dance floor. Terrence excused his way through the crowd, pulling C. J. close to his side as they made their way across the ballroom, past the tables, and toward one of the exit doors.

"Where are we going?" she called out to him.

"Don't know yet," he replied over his shoulder. "But I know we're getting the hell out of here!"

He shoved open one of the steel doors and they entered a darkened, quiet hallway that was far less glamorous than the ballroom with its crystal chandelier and gold wainscoting. The corridor was filled with bare white walls and an antiseptic smell. A cleaning cart sat near one of the doors along with a discarded vacuum cleaner. The soles of their shoes echoed off the linoleum tile and high ceilings as they walked. Terrence tried one door handle, then another, cursing under his breath when he discovered the doors were locked.

"Terry," C. J. whispered, gazing apprehensively around her, "I don't think we're supposed be back here! What are you—"

"Yeah, that's what I'm talkin' about," he said triumphantly as the next door handle he tried turned. The door creaked open, revealing a pitch-black room. He reached blindly along the wall and turned on the light switch, revealing a walk-in closet filled with floor-to-ceiling shelves covered with folded linen, candles, and several other supplies that could be used in the ballroom. A small table for folding linen was in the corner. He guided C. J. into the closet, then closed the door behind them with a *click*.

"Why are we in here?"

He smirked and linked his arms around the small of her back. "Why do you think we're in here?"

She reached for one of the gold napkin holders on the stainless steel shelves and held it aloft. She then cocked an eyebrow. "You really expect me to have sex with you in a linen closet?"

"I admit it's not the best solution, but I had to come up with something fast. I didn't want to lose the momentum." He laughed when she continued to glare at him. He drew her closer. "Do you really wanna wait until we can drive to your place or mine?" he asked as he kissed her chin and her neck with an aching deliberateness he knew she loved.

"It's a *closet*, Terry!" she repeated, but more weakly this time.

"Yes, it's a closet . . . and I still want to make love to you," he whispered in return before lowering his mouth to hers.

C. J. grumbled as he removed the satin straps of her gown, but she didn't shove him away like she had the last time he tried to make love to her. She didn't stomp toward the door in outrage. Instead she returned his kiss with fervor and tugged his tuxedo jacket off his shoulders. She began to hurriedly undo the buttons of his shirt and allowed him to ease her back against the stainless steel shelves as his hand shoved the hem of her dress up her thighs.

Her body missed his touch just as much as he missed hers. She wanted him at that moment just as much as he wanted her, even if it was in a linen closet and two hundred and some odd people were drinking, eating, and dancing less than twenty feet away.

"I love you, baby," he whispered against her lips as they frantically undressed.

"I love you, too," she breathed, kissing him back.

Within minutes, C. J.'s passionate moans filled the room. The hem of her floor-length satin gown was now up around her waist and the sequined top hung precariously off one shoulder as she bent over the folding table. Terrence was crouched behind her, kissing and nipping her neck and shoulders, cradling her breast with one hand and massaging her clit with the other. Though she was usually the louder one, his loud groans and throaty curses eclipsed her moans and yells.

C. J. grabbed onto the table and one of the metal shelves to brace herself as he thrust into her over and over again. He knew that he should probably slow down. The fervent tempo was making the folding table thump against the wall like a jackhammer. It was making the shelves rattle. A sterling silver candelabra from one of the top shelves clattered to the floor. A box of salt and pepper shakers soon followed.

If anyone walked into the corridor, they were bound to hear all the noise the two were making, but Terrence didn't care. He couldn't slow down or stop—and neither could she. They had to ride this wave until it was over.

She came first, holding onto the shelf for dear life and shouting out his name as she did it. He came less than a minute after, hearing his blood whistle in his ears, feeling his heart pound fiercely in his chest, and closing his eyes as it swept over him.

They both collapsed against the linoleum table-top when it was over. Weak-kneed and sapped of energy, they gradually slid down and landed in a heap on the linen closet's cold concrete floor.

Terrence dazedly thumped his head back against a stack of folded tablecloths. C. J.'s head lolled onto his shoulder as they both fought to catch their breaths. He could faintly hear the sound of the band playing another R & B selection on the other side of the linen closet wall.

"Goddamn," Terrence murmured with a crooked grin. "We should break up more often," he said with gulping breaths.

At that, C. J. turned to look up at him, squinted at him in disbelief, then burst into laughter before raising her mouth to kiss him again.

Chapter 24
Evan

Evan gazed out the floor-to-ceiling windows of his office, watching a white charter boat as it slowly cut a path down the Potomac River, sending up a froth of white spray along the way. He had been gazing out the window for the past hour, watching the boats go by and the planes fly overhead on their way to nearby Reagan National Airport. He was unable to focus his thoughts on anything substantive. He had e-mails to write, sales figures to review, and marketing plans he was supposed to discuss with his team later that day, but he didn't care. He couldn't work up the energy to care.

"I fucked up so bad," he muttered to himself for the umpteenth time.

Leila was now living in one of the guest rooms

in the east wing, not far from her daughter's suite. She hadn't exchanged more than a few words with him in that period of time, treating him with a cool demeanor that one would reserve for a perfect stranger. Even Diane had noticed the difference between them.

"What on earth did you do, boy?" she had asked only yesterday as she stood in the doorway of his study. He had looked up from his laptop, startled to find her sternly gazing at him.

"I'm sorry?" he had asked her, confused. He had been staring at his laptop screen, trying to type, but only managing to click out a few sentences.

"What . . . did . . . you . . . do . . . to . . . my . . . chile?" she had repeated slowly, taking another step into the room. "It must be pretty bad, because she won't even tell *me* what you did!"

He had raised his brows in response. "Why do you assume I did something?"

Evan had watched as Diane had crossed her arms over her chest and puckered her lips at him, as if she had just tasted something sour. "Son, don't play with me." She paused. "You didn't cheat on her, did you?"

Would kissing Charisse really qualify as cheating? He had felt a spark, but it was nothing compared to what he felt when he kissed Leila. And he hadn't gone to Charisse's condo with the intention of doing anything out of bounds. He'd had the best of intentions. But that didn't seem to matter very much now.

Besides, what was that old saying? *The road to hell is paved with good intentions,* he had thought.

"You're taking way too long to answer that question," Diane had said, eyeing him from the doorway.

"No offense, Diane, but I really don't think it's appropriate for me to be discussing what goes on between me and Lee with you."

"Uh-huh." Diane's nostrils flared as she released a loud breath. "Well, let's hope for your sake, Evan Murdoch, that my daughter forgives you for *whatever* you did, because we both know you'll be a lot more torn up if *she* leaves *you* than the other way around."

She had then raised her nose into the air, turned on her heel, and walked back into the hall.

"Meddling old biddy," he had muttered to himself.

He had been angry at Diane's words, but he knew she was only telling the truth. If Leila really did follow through with her promise to leave him, he didn't know what he would do. It was one of the reasons why he had lashed out at her, why he threatened her with a custody lawsuit if she left him. It had been a desperate, callous move, and he regretted it just as much as the kiss he and Charisse had shared.

Evan heard a knock at his door, momentarily drawing him from his thoughts. "Come in," he called out, still gazing out the floor-to-ceiling windows.

"Mr. Murdoch," Adrienne said from the doorway, "you have someone here who'd like to speak with you. She wasn't sure if you were busy. She didn't want to interrupt you."

At the reference to "she," Evan snapped out of his malaise. Had Leila decided to come to his office out of the blue and talk to him? Was she finally ready to forgive him?

"No, I'm not . . . I'm not busy," he said, turning away from the windows. He sat upright in his chair and his hand flew to his tie and collar in a hurried attempt to look more presentable. "Who . . . who is it?"

"Your sister, Mrs. Williams, sir," Adrienne said. "Should I send her in, then?"

So it's not Lee, he thought sadly. His shoulders slumped. He had been foolish to expect that it was her.

"Sure," he said softly to Adrienne. "Send her in."

Adrienne smiled and nodded before opening the door wider and waving Paulette inside his office.

Evan was disappointed Leila hadn't come to speak to him today, but truth be told, he was just as surprised that Paulette had paid him a visit. He hadn't spoken to her or Antonio since the baby shower, since she had stormed out with tears in her eyes. Antonio had trailed behind her with a look so tortured that Evan honestly felt for the man, even though he knew what Antonio had done. He had tried calling Paulette, and she had finally answered, only to tell him that she was fine but she didn't want to speak to anyone right now. He had obeyed her wishes. Evan now watched as his sister stepped timidly into the room.

She may have been bad off emotionally, but you couldn't tell it from the way she looked. She wore a camel wool coat with fox fur along the lapel. Her hair was pulled back into a bun atop her head. Her makeup was flawless, but he could still clearly see her withdrawn expression.

"Hey," he said as Adrienne closed the office door. He rose from his desk and walked across the room and opened his arms to embrace her. She seemed to hesitate before stepping into his embrace. She let him hug her but didn't hug him back.

"Hey, Ev," she answered. She then took a step back and looked up at him, fixing him with her dark eyes. "We . . . we need to talk."

He nodded and pointed toward the sitting area on the other side of his office. She removed her coat and tossed it aside, and then sat down on the leather sofa. He took the Bauhaus chair facing her.

"First," she began, staring down at her hands, which were clasped in her lap, "I want to begin by telling you that I'm not angry at you or Terry for not telling me what . . . what Tony . . . well, what he did. I appreciate you not telling anyone else, either. Thank you for not turning him in, Ev."

"I wouldn't do that to you, Sweet Pea."

"I know you wouldn't." She raised her eyes to look at him and gave a pained smile. "You want to protect me—just like Tony does. That's why he did it, you know?"

Evan nodded in silent agreement.

"He told me everything—what he did and why he did it. It wasn't just blind rage, Ev. He said Marques was owed a . . . a punishment. He said that bastard deserved to be punished for what he did to me . . . what he did to *us*." She closed her eyes. "And you know what, Ev, the whole time Tony was telling me all of this, I felt so sorry for him. I was angry at myself because Tony didn't used to talk like that before all of this happened—before I made mistake after mistake after mistake. He was a kind and decent man before I came along, and now he's . . . he's a . . ." She couldn't finish. She couldn't say the word. Instead, she squeezed her eyelids so tightly that they were starting to jitter, like her mind didn't want to see the man her husband had become. "It's . . . it's all my fault!"

"No, it's not," Evan said, reaching out to place his hand over his sister's. "Please don't blame yourself."

Her eyes flashed open. "But who else would I blame, Ev?"

Maybe the man who blackmailed you, Evan thought, *or the man who strangled and beat him to death.* But he said neither aloud, not wanting to upset her.

"You've had to deal with a lot of guilt for the past year, Sweet Pea. Please don't add another thing to feel guilty about."

"That's easier said than done."

He could agree with that one. He of all people knew what it was like to walk around with the heavy burden of guilt.

"So you say Tony told you everything," Evan

ventured. "Did he happen to mention what happened with Dante?"

Evan was still unsure about that one. It had been his suspicion that Antonio had tried to kill Dante, and he thought Dante would point the finger at his brother-in-law as soon as he woke up. But it had been months now, and Antonio still hadn't been arrested. Detective Morris had gone conspicuously silent. What was going on?

Paulette stared at him, confused. "What do you mean, what happened with Dante? Why would Antonio have anything to do with Dante?"

"Well," Evan began, "I told him about what Dante tried to do to you. It made him angry. I wasn't sure if . . . well, if—"

"If Tony went after Dante, too," she finished for him.

Ever so slowly, Evan nodded.

"He didn't do it," she said, quickly shaking her head. "Dante was shot . . . *when?* In late July, right?"

Evan nodded. "July the eighteenth . . . at around nine p.m."

That date, and the date Antonio had made his confession to him, had been burned permanently into Evan's memory.

"We had made up by then! He couldn't have done it," she argued, vigorously shaking her head again, making her large hoop earrings swing and hit her cheeks. "He was home every night, Ev. We were sleeping in the same bed. He wouldn't have had time to disappear and then come back home."

"Are you sure? You're certain?"

"I'd swear on the Bible!" She held up her hand.

"Oh, thank God," Evan said, exhaling with relief and leaning forward in his chair. He didn't know it but he had been carrying the burden of the guilt over Dante's shooting himself, much like his sister mentally carried the burden of Marques's murder. He had wondered if his confession to Antonio had almost pushed the younger man to pull the trigger. Now he knew that it hadn't, and he felt like he had been given a reprieve.

I didn't fuck that up, at least, he thought.

"Well, now that we've settled that, I have one last thing to ask you, Ev," she said, gazing into his eyes again.

"Anything! Go ahead."

"Please continue to keep Tony's secret. I . . . I understand that you told Terry. I even understand if you tell Lee, but don't tell anyone else, please. Definitely don't tell the police."

"I told you, I wouldn't do that to you."

She stared at him for a long time and then finally nodded. "Thank you, Ev."

He watched as his sister rose from the sofa. He followed suit and walked with her to his office door.

"Oh," she said, halting abruptly just before he reached for his doorknob, "please apologize to Lee for me. I felt bad for walking out of your baby shower. I hadn't intended to do that. I didn't want to ruin her day."

"I'm sure Lee would understand if she knew the circumstances."

"But please . . . tell her anyway."

Evan laughed sadly. "I would, but . . ."

"But what?"

"She and I aren't really talking. She's angry at me."

Paulette's serene expression changed. Her brows drew together and she frowned. "What did you do?"

"I'd rather not get into it. Let's just say, I overstepped—greatly."

Paulette slowly shook her head. "You're one of the smartest guys I know, Ev, but sometimes you can be so dumb! When will you ever learn?" she asked, making him frown again.

"Learn what?"

"That the people in your life aren't little pieces on a chessboard for you to shift around and strategize their lives anyway you want. It annoys the hell out of all of us! It makes us feel like you don't really respect us."

At that, he winced. He never knew his family thought of him that way—let alone Leila. But she had said it. She had used those very words.

"I'm not going to be married to or live with yet another man I can't trust . . . who doesn't respect me!"

"Look, we know that you love us," she said, reaching out, rubbing his arm, trying to soften the emotional blow she was giving, "but sometimes you just find it hard to . . . to let go. You think you know everything, and to hell with what all the fools say. But we're not all fools, Ev! That's no way to treat people, even if you have the best of intentions, even if you love them."

He stared at her, dumbfounded. He was only shaken out of his trance when Paulette stood on the balls of her feet and kissed him on the cheek.

"But I know you guys will work through it," she whispered. "If Tony and I can, I know you and Lee certainly can. Just . . . just remember what I said."

He nodded vaguely and watched as his sister opened the door and walked out of his office.

Chapter 25

Leila

Leila knocked on the bedroom door before pushing it open. She found her daughter, Isabel, sitting on her bed underneath the gauzy canopy, flipping the pages of one of her Harry Potter books while humming along to the music playing in her headphones. Leila shook her head and laughed. Isabel had to have read the entire series at least twice.

"Izzy," Leila said with a smile as she walked across the room toward her daughter. "Izzy, it's bedtime, honey. Did you hear me?" She leaned forward and removed one of the headphones from Isabel's ears, startling the eight-year-old. "I said it's bedtime!" she shouted over the sound of a blaring teenybop tune. "It's getting late. I came in to say good night."

Isabel nodded and removed her headphones

before setting them and her iPod on her night table. She yawned and closed her book, placing it on the night table, too.

"I want you to have sweet dreams and a good sleep so you can get up bright and early and have a good day at school tomorrow," Leila said before kissing her on the cheek. "Because you *are* going to have a good day, right?"

Isabel rolled her eyes. "*Yes*, Mommy!"

Since Isabel's week-long suspension, Leila hadn't heard about any more drama at Queen Anne Academy. Leila hoped that the school bullies had backed off of Isabel. She hoped that her daughter could finally peacefully settle into her new school.

Though, when I leave Evan, she'll probably have to change schools again, Leila thought forlornly.

"But still wake me up early if Angelica is about to come," Isabel piped as she climbed underneath her comforter, adjusting one of the silk-sheathed pillows behind her.

Angelica . . . Leila and Evan had chosen the name of their baby girl together, deciding to do a spinoff of Angela, his late mother's name. He had wanted to honor her, and Leila had thought it was a sweet gesture and had been more than happy to appease him.

Leila now nodded at her daughter. "I'll wake you up right away. Don't worry."

"She was supposed to be here already," Isabel said as she sat up in bed. "I marked it on my wall calendar and everything."

"Believe me, honey. I know!" Leila rubbed her belly. "If anyone knows how long she's been in here, it's me."

Leila was now two days past her due date and feeling overly ripe and ready to burst. Her OB/GYN was talking about inducing if Angelica didn't come by the end of the week.

"Some babies are eager to get out," the doctor had said with a laugh at Leila's last appointment. "Some aren't."

And some know when you're ready for them and when you're not.

Perhaps Little Angelica sensed what upheaval lay outside of her mother's womb.

Leila still didn't know whether she should stay at the Murdoch Mansion for a year or so, until Angelica was older and Leila could work full-time while her mother watched her. Or should she leave the mansion sooner and get her own place? And how would Isabel respond to moving to yet another home, starting yet another school, and losing yet another father figure?

Just thinking about all those things made Leila exhausted—and carrying an eight-pound baby around all day made her tired as it was. She wasn't prepared to make weighty decisions like this. She had a hard enough time figuring out where to put her rocking chair in the nursery, let alone what was the next course she should take with her life.

"Time to get out, Angelica!" Isabel shouted, leaning toward her mother's stomach, making Leila laugh again. "We're ready to meet you already!"

Leila kissed her daughter again before rising to her feet with a grunt. "Hopefully, she heard you and will obey your command. Good night, honey."

"Night, Mommy," Isabel replied before sinking

beneath the sheets and comforter. "Hey, Mommy?" she called out just as Leila reached her door.

Leila turned. "Yes, honey?"

"Are you . . . are you mad at Evan?"

Leila paused. That question caught her off guard. "Why do you think that?"

"Well . . ." Isabel gnawed her bottom lip. "You don't really talk to each other anymore. You don't eat dinner together. You sleep in another room now, and Evan seems really . . . sad."

Leila pursed her lips, contemplating whether she should lie to Isabel about what was going on between her and Evan, but if Leila left Evan, Isabel would find out soon enough. And she had witnessed what had gone on between her father and mother two years ago. The precocious eight-year-old was young, but she wasn't naïve.

"Evan and I are going through some . . . some things right now," Leila explained as best she knew how. "We just need some . . . some space from each other."

Permanently, she thought, but didn't add that part.

"Kind of like when Ron left Harry and Hermione when he got mad?" Isabel piped, making Leila frown.

"*Huh?* What are you talking about, baby?"

"In *Harry Potter and the Deathly Hallows*!" Isabel threw up her hands and sighed loudly, like it was obvious what she was talking about. "Ron fought with Harry and left him and Hermione all alone. He was really, *really* mad but it was only because he had the . . . umm, Horcrux locket, though, I guess. Ron always had kind of a temper and he didn't like that Harry and Hermione were getting so close, and the locket made it all worse. Well, anyway," she said, her eyes widening with zeal, "he left them because he didn't want to be around Harry anymore. But after he left, he figured out how much he liked Harry. He figured out that they were really, really good friends. Maybe that's what you and Evan need to do!"

"Get rid of the Horcrux locket?"

"No!" Isabel exclaimed, throwing back her head. "Figure out why you liked each other in the first place so you can come back together!"

Leila gazed sorrowfully at her daughter. If only her life was as simple as Harry Potter's. "Maybe, honey," she whispered. "Sweet dreams," she said before turning off the lights and shutting the door behind her.

Three hours later, Leila lay awake tossing and turning in her bed, commencing another sleepless night. She had tried everything to help her sleep—reading a book, taking a warm bath, and watching the infomercials on television that usually had her nodding off within minutes—but nothing had worked. She told herself that it was her sore lower back and hips that were keeping her awake, or maybe her wide body that made it almost impossible to get into a comfortable position anymore. But she knew it wasn't true. It wasn't how or where she was sleeping that was keeping her awake, it was who wasn't sleeping next to her. She turned and gazed at the empty pillow next to her head. She had gotten used to sleeping with Evan at her side, hearing his soft breath in the dark, feeling his hand resting on her hip.

But climbing in bed beside him wasn't an option.

Leila slowly pushed herself upright and gazed bleakly at her darkened bedroom.

"Well, if I can't sleep, I might as well eat," she murmured before rocking back and forth and rising to her feet.

She walked down the silent corridor of the east wing and down the staircase before heading to the kitchen. She rarely went there since Evan had a hired cook, but every now and then she would raid the refrigerator to make herself a late-night snack.

As she approached the kitchen entrance, she saw through a crack beneath the door that a light inside was on, making her frown. She pushed the door open to find Evan sitting at the steel kitchen island on a metal stool, wearing his robe and pajama bottoms, eating a club sandwich and drinking a soda. He paused mid-chew when he saw her standing in the doorway. His eyes widened and he lowered the sandwich from his mouth.

A flood of yearning surged through her when their eyes met, but she reminded herself that he had lied to her, that he had kissed Charisse, that he had threatened to take her baby away from her. The yearning was quickly snuffed out and replaced with a cool detachment.

"Couldn't sleep either, huh?" she deadpanned, shoving her hands into her robe pockets and casually walking toward one of the industrial-size refrigerators.

She watched as he set down his sandwich, gathered his paper napkins and his can of soda. He rose to his feet. "You can have the kitchen. I was just about to—"

"Finish your sandwich, Ev," she said, waving him back onto his stool. She then opened one of the refrigerator doors and pulled out a carton of cherry vanilla ice cream. "We'll have to sit in the same room together eventually."

He hesitated before gradually lowering himself back onto his stool. She grabbed a spoon out of one of the drawers and took one of the stools facing him on the opposite side of the kitchen island. The two ate in mutual silence.

After a few minutes, Evan loudly cleared his throat, making her look up from her ice cream. "I . . . I've been meaning to talk to you. I wanted to ask you what's the plan for—"

"I haven't decided yet," she said, cutting him off. "I haven't decided if I want to stay here, and if I stay, for how long. I'd leave tomorrow if I could, but I don't have just me to consider anymore. I have the baby and . . . and Isabel. She's started a new school and is settling in. I don't want to bring any upheaval to her life again. Not right now. And I don't know if I'm up for searching for a new place and taking care of a week-old infant at the same time."

"That wasn't what I was going to ask you," he said, pushing his half-eaten sandwich aside. "I was going to ask what's the birthing plan?"

"What do you mean?"

"I mean what's going to happen when you go into labor? It's going to happen any day now. We had a plan, but . . . I don't know if you still wanted to do it that way."

"What would change?"

"I don't know . . . like . . . do you still want me in the delivery room?"

She lowered her spoon from her mouth. "Of course I do. You're the father."

He dropped his gaze to the tabletop. "But if it's going to stress you out. If it's going to make things worse for you while you're in labor . . . while you're in the delivery room, I can wait outside. Diane can be the one to—"

"I want you there, Evan," she said firmly, and he raised his eyes. He nodded.

"Okay, if you want me there, I'll be there."

Silence fell between them again. She resumed eating her ice cream and he pretended to finish his sandwich.

"I fucked up," he said out of nowhere a few minutes later.

"Yes, you did," she replied, feeling a burning ache spread across her chest and knowing that it wasn't heartburn.

"I thought I had it all figured out. I thought I could fix everything and you didn't have to know." He shook his head ruefully. "But the joke was on me, right? I was wrong . . . *so* wrong."

"Yeah, well, you were wrong about a lot of things, Ev, but you were right about one thing: I love you. I still do. I wanted to be with you, but I've never been 'all in,' so to speak. I've always kept a piece of my heart locked up so you wouldn't hurt me like Brad did. I've always prepared myself for the possibility of disappointment, of having to pick up the pieces, but it didn't keep me from being hurt when the disappointment happened. It didn't give me any cushion." She pursed her lips. "You still broke my heart."

"I'm sorry, Lee."

She sighed and closed the lid on her ice cream, no longer having much of an appetite. "I know you are . . . but that's not good enough anymore."

He took a drink from his soda can before crushing it in his hand and lowering it to the countertop. "With everything that's happened, I've been thinking a lot about Dad lately. I wondered how he would handle this situation."

She curled her lip. "He'd probably follow through with the threat to take my baby away if I decided to leave, use it to scare me into staying."

"You're right. He would have . . . because he was a manipulative asshole . . . a sociopath, or so I thought. I used to think Dad didn't care about us, that he didn't care about *anybody*. I thought he was all ambition and ego. He thought it was all about him and what he wanted, and who gives a shit about anybody else." He took a deep breath. "But now that he's gone and each year that I get older, I think I've finally started to figure out the truth about Dad. He *did* care, Lee. He *did* love us. He even loved my mom, in his own fucked-up way. But he didn't love us enough to pull back and let go. He always had to be the one in control. He always had to know what was best for us. He never trusted us to live our own lives. He thought it would draw us closer to him, but it only pushed us away.

"And the worst part is, even though I know all of this about Dad, even though I realize the truth, I . . . I can still feel myself turning into him. That need for control, to assure myself that I really know what's best . . . it's all him. And that anger," he said, clenching his fists on the countertop. "That *rage*. I felt it when I said those things to you that day, when I said I'd come after you with everything I had. I saw you as the enemy and it . . . it scared the shit out of me, Lee! It made me sick to my stomach, but . . . but I couldn't stop it." He closed his eyes and lowered his head. "I couldn't stop it! I can't . . ."

His words faded as he gritted his teeth, like he was in physical pain. She watched as he turned his back to her, so she wouldn't have to see his face, so she wouldn't have to see him crying—something she had never witnessed before in the twenty-plus years she had known him. Watching him become this battered and broken, tears pricked her own eyes.

He hurt me, she reminded herself. *He hurt me so bad.* But she couldn't take it anymore, seeing him like this.

This was Evan: her best friend, the first person she had ever given that title. That was why his betrayal had hurt so much, even more than what Brad had done to her, and she had been married to that bastard for ten years! Her relationship with Evan went deeper than passion or romantic love, and she realized that it always would—no matter what they went through.

Who am I foolin'?

She could never walk away from him, and it had nothing to do with recovering after the baby or finding a new place to live or Isabel's education, though those were all good reasons to stay. She couldn't leave Evan for the most important reason: They completed each other. He was her imperfect other half.

Leila rose from her stool and walked around the kitchen island. She wrapped her arms around Evan. He turned to her and did the same, burying his head against her shoulder.

"You're not your father, Ev," she whispered into his ear, kissing his cheek and brow, blinking through her tears. "You're not him. Trust me."

He clung to her and she clung to him for what seemed like forever. Finally, she pulled back, loosening her embrace.

"I think we should both go to bed, don't you?" she said. "It's late."

He nodded.

They cleaned up the remaining food and turned off the lights in the kitchen before heading to the stairs leading to the east and west wings. They took the stairs slowly, dragging out the moment.

When they reached the top of the staircase, Evan looked over his shoulder, prepared to head their separate ways. He leaned down and kissed her cheek.

"Night, Lee," he said before turning to head in the opposite direction, toward the west wing, but he stopped when she grabbed his hand. He frowned down at her.

"I'm going with you," she whispered.

He squinted at her, as if asking, *Are you sure?*

She nodded and squeezed his hand. She had taken Isabel's advice: She figured out why she and Evan were together in the first place.

They walked down the corridor to their bedroom and walked inside, quietly shutting the door behind them. He removed his robe and so did she. He stood at the bedside, watching her as she threw back the comforter, then the sheets, and climbed underneath them both. He followed suit, climbing into bed beside her. When he did, she rose to her knees and reached for him, tugging his T-shirt over his head and tossing it to the floor. She lowered her mouth to his. He kissed her back eagerly, burying his fingers in her hair, languidly letting his tongue explore her mouth. His hand cradled her breast and he rubbed his thumb over the nipple. His other hand cupped her bottom and she moaned.

Being so late-term in her pregnancy made her feel like an overly ripe fruit, but it also made her sensitive to every sensation. His kisses and caresses felt twice as intense and three times as pleasurable. The lightest touch of his fingertips against her skin left her shuddering.

She shifted aside the waistband of his pajama bottoms and wrapped her hand around his manhood. He grunted as she stroked him, all the while kissing him. When his breathing deepened and she could feel him drawing close, she let go of him. She raised her nightgown to her hips and straddled his lap.

He abruptly pulled his mouth away and shifted her back slightly. He shook his head. "Is that really a good idea, Lee, with you being so . . ." He glanced down at her protruding belly. "I don't think we should—"

He stopped talking when she placed her finger on his lips.

"I'm not a china doll, Ev. I swear to you . . . I

won't break," she said before she lowered herself onto him and he slid inside her.

He groaned as she rocked on top of him, kissing his neck and nibbling his earlobe. Despite his earlier protests, he closed his fingers around her hips to steady her. Gradually, he began to move underneath her, meeting her thrust for thrust.

When they were done, they fell back onto the mattress. Evan closed his eyes and fell asleep first, cradling her from behind and resting one hand on her hip. She fell asleep less than ten minutes later to the sound of his deep breathing. It was the most blissful sleep she had had in weeks.

They slept in late, until sunlight filtered through the parted curtains. Evan woke up first and kissed the back of her neck, making her turn to face him.

He smiled. "And how are you this morning, beautiful?"

"Good. A lot better than I was yesterday," she said with a shaky breath and a grimace as electric bolts of pain shot through her abdomen.

"Are you sure?" he asked, eying her and shifting onto his elbow. "You don't look so good, baby."

She nodded, closed her eyes, and smiled through her Lamaze breathing. "I'm perfectly fine, Ev. I'm . . . I'm just . . . finally going into labor!" she shouted, grabbing his hand. "Oww! Oww! Damn it!"

Chapter 26

Terrence

"You've gotta be kidding, Terry!" C. J. called out.

Terrence glanced up from his bowl of granola and banana nut cereal. He lowered the spoon from his mouth. "What do you mean?" he asked her, mid-slurp. "Kidding about what?"

"I mean there's no damn space for my stuff in here!" She leaned her head out of one of the doors of his walk-in closet to stare at him. "There's no place to put my things!"

He set his half-eaten cereal on his night table. "Yes, there is!"

"No, there isn't!"

"Yes, there is!"

Terrence then rose from his bed and walked across the room to join her in one of his closets to show her the space he had made for her.

Two weeks ago, Terrence had asked C. J. to move in with him. They had both agreed that if they were serious about making their relationship work, they had to take things to the "next level." That involved her giving up her apartment and setting up residence in his condo. They had both agreed to this in theory, but implementing "the next level" was turning out to be a little bumpier than anticipated.

C. J. had already suggested changes to Terrence's bachelor pad that made him raise his eyebrows or outright cringe: colorful throw pillows, new teal curtains, and a few abstract paintings from her apartment.

"Maybe we should get a cat," she had mused while they lay in bed a few nights ago. "A cute little tabby. What do you think?"

Now that she was officially moving in, they both realized that making space for two in a condo that a bachelor had lived in for so long wasn't an easy task.

He walked into his closet to find her pointing to the section he had cleared out for her.

"What's wrong with it?" he asked.

"*What's wrong with it?* Terry, you basically gave me three feet of shelf space. That's all I get in *two* whole walk-ins?"

He sighed. "Babe, you know I've got a lot of clothes."

"So do I!" She gestured through the opened doorway to her pile of clothes now stacked on his bed.

"But not as much as me!" he argued, making her

grumble. "Do you know I even had to get rid of some stuff to make room for you? And I did away with some good shit ... even a few couture pieces from my modeling days."

"Oh, you poor baby," she said dryly.

"Some of them were signature pieces," he continued, making her laugh and shake her head in exasperation. "I made sacrifices! *Big* sacrifices!"

"Yeah, you're a friggin' saint, Terry."

He watched as she walked down the length of the closet and grabbed several pairs of jeans he had neatly hung together. She brandished the jeans at him. "What about these? Are these signature pieces, too? How many pairs of dark-washed denim does one man need?"

He considered the jeans and glanced at the labels. "AG, Diesel, and True Religion."

"*And?* That means what?"

"Different designers and different cuts. I need them all."

"Okay! Okay!" She tossed aside the jeans and turned to a series of shelves where he kept his shoes. She grabbed two pairs and held them out to him. "Are you also telling me you need identical pairs of gray suede hush puppies?"

He squinted. "One is clearly gunmetal gray and the other is dove gray. Those are completely different shoes!"

She dropped his shoes to the closet floor with a thud, then dropped her head into her hands. "Terry, do you really want to do this?" she asked from behind her palms.

"Really want to do what?"

"Do you want me to move in here with you?"

He took a step toward her. "I asked you to do it, didn't I? Of course I want you to move in!"

"You say that, but I'm not seeing it," she said, gesturing again to the space he had cleared for her.

"C. J." He gripped her shoulders. "I *love* you. I want something serious and permanent with you. I've told you that about five thousand times! What else do you—"

"Then *show* me, Terry! Show me that you're as serious about us as I am, and it might involve getting rid of a lot more than just two pairs of shoes and a couple of designer jeans."

He dropped his hands from her shoulders, feeling his hackles rise at her challenge. "You want me to show you I'm serious?"

"I would *love* you to show me."

"You *really* want me to show you?"

She threw back her head and laughed.

"Fine, you asked for it. I'mma give it to you." He then strutted out of the closet.

"Where are you going, Terry?" she called after him.

He didn't answer her. Instead he went straight to his dresser and went rummaging through the drawers, pushing aside stacks of boxer briefs and socks in search of what he was looking for.

He had purchased it a week ago, returning to the same jewelry store where Evan had bought Leila's "push gift" months earlier. Evan had returned with him, except this time *he* was the one advising Terrence. Terrence had known not to loiter too long over his decision because Evan had been in a rush to get back home to his newly expanded family, to his darling infant daughter, Angelica.

"I can't believe I'm doing this shit," Terrence had muttered with a trembling voice as he peered down at the line of solitaire diamond rings displayed in the glass case.

He had felt his heart beating rapidly in his chest and trickles of sweat tumbling down his back as he stood there, trying to decide which ring to buy.

Evan had smiled as he stood beside him. "I can't believe you're doing it, either! I never would've guessed in a million years that my skirt-chasing, commitment-phobic brother would want to ask a woman to marry him."

Terrence had stilled at Evan's words and grimaced. "You think I'm not ready? You think it's too soon, right?"

Evan had shaken his head. "I think no such thing! Besides, it doesn't matter what *I* think, Terry. This is about you and C. J. What do *you* want?"

"I . . . I want her. I want to be with her," he answered solemnly. "I don't want to be without her again."

"Good answer!" Evan had clapped Terrence on the shoulder. "Well, if you think you're ready to build a life with her, I support you. I wish you all the luck in the world."

"That's *if* she says yes," Terrence had mumbled, nervously peering down at the glass case again. "She could say no."

"She won't say no."

"I wish I knew that shit for sure!" He had sighed

before roughly scrubbing his hand over his face. "But first things first . . . I've got to pick out the ring." His eyes had drifted to a seven-carat, canary-yellow diamond that looked big enough to choke a squirrel. He'd pointed at it. "How about that one? That looks good, right?"

Evan had pursed his lips as he stared at Terrence's selection. "It's nice, but word to the wise . . . and I speak from experience. Get C. J. the ring that you know *she* would want, not the one you would want for her. She'll appreciate it more."

Terrence now reached into his dresser drawer and pulled out the black velvet box he had planned to give her later that week at a candlelit dinner in a penthouse suite overlooking the Washington Monument, Jefferson Memorial, and the Potomac. He had even hired a saxophonist to play them one of the jazz hits she liked.

"Ah, well," he muttered with another shrug as he slammed the drawer shut and popped the lid of the box open, revealing a three-carat, emerald-cut solitaire with an understated white gold band. It was simple and elegant—just like C. J. More important, it was something he knew she would wear, that she would want.

"I'm waiting, Terrence Murdoch!" she shouted as he walked back across the bedroom toward the closet.

"Let me guess," she said with laughter in her voice as he rounded the closet door, "instead of me putting my stuff in one of your closets, you're giving me another drawer." She snorted. "Well, at least it's a start! I'm happy you even bothered to . . ."

Her sarcastic quip died on her lips when she saw what he held in his hand. Her eyes zeroed in on the ring and her mouth dropped open. She took a step back, blinking furiously and bumping into one of the closet shelves.

"What the . . . what the hell, Terry," she murmured. "What . . . what are you . . ."

She couldn't finish.

"I told you that I'm serious about us, C. J.," he said, not feeling any of the nervousness or misgivings he had experienced when he had purchased the engagement ring. He was sure now of what he wanted to say and to do. He was completely resolute. "I want to make this as permanent as we can possibly make it, if . . . if you're willing to have me."

"Oh, my God!" She dropped one quivering hand to her stomach and the other to her mouth. Tears welled in her eyes.

He took another step toward her, still holding out the box and the ring.

"This isn't really happening, is it?" she whispered. "I must be dreaming, because it looks like . . . it looks like you're . . . you're a-a-asking me t-to—"

"I'm asking you to marry me, girl!"

She stared at him mutely, openly crying now.

"Will you marry me, C. J.?"

She smiled and slowly nodded. "Yes. Of course, baby!"

Chapter 27

Dante

Dante stumbled out of his bedroom a little after one o'clock to the sound of banging at his front door. He squinted at the bright light streaming through the window blinds and absently scratched his hairy stomach. He realized, grudgingly, that he had developed quite a paunch from all the cheap beer he had drunk in the past few months. If he kept going at this rate, he might develop a full beer gut. He tossed a handful of pills into his mouth as he walked down the hall, as he did every morning, and made a mental note to buy more OxyContin later that week. He was running low yet again.

"Open up!" Kiki shouted as she banged on his front door. "I know you in there! Open up, Daddy!"

No matter how many times his daughter said it, Dante didn't think he would *ever* get used to someone calling him "Daddy." Well, outside of the bedroom, anyway.

"I'm coming!" he yelled back.

Kiki had become a persistent and permanent fixture in Dante's life. She came by the house almost daily now, raiding his fridge, using his phone, and watching his television. She would talk constantly while she was there, filling his ears with a chatter that at least helped him momentarily forget how his life had taken a high dive off a steep cliff. But he still needed a break from her every now and then; she was a teenager with a lot of mouth and attitude, after all. Judging from her banging at his front door, he guessed his break was over.

"Damn!" she exclaimed after he unlocked the door and swung it open. "It took you long enough."

"Good morning to you, too," he murmured dryly.

"You might wanna check your clocks. I think you mean 'afternoon,'" she corrected, sauntering into his living room, throwing her purple braids over her shoulder.

"Morning . . . noon . . . Who the hell cares?" He reached for one of the half-empty beer bottles on the coffee table and rubbed his eyes. "What do you want anyway? You don't usually show up here for another couple of hours."

She grinned. "I came to give you an early Christmas present."

At that, he raised his brows. "Christmas present, huh?"

He hadn't gotten her anything, even though Christmas was in two days. That fact had mentally escaped him in the alcohol- and drug-filled stupor he usually found himself in lately. Plus, he hadn't thought they were the type of father and daughter who would exchange gifts.

"Yep, and you'll *love* what I got you," she said as she tossed her cell phone at him.

"What?" He caught her cell in the palm of his hand and squinted down at the screen. "What is it?"

"Just *read* it!"

The font was small, but even he could clearly see the headline on the mobile news web site.

"'Area woman goes missing. Family and community hold vigil to pray for her safe return,'" he read aloud.

He then saw a close-up picture of Mavis Upton, Renee's mother, with tears in her eyes. Several people stood behind her, holding lit candles. Dante fell back into his recliner and read that Renee hadn't been seen or heard from by family members and friends for more than a week. According to a police report filed by Mavis, Renee was last seen pulling off in her car after dropping off her daughter, Tasha, at Mavis's home.

"Renee's disappeared a day or two before when she went out clubbing, but she's never been gone this long," Mavis said in the article. "I'm really worried about her. I'm worried that something's happened to her."

When Dante read that line, his face broke into a

smile. "Well, I'll be damned," he muttered with a rumbling chuckle. He slowly looked up at his daughter, who was grinning ear-to-ear. "You did it," he said, almost with awe.

"You goddamn right I did it!" she said, hopping to her feet, pumping her fists. "I told you I would do it, didn't I?"

He gradually nodded. "That you did."

But he hadn't believed her. Why would he? She was just a loudmouthed teenage girl with beat-up tennis shoes and ratty purple braids that were badly in need of a touch-up. How the hell could she arrange a hit? Even when he had given Kiki the eight hundred dollars in cash along with Renee's address two weeks ago, he hadn't expected anything to come of it. He had thought it would be money flushed down the drain. Now he was elated to find out that he had been wrong. Turns out it had been the best eight hundred dollars he had ever spent!

Dante gazed at his daughter, assessing her openly now. He had tried in the past to have allies in his schemes—and all had disappointed him. Charisse had been a mistake and Renee had been a disaster of even bigger proportions. How delightful it was to discover that his best and most reliable ally was his own seed, his own daughter. He guessed it made sense. He was a lot like his father, George. Scheming and dirty dealing was in Kiki's blood.

"So can I stay here?" she asked eagerly. "Can I move in the back room?"

"That was our deal. I won't renege on it."

He watched as she shouted and did a mock end

zone dance in his living room, celebrating her victory and Renee's demise. She didn't seem the least bit sorry that a woman was now dead thanks to her.

No remorse. That's good, he thought.

If he refined her a little, Kiki could become a force to be reckoned with. She could be an awesome weapon he could wield.

She paused from dancing and twisted one of her braids around her fingers. "So you'll let me drive your ride? That was part of the deal, too!"

"Sure." He reached for the car keys on his coffee table and held them out to her. "Just bring it back in a couple of hours, and don't break any speed limits."

She giggled and grabbed the car keys from him before racing to the front door. She ran like she wanted to get out of the house before he had a chance to change his mind, but he wouldn't change his mind. She had earned her reward ten times over. Renee was dead. His biggest problem was taken care of.

Dante watched as his door slammed shut behind Kiki. He heard the tires of his Jag squeal seconds later as she drove off to a destination unknown. Dante rose to his feet and walked across the living room. He grabbed the cordless phone and began to dig through his wallet for an old business card.

Now that Renee was taken care of, it was time to go down the list of old scores he needed to settle. And he knew *exactly* who was next in line.

Dante dialed the number on the business card and listened to the phone ring on the other end. The person finally picked up after the fourth ring.

"Detective Morris speaking," a gruff voice answered.

"Hello, Detective Morris? This is Dante Turner."

"Ah, yeah, uh . . . hello, Mr. Turner," the detective said, sounding distracted. "Look, I'm sorry I haven't updated you on the investigation. We've been trying to follow up on that lead you gave me about—"

"Yes, I know. You haven't been able to find her. But that doesn't matter anymore. I had time to think about it . . . to think about that night in more detail, like you said, and my memory is a lot better. I realize now that I had it all wrong. I was mistaken."

The detective paused. "You were mistaken? What do you mean?"

"I mean that I can remember what *really* happened, Detective," Dante said, falling back into his recliner. "I can tell you who really shot me."

"Well," Detective Morris replied, "if that's the case, Mr. Turner, I'm all ears!"

Chapter 28

Evan

It was Christmas morning and the smell of pine and the sharp hint of burning embers in the front hall fireplace filled the air. A series of sounds echoed up the stairs to the east and west wings of the Murdoch Mansion: sterling silver trays and glass dishes being set down on tables for the morning buffet, the groundskeeper using the snow blower to remove the snow that had fallen only the night before from the driveway, and the clamor of feet and rising voices as the Murdochs and their loved ones headed to one of the sitting rooms to open presents around the ten-foot-tall Christmas tree.

And another sound was added to the cacophony that hadn't been there before: the cooing of a baby. It was the most beautiful sound Evan had ever heard.

"I'll head down with the rest of you guys in fifteen minutes," Leila said over her shoulder to Evan before gazing down at their daughter, who was still nursing at Leila's breast. "I just want to give her a chance to get her fill. She's a greedy little one." She laughed.

Leila was sitting in one of the armchairs in their bedroom with her feet propped up on an ottoman. The light streaming through the window played on her and Angelica, making the duo resemble a portrait done by some Dutch Golden Age painter.

"Go ahead without us," Leila said, shooing him away. "We'll catch up."

But he lingered in the bedroom, watching them, enraptured. She felt his eyes on her and smiled.

"Or stay if you want, Ev."

"I think I'll stay," he whispered, lowering himself back onto the bed, watching Leila and Angelica.

They headed downstairs twenty minutes later. He held Angelica on his broad shoulder, gently patting her back as he walked until she released a rumbling burp that made them both chuckle.

"Oh, that was a good one," he said, lowering her from his shoulder, but still cradling her close as they walked into the sitting room.

He was surprised at how natural it felt to hold such a tiny bundle. He had thought he would be awkward with her, not knowing where to hold her head or if he should steady her back or her bottom. But it had all fallen into place, like he was *meant* to do this.

He broke his gaze from Angelica's dark eyes, which drifted toward the Christmas tree, no longer pulled by her daddy but by all the bright lights and decorations. Evan spotted his brother Terrence on one of the sofas with his fiancée, C. J. She kissed his cheek after opening the gift box he had handed her.

"I love it, baby," C. J. gushed.

Paulette and Antonio sat on another sofa. Nate was nestled in his father's lap, wearing a miniature version of the sweater and slacks his father was wearing. Paulette opened one of the boxes and pulled out a baby toy with bright colors and noises that had Nate absolutely riveted.

Meanwhile, Isabel looked like she was in the throes of manic frenzy as she ripped wrapping paper off one of the large boxes beneath the tree. Her grandmother sat off to the side, laughing as she stared at the eight-year-old.

"It's a wand just like Hermione's!" Isabel screeched, pulling the replica out of its velvet-lined box. "Oh, my God! Thanks, Mom!"

Leila leaned down to kiss her daughter's crown before sitting in one of the nearby armchairs. "You're welcome, honey. I'm glad you like it."

Still cradling Angelica in his arms, Evan leaned down and grabbed a small box that had Leila's name on it from beneath the tree. He turned and handed it to her.

"This is for you," he said softly.

"Thank you, Ev." Leila lowered it onto her lap

and began to unwrap it. When she removed the lid and saw what was inside, she paused. Her eyes flooded with tears, and she stared up at him.

It wasn't yet another Tiffany bracelet he had bought her or diamond earrings or the tickets to Fiji for the honeymoon they would *finally* take after they were married at the start of the year. Instead, it was a simple sterling silver picture frame with a picture of them from when they were kids. It was a picture that Diane had taken but long ago forgotten and had finally unearthed, at his request.

He and Leila were ten years old in the photo and both wearing their Queen Anne uniforms. Evan squinted behind his thick glasses and sported a high-top fade. Leila wore her braces and pigtails. Their arms were thrown around each other's shoulders as they grinned at the camera. This was back when he called her Bugs and she called him Magoo . . . back when he knew his emotions better than his home address . . . back when it felt like nothing in the world could come between them.

"To my best friend, my other half, my first and my last . . . I loved you even then, Evan," he'd had inscribed on the picture frame.

"Oh, Ev! Baby, this is so . . ." She held the frame up to her chest and choked up as a lone tear slid onto her cheek. "It's so beautiful!"

He leaned down and kissed her.

"Lord, can someone get me a tissue!" she exclaimed as he pulled away. She wiped at her reddened eyes, laughing and crying at the same time.

No more tears were shed for the rest of that

morning. The family continued to open gifts and snack on the cheese and bacon biscuits and mini quiches, to drink mimosas and hot chocolate.

Evan had just finished opening a gag gift from Terrence that made him burst into laughter when the housekeeper came running into the sitting room, holding her hand to her bosom as she gulped for air.

"I'm . . . I'm so sorry, Mr. Murdoch!" she shouted as all eyes turned toward her and conversation came to a halt. "But they . . . they said they had a warrant!"

"*A warrant?*" he echoed. "What?" He turned back toward the entranceway to find five police officers streaming into the room. Their hands were on their holsters, at the ready to pull out their weapons, like they had just entered a seedy drug den and not a Christmas celebration.

"What the fuck . . ." Terrence murmured, dropping C. J.'s hand and shoving her behind his back.

Leila's eyes widened as she drew Angelica to her chest, cradling their baby protectively against her. Isabel scrambled to the foot of her mother's chair, dropping her box and tissue paper to the floor as she went.

"What's happening?" Isabel shouted to her mother. "What's happening, Mommy?"

Leila shook her head, mute with fright.

"Sorry to interrupt you folks during your gift opening," Detective Morris said as he sauntered into the room, all smiles and not looking the least bit sorry, "but we're here to make an arrest." He then pulled out a set of handcuffs from his pocket.

Paulette clapped her hand over her mouth, stifling a shrill cry.

Half of the room was still confused, but Terrence and Evan knew exactly what was happening. Terrence closed his eyes and turned away from his sister. Meanwhile, Evan watched as Antonio slowly rose from the sofa. Antonio glanced down at his wife, who was already sobbing uncontrollably. He then turned to look at Diane, who was standing nearby.

"Please . . . take our son," he whispered to Diane. He held out the baby to her.

The older woman blinked, then nodded, still looking bemused. She shakily held out her arms to sweep the squirming infant against her chest.

With his head bowed and an empty expression on his face, as though he was resigned to his fate and ready to accept his long overdue penance, Antonio took an unsteady step toward the officers.

"No!" Paulette screamed. Tears continued to stream down her face. She lurched to her feet, reached out, and frantically grabbed her husband's arm to yank him back. "No! No, Tony!"

Antonio turned to look down at her and gave a small smile. "It's okay, baby," he whispered.

But instead of walking toward Antonio, who already held out his wrists to be cuffed, the detective abruptly turned to Evan. His smile widened into a grin.

"I gave you plenty of chances to come clean," Detective Morris said. "Now all your chances are up."

"W-what?" Evan said, frowning in bewilderment.

"Turn around!"

Evan didn't make a move, still stunned.

"I said turn around, dammit!" Detective Morris barked. His round face went crimson with the rage and contempt he could no longer hide. "Don't make us have to rough you up in front of all these ladies, in your own home! Turn your ass around, boy!"

Evan shook his head. "But I—"

He didn't get the chance to finish. Two of the officers charged forward, grabbed Evan, and shoved him down to the sitting room rug. They pressed his face into the thick threads of wool as they twisted his arms behind his back. One officer lowered his knee between Evan's shoulder blades. Evan was too shocked to respond, to even contemplate fighting back. He could barely see anything. He could barely breathe with the weight of two men pressed down upon his back, compressing his rib cage.

"What the hell are you doing?" Terrence shouted. "Get the fuck off of him!"

"Oh, God! Ev! Baby!" he heard Leila call to him. "Please stop! He didn't do anything!"

Evan heard Angelica's angry wails as her mother screamed. He heard more frantic voices that were now unintelligible. He felt the cold clasp of handcuffs on his wrists. He was then roughly yanked back to his feet, gulping for air now that he could breathe again.

Evan could now see that the sitting room, which had been full of laughter and familial love only minutes ago, was now in complete chaos. He glanced to his right and saw that Terrence was being held back by two of the other officers, tussling with them both and cursing as he did it. His brother was well on his way to getting arrested, too. C. J. was yelling at him to stop and screaming at the officers to do the same. Leila, Paulette, and Isabel were openly sobbing. The babies were howling, filling the room with their ear-piercing cries. Meanwhile, Antonio stood immobile, looking dazed, and Diane looked absolutely terrified.

"Terry, stop!" Evan called hoarsely to his brother. "Just . . . just stop." But his brother couldn't hear him over all the noise. Evan swallowed and turned again. His eyes met the icy gray ones of Detective Morris.

"Evan Murdoch, you are being charged with the attempted murder of Dante Turner," he said coolly, making Evan's stomach drop. "You have the right to remain silent. Anything you say can and will be held against you in a court of law. You have a right to an attorney. If you cannot afford an attorney, one will be assigned to you." He inclined his head. "But that shouldn't be a problem for a man like you, should it, *Mr. Murdoch*?"

Evan didn't respond.

"Do you understand these rights as they have been read to you?"

Evan sluggishly nodded.

"Good. Then I guess we can get the hell out of here," the detective said, grabbing his arm and yanking him forward.

Evan's feet were slow to respond. He stumbled

a little as he walked, still muddled. The shouts and cries around him and behind him continued even as he was led out of the sitting room, down the hall, and finally out the door to the police cruiser that awaited him in his driveway to take him to jail.

Connect with Us

Visit us online at
KensingtonBooks.com
to read more from your favorite authors, see books
by series, view reading group guides, and more.

Join us on social media

for sneak peeks, chances to win books and prize packs,
and to share your thoughts with other readers.

facebook.com/kensingtonpublishing
twitter.com/kensingtonbooks

Tell us what you think!

To share your thoughts, submit a review,
or sign up for our eNewsletters, please visit:
KensingtonBooks.com/TellUs.